UPS AND DOWN OF

UPS AND DOWN
OF LIFE IN THE INDIES

P.A. DAUM

PERIPLUS

Paperback edition published in 1999 by Periplus Editions (HK) Ltd.
ALL RIGHTS RESERVED

ISBN 962-593-512-6
Printed in Singapore

Publisher: Eric Oey

Distributors

Asia Pacific	Berkeley Books Pte. Ltd. 5 Little Road, #08-01 Singapore 536983 Tel: (65) 280-1330 Fax: (65) 280-6290
Indonesia	PT Wira Mandala Pustaka, (Java Books – Indonesia) Jl. Kelapa Gading Kirana Blok A14 No.17, Jakarta 14240 Tel: (62-21) 451-5351 Fax: (62-21) 453-4987
Japan	Tuttle Publishing RK Building 2nd Floor 2-13-10 Shimo Meguro, Meguro-Ku Tokyo 153 0064, Japan Tel: (03) 5437-0171 Fax: (03) 5437-0755
United States	Tuttle Publishing Distribution Center Airport Industrial Park 364 Innovation Drive North Clarendon, VT 05759-9436 Tel: (802) 773-8930, (800) 526-2778

Preparation and publication of this work were supported by the Translation and Publication Programs of the National Endowment for the Humanities, the Foundation for the Promotion of the Translation of Dutch Literary Works, the Prince Bernhard Fund, and the Dutch Ministry of Welfare, Health, and Culture (Ministerie van Welzijn, Volksgezondheid en Cultuur), Department for International Affairs, The Netherlands, to which acknowledgment is gratefully made.

Contents

Preface to the Series

This volume is one of a series of literary works written by the Dutch about their lives in the former colony of the Dutch East Indies, now the Republic of Indonesia. This realm of 13,670 islands is roughly one quarter the size of the continental United States. It consists of the four Greater Sunda Islands—Sumatra, larger than California; Java, about the size of New York State; Borneo, about the size of France (presently called Kalimantan); and Celebes, about the size of North Dakota (now called Sulawesi). East from Java is a string of smaller islands called the Lesser Sunda Islands, which includes Bali, Lombok, Sumba, Sumbawa, Flores, and Timor. Further east from the Lesser Sunda Islands lies New Guinea, now called Irian Barat, which is the second largest island in the world. Between New Guinea and Celebes there is a host of smaller islands, often known as the Moluccas, that includes a group once celebrated as the Spice Islands.

One of the most volcanic regions in the world, the Malay archipelago is tropical in climate and has a diverse population. Some 250 languages are spoken in Indonesia, and it is remarkable that a population of such widely differing cultural and ethnic backgrounds adopted the Malay language as its *lingua franca* from about the fifteenth century, although that language was spoken at first only in parts of Sumatra and the Malay peninsula (now Malaysia).

Though the smallest of the Greater Sunda Islands, Java has always been the most densely populated, with about two-thirds of all Indonesians living there. In many ways a history of Indonesia is, first and foremost, the history of Java.

But in some ways Java's prominence is misleading, because it belies the great diversity of this island realm. For instance, the destination of the first Europeans who sailed to Southeast Asia was not Java but the Moluccas. It was that "odiferous pistil" (as Motley called the clove), as well as nutmeg and mace, that drew the Portuguese to a group of small islands in the Ceram and

Banda Seas in the early part of the sixteenth century. Pepper was another profitable commodity, and attempts to obtain it brought the Portuguese into conflict with Atjeh, an Islamic sultanate in northern Sumatra, and with Javanese traders who, along with merchants from India, had been the traditional middlemen of the spice trade. The precedent of European intervention had been set and was to continue for nearly four centuries.

Although subsequent history is complicated in its causes and effects, one may propose certain generalities. The Malay realm was essentially a littoral one. Even in Java, the interior was sparsely populated and virtually unknown to the foreign intruders coming from China, India, and Europe. Whoever ruled the seas controlled the archipelago, and for the next three centuries the key needed to unlock the riches of Indonesia was mastery of the Indian Ocean. The nations who thus succeeded were, in turn, Portugal, Holland, and England, and one can trace the shifting of power in the prominence and decline of their major cities in the Orient. Goa, Portugal's stronghold in India, gave way to Batavia in the Dutch East Indies, while Batavia was overshadowed by Singapore by the end of the nineteenth century. Although all three were relatively small nations, they were maritime giants. Their success was partly due to the internecine warfare between the countless city-states, principalities, and native autocrats. The Dutch were masters at playing one against the other.

Religion was a major factor in the fortunes of Indonesia. The Portuguese expansion was in part a result of Portugal's crusade against Islam, which was quite as ferocious and intransigent as the holy war of the Mohammedans. Islam may be considered a unifying force in the archipelago; it cut across all levels of society and provided a rallying point for resistance to foreign intrusion. Just as the Malay language had done linguistically, Islam proved to be a syncretizing force when there was no united front. One of the causes of Portugal's demise was its inflexible antagonism to Islam, and later the Dutch found resistance to their rule fueled by religious fervor as well as political dissatisfaction.

Holland ventured to reach the tropical antipodes not only because their nemesis, Philip II of Spain, annexed Portugal and forbade the Dutch entry to Lisbon. The United Netherlands was a nation of merchants, a brokerage house for northern Europe, and it wanted to get to the source of tropical wealth itself. Dutch navigators and traders knew the location of the fabled Indies; they were well acquainted with Portuguese achievements at sea and counted among their members individuals who had worked for the Portuguese. Philip II simply accelerated a process that was inevitable.

At first, various individual enterprises outfitted ships and sent them to the Far East in a far from lucrative display of free enterprise. Nor was the first arrival of the Dutch in the archipelago auspicious, though it may have been symbolic of subsequent developments. In June 1596 a Dutch fleet of four ships anchored off the coast of Java. Senseless violence and a total disregard for local customs made the Dutch unwelcome on those shores.

During the seventeenth century the Dutch extended their influence in the archipelago by means of superior naval strength, by use of armed intervention which was often ruthless, and by shrewd politicking and exploitation of local differences. Their cause was helped by the lack of a cohesive force to withstand them. Yet the seventeenth century also saw a number of men who were eager to know the new realm, who investigated the language and the mores of the people they encountered, and who studied the flora and fauna. These were men who not only put the Indies on the map of trade routes, but who also charted riches of other than commercial value.

It soon became apparent to the Dutch that these separate ventures did little to promote welfare. In 1602 Johan van Oldenbarneveldt, the Advocate of the United Provinces, managed to negotiate a contract which in effect merged all these individual enterprises into one United East India Company, better known under its Dutch acronym as the VOC. The merger ensured a monopoly at home, and the Company set out to obtain a similar insurance in the Indies. This desire for exclusive rights to the production and marketing of spices and other commodities proved to be a double-edged sword.

The VOC succeeded because of its unrelenting naval vigilance in discouraging European competition and because the Indies were a politically unstable region. And even though the Company was only interested in its balance sheet, it soon found itself burdened with an expanding empire and an indolent bureaucracy which, in the eighteenth century, became not only unwieldy but tolerant of graft and extortion. Furthermore, even though its profits were far below what they were rumored to be, the Company kept its dividends artificially high and was soon forced to borrow money to pay the interest on previous loans. When Holland's naval supremacy was seriously challenged by the British in 1780, a blockade kept the Company's ships from reaching Holland, and the discrepancy between capital and expenditures increased dramatically until the Company's deficit was so large it had to request state aid. In 1798, after nearly two centuries, the Company ceased to exist. Its debt of 140 million guilders was assumed by the state, and the commercial enterprise became a colonial empire.

At the beginning of the nineteenth century, Dutch influence was still determined by the littoral character of the region. Dutch presence in the archipelago can be said to have lasted three and a half centuries, but if one defines colonialism as the subjugation of an *entire* area and dates it from the time when the last independent domain was conquered—in this case Atjeh in northern Sumatra—then the Dutch colonial empire lasted less than half a century. Effective government could only be claimed for the Moluccas, certain portions of Java (by no means the entire island), a southern portion of Celebes, and some coastal regions of Sumatra and Borneo. Yet it is also true that precisely because Indonesia was an insular realm, Holland never needed to muster a substantial army such as the one the British had to maintain in the large subcontinent of India. The extensive interiors of islands such as Sumatra, Borneo, or Celebes were not penetrated, because, for the seaborne empire of commercial interests, exploration of such regions was unprofitable, hence not desirable.

The nature of Holland's involvement changed with the tenure of Herman Willem Daendels as governor-general, just after the French revolution. Holland declared itself a democratic nation in 1795, allied itself with France—which meant a direct confrontation with England—and was practically a vassal state of France until 1810. Though reform, liberal programs, and the mandate of human rights were loudly proclaimed in Europe, they did not seem to apply to the Asian branch of the family of man. Daendels exemplified this double standard. He evinced reforms, either in fact or on paper, but did so in an imperious manner and with total disregard for native customs and law (known as *adat*). Stamford Raffles, who was the chief administrator of the British interim government from 1811 to 1816, expanded Daendels's innovations, which included tax reform and the introduction of the land-rent system, which was based on the assumption that all the land belonged to the colonial administration. By the time Holland regained its colonies in 1816, any resemblance to the erstwhile Company had vanished. In its place was a firmly established, paternalistic colonial government which ruled by edict and regulation, supported a huge bureaucracy, and sought to make the colonies turn a profit, as well as to legislate its inhabitants' manner of living.

It is not surprising that for the remainder of the nineteenth century, a centralized authority instituted changes from above that were often in direct conflict with Javanese life and welfare. One such change, which was supposed to increase revenues and improve the life of the Javanese peasant, was the infamous "Cultivation System" (*Cultuurstelsel*). This system required the Javanese to grow cash crops, such as sugar cane or indigo, which, although profitable on the world market, were of little practical use to the Javanese. In effect it meant compulsory labor and the exploitation of the entire island as if it were a feudal estate. The system proved profitable for the Dutch, and because it introduced varied crops such as tea and tobacco to local agriculture, it indirectly improved the living standard of some of the people. It also fostered distrust of colonial authority, caused uprisings, and provided the impetus for liberal reform on the part of Dutch politicians in the Netherlands.

Along with the increased demand in the latter half of the nineteenth century for liberal reform came an expansion of direct control over other areas of the archipelago. One of the reasons for this was an unprecedented influx of private citizens from Holland. Expansion of trade required expansion of territory that was under direct control of Batavia to insure stability. Colonial policy improved education, agriculture, and public hygiene and expanded the transportation network. In Java a paternalistic policy was not offensive, because its ruling class (the *prijaji*) had governed that way for centuries; but progressive politicians in The Hague demanded that the Indies be administered on a moral basis which favored the interests of the Indonesians rather than those of the Dutch government in Europe. This "ethical policy" became doctrine from about the turn of this century and followed on the heels of a renascence of scientific study of the Indies quite as enthusiastic as the one in the seventeenth century.

The first three decades of the present century were probably the most stable and prosperous in colonial history. This period was also the beginning of an emerging Indonesian national consciousness. Various nationalistic parties were formed, and the Indonesians demanded a far more representative role in the administration of their country. The example of Japan indicated to the Indonesians that European rulers were not invincible. The rapidity with which the Japanese conquered Southeast Asia during the Second World War only accelerated the process of decolonization. In 1945 Indonesia declared its independence, naming Sukarno the republic's first president. The Dutch did not accept this declaration, and between 1945 and 1949 they conducted several unsuccessful military campaigns to re-establish control. In 1950, with a new constitution, Indonesia became a sovereign state.

I offer here only a cursory outline. The historical reality is far more complex and infinitely richer, but this sketch must suffice as a backdrop for the particular type of literature that is presented in this series.

This is a literature written by or about European colonialists in Southeast Asia prior to the Second World War. Though the literary techniques may be Western, the subject matter is unique. This genre is also a self-contained unit that cannot develop further, because there are no new voices and because what was voiced no longer exists. Yet it is a literature that can still instruct, because it delineates the historical and psychological confrontation of East and West, it depicts the uneasy alliance of these antithetical forces, and it shows by prior example the demise of Western imperialism.

These are political issues, but there is another aspect of this kind of literature that is of equal importance. It is a literature of lost causes, of a past irrevocably gone, of an era that today seems so utterly alien that it is novel once again.

Tempo dulu it was once called—time past. But now, after

two world wars and several Asian wars, after the passage of nearly half a century, this phrase presents more than a wistful longing for the prerogatives of imperialism; it gives as well a poignant realization that an epoch is past that will never return. At its worst the documentation of this perception is sentimental indulgence, but at its best it is the poetry of a vanished era, of the fall of an empire, of the passing of an age when issues moral and political were firmer and clearer, and when the drama of the East was still palpable and not yet reduced to a topic for sociologists.

In many ways, this literature of Asian colonialism reminds one of the literature of the American South—of Faulkner, O'Connor, John Crowe Ransom, and Robert Penn Warren. For that too was a "colonial" literature that was quite as much aware of its own demise and yet, not defiantly but wistfully, determined to record its own passing. One finds in both the peculiar hybrid of antithetical cultures, the inevitable defeat of the more recent masters, a faith in more traditional virtues, and that peculiar offbeat detail often called "gothic" or "grotesque." In both literatures loneliness is a central theme. There were very few who knew how to turn their mordant isolation into a dispassionate awareness that all things must pass and fail.

E. M. Beekman

Introduction

Before he was thirty, P. A. Daum was able to escape the restricting conservativism of his native Holland and exercise his bold talents in the colonial Indies. Although of the lower class, he did not permit the circumstances of his birth to keep him down; rather, they seemed to serve as a stimulant for the latent virtues of his character.

He was born Paulus Adrianus Daum in The Hague in 1850, the illegitimate child of a lower-class mother. Having apparently educated himself, he worked his way up the social ladder. He was twenty when he married, and somewhat later, in 1876, he found his true vocation when he began working as a journalist for the rather stodgy newspaper *The Fatherland* (*Het Vaderland*) in The Hague. True to the image of a self-made man, Daum was too enterprising, spirited, and independent to be constrained by the cautious Dutch society of his time.[1]

Daum arrived in Java in 1878 and continued in journalism as an editor for the popular newspaper *The Locomotive* (*De Locomotief*) in Semarang, a city in central Java. By the time he was thirty he had become its managing editor. The tone and disposition of the colonial press were far different from those of their counterpart in the Netherlands. Here there was an opposition press, sharply critical of colonial policies and openly on the side of private enterprise. Its style was immoderate and virulent, shaped by individual temperament rather than by editorial guidelines, and was distinctive enough to become known as the "tropical style."[2]

Daum was in his element. His vociferous articles soon brought him in conflict with the authorities. Since 1856 the government had been able to prosecute journalists and newspapers it disagreed with. In May 1882 Daum was sentenced to jail for the first time, and he also found himself at odds with his employers. To ensure his independence he quit his job and bought a defunct paper called *The Indies Fatherland* (*Het In-*

dische Vaderland), which was also published in Semarang. Because he had little money, he was forced to produce most of the copy himself, and in order tó attract more readers he began to write novels under the pseudonym of "Maurits" and publish them in his paper as feuilletons. He began doing this in 1883 and it was ten years before it was discovered who "Maurits" was. Daum had a practical reason for his secret: he didn't think that his readers would like the idea of one man's writing everything.[3]

In this fashion, Daum produced ten novels in ten years. His energy and diligence is astonishing when one considers that, besides running his paper, he wrote the lead articles, did the reviewing and other routine journalistic tasks, and supplied the regular installments of his serialized novels. In 1883, at the beginning of his independent career, he printed an article that contained something of a credo: "What we submit in this article belongs to 'realistic politics,' which we support and which wants to see social issues regulated as little as possible according to sympathies or antipathies or, generally speaking, by emotions, but according to the dictates of reality. Nor will it fantasize about ideas or general circumstances but will accept them first and foremost such as they are."[4] Daum pursued this realistic view of society for the rest of his life in both his journalism and his fiction.

Despite the lack of what we would call constitutional rights, Daum continued to lambast the "autocratic" colonial administration. In October 1885 his paper was shut down and he was sentenced to a year and a half in jail. This sentence was subsequently reduced in Superior Court to one month, a term he didn't serve until 1887, in the colonial capital of Batavia. He had moved there after the demise of his paper in Semarang, and within two months had launched a new one called *The Batavian News* (*Bataviaasch Nieuwsblad*), which very quickly became one of the most widely read papers in Java. Always a practical businessman, Daum printed it in a reduced format for easier handling and sold it at half the subscription price of his competitors. The first issue of *The Batavian News*, dated 1 December 1885, printed the first installment of his fourth novel, *L. Van Velton-Van der Linden*, and subsequently ran the remaining six.

After fifteen years of constant hard work, Daum achieved

sufficient success to allow him to take time off, and he returned to Holland in 1894 for a vacation of several months. Several years later, back in Java, he contracted a liver ailment which, next to malaria, was the most common tropical disease to afflict Europeans.[5] At the time this malady was practically incurable, and when his health did not improve Daum hastily returned to Holland in 1898 to obtain better medical treatment. To no avail. He died in the country of his birth on 14 September 1898.

Daum's pseudonymous fiction was quite popular at the time. His contemporary audience considered all ten novels romans à clef, and it has been proven that most of the plots and characters had their counterpart in reality.[6] Daum invented very little. According to his daughter, her father combined aspects of colonial actuality with his own experience to form a fictional alternative that was original only in its arrangement and delivery.[7] Dutch critics in Europe did not always believe that some of the bizarre events were bona fide, but colonial reaction testified to their veracity.

Praised as "a mirror of colonial life,"[8] Daum's fiction presents us with a picture that has been confirmed generally as well as particularly. It is precisely this authenticity that, quite apart from the novels' literary merit, preserves them as a valuable "source for colonial history" of the last three decades of the nineteenth century.[9] Using them in that sense, as an instructive collective, one can rehabilitate the quotidian reality of that vanished community.

After scrutinizing Daum's narratives, one realizes that, *mutatis mutandis*, the colonial society living in Java toward the end of the nineteenth century had many things in common with the white upper class living in the Old South.[10] In presenting some of these analogies I am primarily interested in cultural psychology. This means that for the two regions things cannot be neatly aligned chronologically or divided into distinct areas of investigation. Facts merge with legend, and legends can sometimes look remarkably like reality. Within this brief context I cannot adduce all the evidence available from the two areas; the testimonial weight would daunt speculation. Although the differences are obvious, the similarities between Dutch colonial society and literature and the society and literature of the Old

South of the first half of this century may not be common knowledge. Finally, my case for the colonial Indies is mainly based on Daum's fiction, so it is roughly limited (though with some inevitable excursions) to the last three decades of the nineteenth century. This was an era that for many colonial writers came to be synonymous with the Malay phrase *tempo dulu* ("the time of yesteryear"), a chronological era that with the passage of time and the onslaught of historical necessity came to represent something perhaps far better than what had actually existed and that in its passing nurtured a characteristic literature of nostalgia on both sides of the Pacific.

If one examines W. J. Cash's celebrated study, *The Mind of the South*, some likenesses between the two cultures become instantly noticeable. The famous "Southern gregariousness" was easily matched by that of the Indies. In Daum's first novel, *From Sugar to Tobacco*, the narrator's reception in a strange house was "well, [that's] the way it was then in Java's hinterland: 'Here's your room, make yourself comfortable, have a cigar; I'll have some tea brought; if you need anything just call one of the servants; and above all, do as you please' " (1:85). Another example is the huge feast described in chapters eleven and twelve of the present novel. The Indies colonial, like his American counterpart, was "discriminately hospitable," as Samuel Eliot Morison expressed it. He was also known for his courtesy to women.[11] The amiable hedonism and extravagance Cash found so typical of his confreres were equally proverbial of the colonials when they came to Holland either on leave or to retire, and offended the more restrictive sensibilities of the continental Dutch quite as much as those of the "Yankees."

In a recent study by the same name, Bertram Wyatt-Brown made "southern honor" central to his investigation of the Old South.[12] A similar code of conduct was brought to bear on the children of the upper class in the Dutch colonies which produced, according to Daum, as weak a crop of men as in the South. A peculiar manifestation of that code, according to Wyatt-Brown, was dueling, an anachronism in Europe and the rest of the United States, but a romantic affectation that was still indulged in the South and in the colonial Indies. Duels are either threatened or actually fought in half of Daum's ten novels. And even though the men may think it an unsatisfactory way of settling disputes, because of their volatile temperaments and

4

irascible sense of honor, they ignore their better judgment (1:139–49; 2:60; 3:63; 6:175, 202–4; 7:192–95). Multatuli, perhaps the most influential of Dutch colonial writers, is said to have fought with sabers in Sumatra as a young man without, as he put it with ironic bravado, "ever letting his cigar go out"; in 1881, at the age of sixty-one, he still thought that "the principle of dueling is useful in a society that does not have a sense of honor." He was referring to Holland, not to the Indies.[13] This chivalric relic may have been inspired, as was certainly the case in the American South, by the work of Sir Walter Scott, a novelist and poet greatly admired both by Multatuli (he called him his "great master") and by the nineteenth-century Dutch reading public.[14] Another important colonial writer, E. Du Perron, was a loyal admirer of Dumas's *Three Musketeers*. Furthermore, there was a veritable d'Artagnan cult in the Indies during the twenties, and fencing returned as the most favorite sport.[15]

Such a solution to conflict is highly individualistic; one cannot conceive of an organization man or a company man risking his career in a duel. Cash found "an intense individualism" to be "the dominant trait" of the Southern mind.[16] The same is true of the characters in Daum's fiction (including the women), and also was obvious in the private sector in the colonial Indies.[17]

The reason for this combative individualism can be found in the structure of colonial society. One needs to know that Indies society recognized three "classes"; they were comprised of the bureaucratic elite, the military, and private individuals. The last, known contemptuously by the bureaucrats as *tjuma partiklir sadja* ("merely private individuals"), included professional people and those pursuing private enterprise: the planters, merchants, cultivators, settlers, and anyone else contractually employed by private enterprise (e.g., mining engineers). In short, those whom the French used to call *colons*.

The colons were always at odds with colonial government, a vast network of officials of the colonial civil service known as "the B.B.," the acronym for *Binnenlands Bestuur*, or the "Interior Administration." This corps was known as "the wellnigh all-powerful 'demi-gods' of the colonial realm," and everything that the private sector (always a relatively small group) sought to accomplish was dependent on that administration.

These demi-gods, ruled by the governor-general on "the throne in Buitenzorg" (the city in Java where his residence was located), had complete autonomy in Daum's time and were in constant conflict with the *partiklir sadja* (see 5:26–7 or 2:159). The B.B. wanted to place itself "above the persistent economic and political demands of mammon's spokesmen in the colony," though this was seldom the case.[18] Daum described this contraposition during the dynamic last two decades of the nineteenth century: "There was an urge to expand. In both craters of commerce were two gigantic plugs; the first would erupt by itself and spread the competition in commodities all over the Indies; the second was still held in check by the government, but the inner force was powerful and people were expecting an eruption very soon which, in the form of agrarian laws, would help them obtain land and promote agriculture" (2:77). The latter did in fact happen in 1870, when the so-called Agrarian Law van de Waal allowed a greater flow of private capital to the Indies in order to revitalize a stagnant colonial economy.[19]

Such a civil body hardly fosters independence, but the civil service felt itself to be far superior to any individual endeavor. Nonetheless, the Indies, like other colonial empires, attracted the more self-reliant spirits of the mother country, men like Daum who, as was clear from the biographical sketch, refused to be coerced by anything except the demands of practicality. Daum's narratives are energized in part by this incessant clash between decree law and reality, and they primarily champion the cause of the colons. As a realist, however, Daum was well aware that the ascendant minority had a secret desire to emulate their masters (4:5).

The world of Daum's colons was like that of Cash's Southerners in that its members also regarded themselves as "an aggregation of self-contained and self-sufficient monads, each of whom was ultimately and completely responsible for himself."[20] Rob Nieuwenhuys, one of the finest interpreters of Dutch colonial society, expressed a similar opinion by writing that "Indies society was atomic; 'everybody [in Java] live[d] by and for himself.' "[21] The colonial shared the Southerner's distrust and dislike of governmental authority,[22] which he could only see as a force that was bent on depriving him of his rights and of stifling individual enterprise. A good example of this view can be found in the more recent work of Beb Vuyk—her novel *The Last House in the World* (1939) is published in this series—where this strife expresses itself as an almost ferocious passion.

The South's dislike of the North or the federal government, personified as the "Yankee," bears some resemblance to the colonial hatred for The Hague, which became synonymous with governmental interference directed by distant strangers, with, it was felt, no direct knowledge of the reality of the Indies, who imposed their illogical notions by force. The "North" and "The Hague" both came to represent progressive, "modern" ideas that were hated and distrusted by defiantly conservative and regressive sectarians. An instance, somewhat similar to the emancipation doctrine, was what came to be known as the "Ethical Policy," perhaps best formulated in a phrase from Queen Wilhelmina's speech in 1901 in which she spoke of a need "to permeate the entire governmental system with the realization that the Netherlands has to fulfill a moral obligation toward the population of these areas."[23] This liberal sentiment had been heard and argued since about 1870. In 1884 the journalist Brooshooft wrote in *The Locomotive* (the paper Daum had left scarcely two years before) that "so much blood has been drawn from the patient [i.e., Java] over the years that he is in danger of succumbing to an advanced case of [economic] anemia."[24] One of Daum's most offensive characters, Kees van den Broek in *How He Became a Councillor of the Indies*, dismissed this sentiment as a "philanthropic mood" (2:6). In another novel it provoked the following exchange:

" . . . and furthermore you'll hear a phrase nowadays that has become quite popular in Holland; they're talking about the sweat and blood of *the* Javanese and *we* are the ones getting fat off it."

"Damn it, Koorders, who dreamed that one up?"

"I don't know. Nervous blowhards who were in need of that blood and sweat to make a name for themselves, or candidates for a job in The Hague who made political hay with it."

"And it's really caught on too. I assure you that the people in Holland think that we are some kind of parasites living off the Javanese." (1:322)

"The colony" as it existed in Daum's day was primarily Java. It is that island that forms the background for most of his books, and it was that island that was identified in Europe with the

Dutch East Indies (although this changed after Daum's time). Like the American South, Java's economic pattern was largely agrarian. If one includes the cultivation of raw materials, one can safely say that during Daum's time (and for many years to come) "Indonesia supplied agrarian products and raw materials, none of which were processed more than was necessary for their dispatch to the manufacturing countries of Europe and America." Daum's era was probably that last heyday of rugged individualism personified by the private planter, "a pioneer working at his own risk...the typical exponent of free enterprise." But, as was true for the South, independent effort was doomed. The plantations where cash crops like sugar, tea, coffee, and tobacco were grown were gradually taken over by corporations so that by the 1920s "the plantations were all brought under a coordinating superstructure of large syndicates and cartels working in close cooperation with the government authorities."[25] The analogy with the South is not unwarranted.

The South has often been characterized as being similar to "a European colony set down in a nation."[26] C. Vann Woodward, the renowned Southern historian, devotes an entire chapter to the "colonial economy" of the region, quoting an expert who characterized the Northeast as acting "like the mother country in an empire" and treating the South like its territory.[27] As late as 1977 Robert Penn Warren denounced "a hundred years of internal imperialism."[28] A study of the economics of the two cultures would be more than is needed for our present purposes, but clearly one can speak of some fundamental resemblances— an agrarian economy, resistance to or lack of industrialism, and the concentration of power and interest away from the regional centers, with the imperial home country acting as an absentee landlord. Such dislike for industrial progress can also be found in Daum's work.

Where used to be only ricefields once, now waved the elegant plumes of the sugar cane; where the tall coconut palms had once represented "the highest good" they were now humbled by taller white factory stacks which never, day or night, stopped sending up clouds of smoke from their black openings. And straight through the once unspoilt fields you could now see limitless rails, here rusty, over there glistening dully from friction in the fierce light of the sun. Money had been introduced to the population, and with the white "filthy lucre" another "filth" had arrived. Near the railroad stations lived the Chinese and Arabs who were now in business, had opened *warongs* [small shops], smuggled opium, ran gambling houses; this was the field train of Western civilization in the East. (6:10)

At any rate, one can state that both the South and the Indies "were caught between two worlds—the old and the new—and two traditions—the regional and the national."[29] This was not only the case with social structures, political fortunes, and economic reality; this "double focus" was also, according to Allen Tate, "the precondition" for Southern literature.[30] The same thing can be said of Dutch colonial literature, particularly that written after the First World War.

Summaries of the best and the worst qualities of these two regions on opposite sides of the Pacific often echo one another. An instance is Cash's summing-up of his investigation in *The Mind of the South*, a description that suits the Indies as well.

Proud, brave, honorable by its lights, courteous, personally generous, loyal, swift to act, often too swift...such was the South at its best ...[while its characteristic vices were] violence, intolerance, aversion and suspicion toward new ideas, an incapacity for analysis, an inclination to act from feeling rather than from thought, an exaggerated individualism and a too narrow concept of social responsibility...too great attachment to racial values and a tendency to justify cruelty and injustice in the name of those values, sentimentality, and a lack of realism....[31]

Nieuwenhuys's analysis of Daum's era strikes a similar note. The dark side of colonial society he finds expressed by "easy sexual relations, the passion for gambling and gossip, the preoccupation with prestige, the materialism and the lack of culture ...but on the other hand there was hospitality, geniality and joviality, readiness to help and cordiality, a more open way of life....."[32] These epithets held true for both societies well into the present century.

King has argued that society in the Old South was patriarchal.[33] This is true of the colonial Indies as well, and of colonialism in general. In *Ups and Downs* Daum clearly states that the "generally current notion" subscribed to the fact that "the husband was the *tukang*, the boss. He was at the head of the business as an absolute ruler and what he wanted or said was the way it would be." This power was often subverted and undermined, to be sure, but Daum's novels demonstrate that colonial society of his day was ruled by a strong patriarchy, its authority determined by money and social position.

King speaks of the father as central to the "family romance, Southern style," and argues that one of the main themes of Southern literature is the conflict between father and son.[34] One could view the Civil War not only as a fraternal strife but also as the South's defiant assertion of filial rights against a distant and overbearing Northern or "Yankee" father. The parallel of the subordinate son as private enterprise and the government as a patriarchal authority that proclaims and enforces strictures with severity and impunity, can also be found in nineteenth-century Java. In one novel the identification of colonial government with an obdurate father is clearly intended (5:184) and throughout Daum's work one will find many instances of this "generational" conflict.

In his first novel Daum portrays a resident, who in practical terms was probably the most influential of colonial officials, except for the governor-general, as a patriarchal deity (1:8, 198–99). His approval is sedulously courted in Daum's second novel by a young official whose wife uses her culinary and flirtational skills as if she were a daughter-in-law trying to please her husband's father (2:33–42). One will find this relationship throughout Dutch colonial literature, from Multatuli's *Max Havelaar* whose central character rebels against the considered opinions of his cautious and older superior, to Couperus's insensitive resident in *The Hidden Force*, to Beb Vuyk's frustration and furious impotence when confronted by a stolid bureaucracy that stifles the free expression of her husband's pioneering skills as if he were a truculent child. Daum shows in *Engineer H. van Brakel* that government service meant a steady income for its staid servants, in contrast to the chanciness of free enterprise, where one risked security as if gambling away a god-given patrimony. It should also be noted that the colonial government insisted on more tyrannical power than ever would have been permitted in Holland. It was as if it were permanently at war—which an overseas colony to some degree always was—and, as if under siege conditions, denied its own citizens such basic freedoms as the right of free speech (as Daum experienced to his chagrin) and the right to vote.

All aspects of life in colonial society were part of a family affair, as also was true in the American South. Merit was less important than who one knew or was related to, a situation similar to Southerners putting their faith in "kin." The coffee planter Charles Prédier in *Guna-Guna*, is only able to negotiate a profitable deal because of his brother-in-law's influence in the capital and because his aunt knows the resident very well (6:9). In the present novel, Clara knows that "*family* takes precedence," regardless of domestic bickering or disputes, and in *Number Eleven* (an Indies euphemism for poisoning somebody), a character is advised that "if you want to have a private business you have to be able to count on blood relations. If that's the case you can get anything done, no matter how crazy it might be; but if you don't, they'll oppose you systematically and you'll get nothing done, no matter how reasonable it might be" (8:76).

The family was a bulwark against the world at large, a haven of comfort and refuge from reality, but there was more to it than that. European society as a whole was an extended family that would help and defend its own as if blood kin. One gets the impression of a siege mentality, which is understandable because, especially in the interior, European holdings were like outposts on a hostile frontier. This is suggested by the reaction in the second chapter of *Ups and Downs* to the *ketju*, or murder, of the overseer at Geber's Kuningan plantation. In *From Sugar to Tobacco* the narrator realizes at one point that everything he has accomplished has been due to his uncle and aunt (1:78), but they do not restrict their help to immediate family. His uncle writes about his efforts to help a white woman, Mrs. van Heert, despite the fact that she is hated by just about everybody. "She isn't worth it; she is a nasty woman; I've always detested her, but you just can't let a European woman who used to be married to a confrere and had her own factory, have a woman like that live in the *desa* [native village]" (1:78).

This kind of communal blind loyalty that extended beyond the household or lineage to include race is as pervasive in Daum's portrait of colonial society as it was in the American South. Almost all of Daum's novels are domestic dramas enacted against a political background that enters into the narrative only when it infringes on the more immediate concerns of kindred and kin. This situation is true of most literary works written by people who were born or raised in the tropics and who knew themselves to be descendants of colonial stock. Authors who, despite many years of colonial service, remained interlopers, born and bred in Holland, a country that for the genuine colonials was as alien a place as New England was to a Southerner, might present the situation differently. It should come as no surprise that the colonial, like the Southerner, "saw society as the family writ large,"[35] or that he too looked upon his relationship with the native population as the Southerner did at his relationship with the blacks: as parents in charge of children. This "parental" role, which was often benevolent though always condescending, could become tyrannical when exercised by a character such as Kees van den Broek in the novel *How He Became a Councillor of the Indies*.

Van den Broek is an utterly useless and weak man who is ruled by his wife. His weakness may explain why he is quite vicious when he can exercise his bogus superiority as a colonial official on the Javanese population. His wife, Corrie, is a true Indies person, born in Java; she tells him to beat the natives if they're troublesome. "They're just children; they won't listen but have to *feel*" (2:6). She herself hates children, abhors pregnancy, and is terrified of childbirth and sexual intimacy. Corrie is much stronger than her husband, and it is he who yearns for a male heir to "preserve the patriarchal name" (2:5). He can answer his wife's comment about beating the Javanese "with a smile," saying that he "is a good father who does not spare the rod" (2:6), while he maligns the "philanthropic mood" that pervades Batavia and The Hague. For such weak personalities the chance of lording it over the native population was a dream come true, and even the normal and decent members of colonial society maintained an overbearing attitude. But no matter how one chose to act, interaction with the native population was unavoidable. Because some contact was inevitable, the Indies were able to take revenge in a peculiarly gentle way, although in a way that could not be denied and that was indelible.

In his classic study of the Old South, Cash noted that the relationship between the whites and blacks was "nothing less than organic. Negro entered into white man as profoundly as white man entered into Negro—subtly influencing every gesture, every word, every emotion and idea, every attitude."[36] This propinquity was even more intimate in the colonial Indies, was feminine in origin, and began at birth. Like the erstwhile black "mammy," the *babu* of the colonial Indies took care of the children of her masters. It was the *babu* who was the nurturing influence, who did the mothering, almost to the exclusion of the legal parent. She cared for the child from birth to early adolescence or, if the child was not sent to Holland to be educated, even into young adulthood. She never left it alone; she cradled it, comforted it, carried it anywhere she went on her hip in the sling called a *slendang*; she fed it native food, crooned to it in her native tongue, told it native stories, and brought it up in the native way, a way far more permissive and indulgent than could be possible in Europe.

The child entered a world that was, in the case of Daum's fictions, Javanese. Only much later was it inducted into European society. Therefore, in the most vital sense, the European patriarchy was lovingly subverted by an Asian matriarchy. It would seem that the heartbeat the child knew as its own was Javanese, that its emotional seedbed was native, that it would grow up fed by a native subsoil that held its roots no matter how the plant would later be cultivated by its European, parental overseer when it was ready to be brought to intellectual fruition.[37] One must emphasize that the *babu* was *always* with her charge, even when the family went on furlough to Holland (4:187), because if the child came from a prosperous family, the woman had no other duties and was in fact the child's private servant (his *lijfbaboe*). Although the *babu* was considered the second mother, she was, in fact, the first, because the child's relationship with the *babu* was far more intimate than with its own mother. The child would never forget the way its Javanese mother smelled or how she felt; in other words, the emotional hunger of the colonial child was satisfied by the maternal Indies.

One will find moving testimonials to the unforgettable presence of the *babu* in the life of many colonial authors. Such a woman was recollected by Du Perron in the character of Alima in *Country of Origin*, or by G. J. Resink in a fine poem that opens with the line "She was my very first love."[38] But a *babu* was perhaps most poignantly remembered by Rob Nieuwenhuys, who is the foremost authority of Dutch colonial life and literature and is represented in this series by his novel *Faded*

Portraits and by his history of Dutch colonial literature, *Mirror of the Indies*. He has eulogized his *babu*, Nènèk Tidjah, both privately and in print, most recently in a book of rare photographs from the colonial era. He prints a picture of himself as a child held by his father. The family resemblance is undeniable and the man, dressed in white, dominates the picture. But behind his back is a smaller figure, dark and indistinct, almost obliterated by the prominence of her employer, but Nieuwenhuys made no mistake about who held the true dominion.[39]

> Nènèk Tidjah was my *lijfbaboe* at least until I was five, and therefore my first mother. I have been told that the first words I spoke were Javenese. Later I talked with her in a strange lingo of Javanese and Malay, interspersed with Dutch words. She always called me Lih, pronounced with a long drawn-out vowel, which was an abbreviation of *lilih*, which means darling in Javanese. When my parents were out visiting or went to the opera . . . Nènèk Tidjah had to take care of us. That was always a party. She installed herself in front of our beds with her sirih apparatus (oh that sharp scent of bruised sirih leaves, chewing tobacco, gambir and pinang, I can still smell them in my mind) and she began her breathtaking stories about gods and goddesses, about petrification and metamorphoses. Sometimes she performed long sections from the *Ramayana* using two different voices, and when it began to rain during the west monsoon, accompanied by thunder and lightning, I knew that "up there" the powers of good and evil were engaged in noisy combat with one another. Then I was allowed to sit in her lap. I must have inhaled the smell of her body and her clothes, especially her sarong, quite intensely, a kind of preeroticism. She caressed me by pressing me close to her and by stroking me. I still remember those smells, because smells can be remembered. I can also still experience the atmosphere of that room, with the clear stars and sometimes the moon out beyond the window. When I was seven years ago in Solo [sometime in the 1970s], the native town of my mother and my Javanese grandmother, I had myself *pidjit* (massaged) by a blind, old Javanese woman, probably to reestablish that skin contact. And God forbid, that blind woman resembled Nènèk Tidjah. And thanks to Nènèk Tidjah's stories, Indies nature is angker for me, that is to say holy, alive, peopled by living creatures which you had to learn to manipulate by murmuring holy formulas or by giving a *selamatan*. I was raised as a child in a magic world—and that means a lot, even when you're an adult already who has lived for many years in Holland.[40]

And yet, though the *babu's* loyalty and devotion were maternal rather than servile, her social position remained subordinate. As the child's servant she was often known only by the child's name, for instance "babu Non," or "babu Han."[41] This peculiar mixture of intimacy and subservience that characterized the relationship between the *babu* and her charge was unique to the colonial Indies, and its presentation in a story acted as a hallmark (*tjap*) to check the authenticity of a narrative. Du Perron considered Daum's description in *Guna-Guna* of the bond between Betsy and her aged *babu* Sarinah particularly masterful and true to type.[42] Daum notes that, like a true colonial child, Betsy treats the old servant in a manner that "alternated between cruelty and endearment" (6:34). The old woman sleeps in the same room as Betsy on a *tikar*, or woven mat, in front of Betsy's bed. She dresses and undresses Betsy as if she were still a child, when in fact she is a married woman who is too thoughtlessly indolent to lift her leg when the old woman removes her stockings for her (6:34). There was a symbiotic relationship between the *babu* and her perennial ward that was impervious to husband or society, and when Betsy contemplates the demise of her feckless husband, it is Sarinah who responds to Betsy's insinuations and is ready to use native skills to turn them into reality. And although Betsy can't function without Sarinah, she treats the old retainer with insouciant heartlessness on the one hand, and like a favorite sister on the other.

The other way the Indies insinuated itself into white society has no parallel with the South. In Daum's day a newcomer to the Indies was typically a young inexperienced male, completely befuddled by an alien environment. He was known as a "baar" or greenhorn, after the Malay word *baru* for "new." The customary way for this *totok* (or fullblood Dutchman) to familiarize himself with the Indies was to engage a *njai* (housekeeper). She would take care of him and his house, oversee the inevitable entourage of servants, manage the domestic economy, and teach him about her people. It was accepted that the *budjang*, or bachelor, would also look to her for fulfillment of his sexual needs, and desired her presence to ward off boredom and loneliness. "Keeping a *njai*" was a common and accepted practice; in 1880 (i.e., in Daum's time) a resident still advised every young official to live with a *njai* before marrying a European woman so "he could learn the language, the mores, and the customs of the native population."[43]

The practice was abetted by the realistic fact that there were few European women a man could court with the notion of marriage. A colonial report from 1860 estimates that there was a total European population, including the military, of about 43,000. About 22,700 of them (excluding soldiers) lived in Java. Of that number, 7,602 were men, 5,265 women, and 9,796 children. The report breaks the adult civilian population into those born in the tropics and those born in Europe, and it is interesting to note that the former, the "Indies" population, far outnumbers the latter. Even among upper-class women, the majority were of mixed blood, presenting a society that had "a very strong predominance of the Eurasian element."[44] One will find this corroborated by colonial literature. And, finally, if one considers that those nearly 23,000 Europeans and Eurasians lived amidst a native population of about 13 *million*, it is not surprising that the *njai* was as common a figure as the *babu*.

There is, in fact, a psychological similarity between the two. Both the *njai* and the *babu* were in a subordinate position despite the highest degree of personal intimacy; the *babu* fulfilled the emotional needs of the male child without being its mother, while the *njai* fulfilled the same function for the adult male without being his wife. Both permitted the European male to gain entry to a society that Europeans had subjugated but did not know, and both unwittingly seduced the European to relax his occidental vigilance and enticed him to accede more to the Indies than he ever realized. At both the beginning of life and at the threshold of manhood, the Indies influenced the affective character of the European male more profoundly than Europe ever had. This is not meant to imply an idyllic existence but merely to emphasize the importance of the *babu* and the *njai* in the colonial society of Daum's time because together they mitigated a mutual hostility and created an alternative society that was far more like them than like their masters.

Of course, the colonial patriarchy always exercised its prerogatives, although in doing so it did not differ from the rest of the Western world, British society in Victorian England, for instance.[45] The children of mixed unions could only be legitimized by the father. He could do so either by marrying the mother or by entering their names in the registry of births. If he did the latter he ostensibly needed the mother's permission but in reality this hardly mattered. After she had so consented, the children became his, and the mother had no legal rights to them anymore. As late as the 1920s an Indies woman bemoans the fact that her children do not belong to her but to their father. The author adds: "In this case the father must have 'acknowledged' the child. Though this happened with a signed agreement from the mother, it was in reality nothing more than a formality. With acknowledgment the mother lost her rights to her child. A juridical position that has caused, whether hidden or not, much human suffering."[46] If the European father died, the native mother had no rights of guardianship,[47] and if the father was in default it was the colonial government that decided whether a child was "European" or "native." Daum provides an example of this in his last novel, *Abu Bakar*. Bakar's father was not Dutch but Eurasian, or "Indo" as this group was known in the Indies. He lived with a *njai*, but never married her. When Abu Bakar returns to the Indies from Holland where he was sent to be educated, he discovers that his father had purposely never registered his birth with the colonial authorities, as he had done with his other three sons. This means that Bakar is merely the son of a native woman, hence a "native," while his three brothers are "Europeans," although all four had the same mother (10. 1. 120–21; 2. 2).

The other obvious hazard for the *njai* was when the European man either returned to Holland or decided to marry a white woman. In either case, the *njai* was at the losing end. Daum portrayed this common dilemma in *Number Eleven*, when George Vermey's *njai* Yps must give way to a European woman, Lena Bruce, and is "sent away, like a servant, like a doormat, like a piece of equipment, after proper use" (8:18). George did not decide to marry the European woman out of love. He was thirty-two, had always lived with a *njai*, been perpetually in debt, and enjoyed the irresponsible life of a *budjang*. Lena is twelve years younger, a kind and good person, not physically attractive, but with practical virtues. In contrast, Yps is lazy, self-indulgent, temperamental, but also pretty and far more sensual than Lena could ever be (8:8, 44). In fact, George is afraid of marriage and considers it a "partial suicide" (8:20). Another male character reflects that as soon as a colonial woman acquired a family and children, the husband became a "servitor" she paid little attention to. If she did so at all it was only because he provided her with "a financial and social position" (1:196).

One husband considers his marriage "a chain" and notes how his wife no longer cares if he finds her attractive or not (6:147). An older man marries for "hygienic" reasons (3:157), while Betsy's marriage with Den Ekster in *Guna-Guna* is sheer torture for both of them but maintained to keep up appearances (6:19–20, 24, 33). Marriage between Europeans was clearly a social contract: to insure proper offspring, for economic reasons, or to reassert identification with one's own kind (1:135–36). The prerogative for matrimony was the man's. In Daum's colonial world it was the man who negotiated with the woman's father. An eligible woman remained at home waiting for a suitable prospect, and her reputation had to be spotless, although more than likely the prospective husband had been living with a *njai* for many years.

Lena Bruce in *Number Eleven* rebels against this moral double standard and against the proscribed role of a colonial wife. While thinking about the man who proposed to her she realizes that "her father, her brothers, her nephew, all of them lived as if what was known as morality and chastity didn't apply to them. She was the only one who was respectable; everybody else around her, down to the lowest servant, was lewd and corrupt. And again she thought of Vermey whom she had refused because, in her opinion, he had behaved indecently [i.e., lived with a *njai*]. And while she had been choosy like that, the rest of them lived like a bunch of animals; and while she had been brought up to be extremely decent and proper, everybody around her did precisely the opposite just as calmly as if that were the way it was supposed to be" (8:120). Furthermore, she wants to be something more than "a living tool that is lawfully patented" for procreation (8:53). Yet she marries Vermey anyway and as a result is poisoned by his jealous *njai* Yps. It is not surprising that in Daum's colonial world extramarital affairs were rather common and that divorces were, relatively speaking, routine and did not stigmatize the dissenting partners (7:82) as was the case in continental Holland. One could say, as Michael Ondaatje characterized Ceylonese colonial society, that "marriage was the greater infidelity."[48]

The plight of the European wife in the colonies bears some resemblance to that of the white woman in the South. King acknowledges that "the Southern woman was caught in a social double-bind: toward men she was to be submissive, meek, and gentle; with the children and slaves and in the management of the household, she was supposed to display competence, initiative, and energy." She was also denied sexuality or erotic appeal, and this ardency was transferred to the black woman. "The white women's idealization and etherealization meant that husbands and children, particularly sons, looked to black women as the source of warmth and security, of sensuality and the pleasures of the body." As the *babu* was similar to the "nurturing mammy," the *njai* resembled the "sultry [black] temptress."[49]

In the colonial Indies the married European woman was similarly faced with a great deal of responsibility. She had to become a competent administrator of a large household, an energetic manager of a considerable number of servants, and was liable for producing "the lawfully patented" offspring. She resented the unfair advantage of the "native cattle" (5:148) whose easy sexuality held far more appeal than the burdens a "proper" woman represented to her husband. Daum makes this very clear in *Engineer H. van Brakel* where Ceciel, living on the margin of European society, is afraid that the presence of a *njai* might subvert her attempts to marry a Dutchman who would guarantee her "respectability."

> Something glistened in her beautiful eyes when she thought of those infernal brown women whose easy outlook on life doomed so many European girls in the Indies to a future as a spinster.[50] She could kill them if she'd get away with it; she hated those creatures with immitigable hatred; *they* were the ones who *robbed* the Indies girls of prospective husbands; who reduced the ardor of the young men to the ashes of cynicism and indifference; *they* were the cancer of European society because of their surrogate marriage without obligation." (5:145)[51]

The implication of this passage, of course, is that this was a real threat, and it is in this respect that sexual life in the colonies differed from that in the American South. White males commonly had relationships with "colored" women; mixed marriages occurred more often than one might think; and illegitimate children of mixed blood were legally adopted. Hence, as compared to British India for instance, there was a pervasive blending of the races in the upper classes of colonial society. The male prerogative was duly maintained, of course; almost without exception native blood could only be traced to the matriarchal line in a family. What Europe considered "the exotic cachet" of the colonials was a feminine contribution, and its particular nature was said to be characterized by a volatile temperament, a less restrictive libido than was acceptable in Europe, a sybaritic attitude to existence, and an ardent sensuality.

This racial admixture was one of the distinctive characteristics of a society that was known as "Indisch." Different from both native and European modes of existence—though closer to the former than to the latter—it is this "Indisch" society that Daum portrays in his novels. In tone and temperament such colonial societies all resembled one another, no matter where they were. But all considered themselves to be a kind of regional aristocracy above and beyond both the Europeans and the indigenous population. The Indies was no different from colonial Ceylon in the twenties or thirties of the present century, at least the way Michael Ondaatje describes it in his fine memoir:

> Everyone was vaguely related and had Sinhalese, Tamil, Dutch, British and Burgher blood in them going back many generations. There was a large social gap between this circle and the Europeans and English who were never part of the Ceylonese community. The English were seen as transients, snobs and racists, and were quite separate from those who had intermarried and who lived here permanently.[52]

It was in many ways a paradoxical society. I mentioned that the "sultry [black] temptress" of the American South could be easily identified with the colonial *njai*, yet from the point of view of the *pur sang* Dutch society (the *totoks* as they were called), it was the "Indisch" people who were considered passionate sensualists, the stereotype assigned to blacks in the South.[53] This ironic extension is very much part of Daum's portrayal of colonial society. For instance, real Indies colonials are said to be sexually precocious (10.1.72–73; 7:8), more broadminded (9:200; 7:71, 82), and with a more flexible attitude to divorce (7:82). In one novel the admission of an Indies boy to a Dutch household is rejected because, by his mere presence, he would have "corrupted" the morality of the Dutch offspring (10.2.89).

Prejudice was obviously rampant. Social prejudice has been intimated in various contexts, but racial prejudice was far more pernicious. There was the physical and moral superiority the white community felt toward the indigenous peoples of the archipelago (1:6–7, 34; 4:2; 8:103; 6:76; 1:18–9, 61, 122; 10.1.134 and 2.67). Daum made no bones about the plight of the native peoples. In *Abu Bakar*, for instance, one reads:

> They always have to work for others, and everybody speaks evil of them. They're always treated like dogs, and nobody asks what gave them [the Europeans] the right to treat them like that; they always have to be polite and submissive but everybody else treats them insolently; they always have to be satisfied with very little and yet have to part with the greater part of that even; the lowliest European assumes the attitude of a master where they are concerned; they have to be submissive, and if they aren't sufficiently so, it is said to be worse than an insult to be as impolite as that. (10.2.12)

In the same novel the list of insults the *njai* Peraq directs at the *blandas*, the Europeans, is devastating (10.1.138–39).

In psychological terms the fate of the Eurasian, the "Indo," was even worse, because he lacked a clear identity. Reminiscent of the "tragedy of the mulatto" in the South,[54] the Indo who had failed in upward mobility was expropriated from colonial society. The Indos lived in an entirely different world, which was perhaps best described in Victor Ido's novel *De Paupers* (1915) and in the fiction of Tjalie Robinson.[55] Daum also wrote about their plight. In *Abu Bakar* an Indo confesses that though he had a native woman for a mother and looked more Malay than Western, he would prefer death to being put on the same level as a native (10.1.123). *Number Eleven* is Daum's novel that portrays the world of the Indo most comprehensively. He observes the common habit of the white male who, if and when he legitimized his mixed-blood offspring, often picked names that were no more than absurd inversions of his own name, coupled to preposterous first names. Yps for example, is short for Ypsilanti, and her last name is Nesnaj, an inversion of the common Dutch name Jansen (8:8–9). A clerk works in Vermey's office who is "as skinny as a rail, a gray-brown young man, one of those Indo-Europeans who never sweat and always have cold hands, but are usually clever enough." His name is Eresteip, which is the simple Dutch name Pieterse turned around; consequently he is always referred to as the "inverted Pieterse" (8:10–11).

But Indies society found itself similarly treated when it confronted the *totoks* on their own turf in *Negeri Blanda*, or continental Holland. In Holland "Indisch" individuals are simply inferior (10.1.82), and in one Daum novel that takes place in The Hague, an aristocratic lady dismisses them as "those blacks." A perfectly respectable, wealthy, and beautiful Indies society woman is, despite her money, "that black creature" (7:62–63), and when in the same novel the wife of a destitute colonial officer dies—mostly from misery and longing for the Indies—the Dutch women who prepare the corpse for burial find their task "scary" because of the dead woman's "dark hide," which reminds them of the devil, "who's as black as that" (7:102). The colonials' accustomed display of emotion in public—hugging and kissing—was considered immoral by the Dutch (7:9), who felt threatened by what they considered a kind of hedonism, a quality Cash also found characteristic of the old American South. There is a fine satirical scene in Daum's first novel that tellingly informs the reader how petty but also how unaccommodating this gulf was between the Dutch in Europe and the colonial "Indisch" people during the last quarter of the nineteenth century. A colonial couple on leave in Holland shock their hosts by wanting to eat dinner at eight, and by having a drink at noon, laughing out loud, talking vehemently, not going to church on Sunday, walking barefoot ("even women ... and even in front of strange men"), and taking a bath every day (1:251–55). They perceive themselves as strangers in a strange land and feel smothered by a moral and physical claustrophobia. Holland has little to offer these people and Daum sums it up in the fine phrase: "You're soon finished with a Dutch city, even if it is called Amsterdam" (1:254). Colonial high society found the Dutch upper classes implacable. Because she is the daughter of an "Indisch" doctor, Louise Van Velton-Van der Linden, for instance, cannot gain entry to fashionable society in The Hague despite her fabled wealth and beauty. But her former suitor Fournier, a man in everything her inferior, does so very easily simply because he is the scion of an upperclass Dutch family with important connections in the highest circles of government (7:58). Yet another form of reverse prejudice.

Daum, who was never unsure about his allegiances, intimates that the snobbery of the Dutch in Holland was rather hypocritical. "Indies money" was suspect, it "smelled" (10.1.75), but all were willing to profit from rich relations even if, with perfect sanctimoniousness, they did so condescendingly. The Van der Lindens on leave in Holland find their kin

> stiff, dull folks, not to mention narrow-minded and stingy. But they [the Dutch relations] came to visit frequently and gladly drank the doctor's good sherry, loved to smoke his Havanas, were perfectly eager to accept Louise's presents, including those for their wives and children; but not one of them ever thought of paying the Indies family members any other attention than to borrow money from them for an unspecified length of time. This heartless egotism was especially repugnant to Louise. She would have given a present worth a thousand guilders to anyone who, from his or her own free will, presented her child with a doll that could have cost no more than two-and-a-half guilders. But that didn't happen; the 'good' people wouldn't think of it. The Indies shouldn't cost a cent. On the contrary. That was according to Dutch tradition, and that notion had become flesh and blood. (4:189–90)

Daum's colonial world, like Cash's South, is extravagant, ardent and hedonistic—an extroverted world that was the complete antithesis of restrictive Dutch society. And although Daum was never blind to its folly or excesses, his loyalty to colonial Java is forthright and affectionate. The casual hedonism was certainly not anathema to him and he was a master at describing it, for example, with such telling details as the Indies women in The Hague who gamble with dice on the floor because that was more comfortable (7:49); *njai* Yps's plump fingers with "dimples above the invisible knuckles" as a "cachet of laziness" (8:20); Betsy's indolence fostered and encouraged by her *babu* Sarinah (6:34); the peculiar and offensive neatness of a fullblood Dutch women who keeps her house spotless but is secretly pitied for her display of "coolie-work" (6:16–17); or a child's *babu* in Europe who is "sweating from the pain" of wearing shoes for the first time in her life (4:187). In fact, one of Daum's most affecting novels is about the unabashed hedonist *Engineer H. Van Brakel*. Though he is meant to illustrate the always present danger of deterioration and decline, Van Brakel is Daum's most engaging creation and his story Daum's most affectionate. When he is introduced in the first novel of a tetralogy that describes the fortunes of a group of Indies people from various levels of colonial society, there is no doubt about Van

Brakel's proclivities so atypical of continental Dutch ideals. "To make life as pleasant and as easy as possible, that's the *only* ideal. There's nothing else. The Orientals got it right. Loafing in a luxurious environment, beautiful women, fine cooking, delicious drinks, and not to move more than what is agreeable for your body and as an aid for digestion" (3:7–8).

Van Brakel pursues his ideal with genial devotion. He has a good job working as an engineer for the colonial government, a position that guarantees a steady income, and he performs his duties well. He marries Lucie Drütlich, the blond daughter of a German administrator of a coffee plantation. She loves him, is a kind wife and indulgent mother, and knows how to run a colonial household. Despite subsequent tribulations, their marriage is one of the rare successful ones in Daum's fictional world. The engineer has two major faults: liquor and gambling. He spends most of his spare time in the ubiquitous local club and loses great sums of money. His debts finally force him to become unfaithful because he borrows money from an Indies widow, called Du Roy, who coerces him into an affair. Again, there's no ill will here: Van Brakel bumbles into a relationship he neither cherishes nor enjoys, but one that he feels obligated to honor until the predatory widow throws him out. Finally, Van Brakel commits the ultimate sin for a colonial official: he accepts bribes from a Chinese. Gossip finds him out, he is dismissed from the service, works for himself for a while, and finally is reduced to working as a construction foreman, a *mandur*. This was a subordinate position normally held by a native man, and a disgraceful position for a man of Van Brakel's former status.

The novel is a cautionary tale but it is a story more tinged with sadness than with Daum's customary acerbity. Van Brakel is a fool but he is not evil; he simply is not man enough to control the vices he shared with almost all males in colonial society. Lucie and Van Brakel are genuinely fond of each other, and their marriage is secure enough to withstand onslaughts that would have destroyed any other marital relationship in the Indies. It is, of course, also a measure of Daum's novelistic excellence to present his complacent victim as a good-natured slob, but Van Brakel's demise is touching nevertheless.

Engineer H. Van Brakel is unusual in this respect because Daum was a combative realist who scorned sentimentality, though he presented it as an essential element of the society he lived in. That society he saw as one ruled by money, social position, and sensuality. As I have said, like Cash's South it was staunchly paternalistic and had no trouble living with a double standard it exploited habitually. The most interesting aspect of Daum's work is that he subverted this intransigence mercilessly, but what is perhaps more amazing is his sympathy for colonial women. Like Van Brakel, most of Daum's male characters are weak ineffectual men or boring drones enslaved by work. And they worked very hard indeed, often to the exclusion to everything else in their lives. This is a constant theme in colonial fiction.[56] But it is also clear from Daum's work that to be a man was a simple task. One had to be able to drink a great deal, to gamble a lot and for high stakes, and to fight when honor had been compromised. Examples of men ruined by liquor and gambling are too numerous to mention—they are in just about all of Daum's novels. The colonial male's credo was not much different from the one Cash formulated for the South. "Great personal courage, unusual physical powers, the ability to drink a quart of whiskey or to lose the whole of one's capital on the turn of a card without the quiver of a muscle—these [were] at least as important as possessions, and infinitely more important than heraldic crests."[57]

Daum's female characters are far more interesting than his men. In seven of the ten novels the protagonist is a woman who, without ignoring her femininity, exemplifies all the virtues colonial society would normally have attributed to males. Not surprisingly, in eight of the novels the marital alliances are disastrous or fraudulent. In his second novel, *How He Became a Councillor of the Indies*, Daum narrates the career of Kees van den Broek, whose rise to an eminent position in the colonial hierarchy is entirely due to his two wives. A model civil servant (2:8, 225), he is a spineless man. His first wife, Corrie, marries him because she was afraid she was going to remain single (2:22–23) and his second wife, Louise, marries him for purely physical reasons. Neither woman loves him very much but each wants him to succeed in order to improve her own status. They are decisive, even ruthless, ambitious, have violent tempers, and harbor no illusions about either the world or love. Corrie Rivière—an unusual creation for the final quarter of the nineteenth century—hates sex, physical intimacy, pregnancy, and children:[58] "Didn't she have enough of a child in her husband? Heirs? She wished them all to go to the devil. It really wasn't worth the trouble to suffer so much pain and so much grief for a thing like that. She wanted to take care of Kees, but she declined to help his heir into the world. If he wanted it *that* much he could try it himself, as far as she was concerned" (2:63; also 4, 101). When she gives birth to her first child, the all important boy, Corrie bites and scratches her husband (31), and is relieved when the baby subsequently dies (63). With bitter irony, Corrie dies some years later while giving birth to another proper heir, one who lives (119).

As if to emphasize the negative side of vaunted tropical sensuality, Daum introduces Mr. and Mrs. Herwijnen. Herwijnen is an impractical blusterer full of unrealistic ideas who always "has a future [but] never a past" (80). He lives a life of debauchery (17) despite being married to a kind, loving, and loyal woman (81–83) and manages to get rid of her and his children by sending them to Holland on a pretext. This leaves him free to engage a *njai* (155). Daum typifies Herwijnen with what at that time was a daring detail: he presses himself against the attractive and very "Indisch" Mina Jansen who, though she does not make a scene because of her kind feelings for Mrs. Herwijnen, is disgusted by this *kakeh* ("old man") as she calls him (13–14).

The shallow, vainglorious, and specious male world is adroitly manipulated by the two female protagonists. Corrie gets Kees promoted by cooking three "Lucullian" meals for a high Dutch official on tour (38–40; 108–9) while directing her husband's conversation from behind a curtain like a prompter in a theater (40). She is rightly convinced that it is *she* who runs things, who directs life not only for her husband but for her own family as well (103). There is little doubt that in the Rivière family the women are the strong ones (46, 52, 72, 100), surrounded by male mediocrity typified by mother Rivière's remark that "there are already far too many ordinary people in the world" (175).

Daum suggests the inversion of customary gender attributes by the word *kranig* (*brani* in Malay). In his day this was an adjective primarily associated with males, meaning "resolve," "will," "pluck," "spunk," "grit," "guts." *Kranig* is Corrie's favorite word to indicate proper behavior. She recognizes it as one of her own virtues while the word also intimates her identification with masculinity. Pregnancy and childbirth are not kranig (4), but keeping the family's patrician name alive is (5). Drinking champagne in the morning is kranig (5), but suffering from seasickness isn't (69). Kranig is also being able to ride a strong, temperamental horse. Corrie's father presented her husband with Bop, a large black stallion. The horse can't stand Kees and he can't control it, but Corrie loves the animal (1–3). As is often true of weak men, Kees is a bully who takes out his frustrations on those who cannot fight back. When in such a mood he revenges himself on innocent natives (7, 62) and on the horse. After Bop has thrown him, Kees whips both the horse and a Javanese stableboy with enough fury to draw blood. Corrie does not care about the physical condition of either her husband or the servant, but, brimming with tender mercy, she comforts the horse with genuine affection (42–43).

Louise, Kees's second wife, is basically similar to Corrie in terms of her resolute character and decisiveness, except that she does not disdain sex. In fact, she uses her glamour and sex appeal to seduce high officials, obliging them to promote her passive husband who lives, as she puts it, in a world "that reeks of tobacco and pessimism" (252). By managing her body cleverly and by manipulating the colonial male's "sexual vanity" (6:134), Louise succeeds in creating an atmosphere of obligation on the part of her lovers. When Kees finally occupies the highest position he could ever hope to attain, she renounces her ways, becomes a regular churchgoer and proceeds to change the image of the Van den Broek family until it is known as one of Batavia's nicest and most decent households.

Another female character, one who figures prominently in three of Daum's novels, seems to be an amalgamation of Corrie and Louise. Louise van der Linden is also blessed with true grit: like Corrie she is competent, practical, and tenacious, but she is also as alluring and seductive as Louise van den Broek. With the exception of her father, a physician, Louise also finds herself in a world of attenuated males, even if they are sympathetic characters such as Fournier, a lawyer Louise once loved, who was not man enough to surmount her aggressive personality. Fournier is so completely at her mercy that Louise literally orders him to marry her stepdaughter Hortense (4:131,

139, 183, 222). Louise could be said to express Daum's view of the world when it is she, the woman, who rebukes the male for his sentimental illusions about happiness: "You think that happiness is an elephant that will become a hundred years old ...[but] it is a little butterfly that you should grab when you can...but don't hold it too long or it'll die" (4:230). She also voices a discovery about men that was true of Daum's colonial Java and was also a major theme of nineteenth-century European literature: "I thought you were a swallow but I found a house sparrow" (4:231).[59]

It is a measure of Daum's integrity and unusual point of view that he made the Indies woman central in his fiction. In his refusal to sentimentalize her—as the American South did—or to condescend to her, Daum countermanded patriarchal claims. But the illusions shattered by Daum's salubrious realism do not make for oppressive gloom. Daum had a keen sense of the ridiculous and could detect posturing and pomposity no matter how gussied up it was with privilege and pretension. One will find that, besides being critical examinations of colonial society, at least half of his novels are also sexual comedies.

King observed that in the South "the realm of culture, the life of the mind and of sensibility, such as it was, became the province of white women." But this also meant that, "because it was identified with women, culture lacked prestige or public relevance and became crabbed, genteel, and sentimental."[60] The same can be asserted about culture in the colonial Indies. Men were devoted to money, business, gambling, drinking, and male companionship. The usual leveling down to the intellectually lowest common denominator combined with the enormous physical distance between the colonies and Europe to create a cultural wasteland in the Indies. It is true that the area also produced some writers of genius, but they were the exception, not the rule. In an environment that cherished indolence, hedonism, social position, and money, the life of the mind could find little sympathetic response. In *L. Van Velton-Van der Linden*, Daum states that reading material was pretty much restricted to "newspapers, brochures, French novels and financial reports" and that the verb "study" was a word that had been erased from the colonial dictionary (4:137). The French novels he mentions are not French literature but the sentimental kitsch or mild pornography of such writers as Catulle Mendès, who is avidly read by the resident's wife in Couperus's *Hidden Force*. The standard bearer of literature was the *leestrommel*, a tin container that resembled a small suitcase filled with popular magazines. This "reading box" circulated among the European community and was a particular godsend for those people who lived deep in the interior and were devoid of all European intercourse.[61] For those living in relatively large towns the favorite cultural indulgence was creating tableaux vivants, described in detail in Couperus's *Hidden Force*. There were also musical evenings and operas staged with local amateur talent, but in general one can apply Cash's judgment of intellectual life in the Old South to the Indies: it was "a superficial and jejune thing."[62]

Gerard Brom in his study of Indies literature published in 1931 makes it quite plain that this barren waste undeniably existed in Daum's time, and that it remained for most of the colonial era. Brom reports that Daum's work was impossible to find; the Royal Library in Batavia had a complete set of his novels but only because the Justice Department deposited them there in accordance with an administrative regulation. Individual copies were worth their weight in gold. Brom clearly indicts the mercantile spirit for its anti-intellectual bias: "Holland only expected high interest from the Indies, not books." He alleges that in Batavia, which was considered the most "cultured" of all the colonial cities, he found "a definite hatred for anything that so much as smacked of civilization," and that the intellectual could never vie with the officials of the civil service or with the entrepreneurs of private enterprise. Not until 1834 did the first bookshop open for business in the colonial capital, while at the customary auctions for transferred personnel, books fetched lower prices than empty bottles. A doctor from Djokja is quoted as intoning: "Reading? All nonsense. They should print only catalogues and banknotes. Everything else is only useful as waste paper."[63]

And to be sure, one never catches any of Daum's characters involved in anything more taxing than adding up rows of ciphers. Spare time was to be consumed by diversions not mental stimulation. There were, of course, exceptions—one will find some in the anthology in this series—but they are not part of Daum's fictional world. The closest thing to an intellectual is the planter Drossaarts in *From Sugar to Tobacco*: he scares the narrator, James van Tuyll, because he likes to ruminate aloud about the relativity of the world and human actions. He reads Kant (1:66), is cynical about human motives, white marriages (205), and the life of a planter, and for the most part impresses the narrator as a devilish bohemian.

A Western reader might assume that because of the cultural destitution the colonial upper classes would turn to worshipping the ineffable majesty of tropical nature, or profit from the refined and ancient Javanese civilization, which had its own music, shadow plays, puppet theater, and dance. But this was hardly the case. In Daum's novels, nature is only indicated in perfunctory terms to present place and time or to show its implacable disdain for human folly. Consider, for instance, the superb last sentence of *Number Eleven*: "In the Indies the trees are always green." Appreciation for sophisticated Javanese civilization was only to be found in the work of a rare scholar or official, as with Raffles, the British ruler during the Napoleonic era. To have been a sensitive person in nineteenth-century Java, especially a sensitive male, must have been a cruel fate in what a French observer characterized as "une société sans art, sans haute culture, sans religion, sans idéal."[64] He would have commiserated with the despair and loneliness of the Southern poet Sidney Lanier, who could not find any encouragement for his literary endeavors, and who wrote to a friend in 1875: "I could never describe to you what a mere drought and famine my life has been . . . pretty much the whole of life has been merely notdying." Lanier's hatred of Southern commercialism matches Multatuli's: "A man cannot walk down a green alley of the woods, in these days, without unawares getting his mouth and nose and eyes covered with some web or other that Trade [or Multatuli's Droogstoppel in *Max Havelaar*] has stretched across, to catch some gain or other. . . . You know what the commercial spirit is: you remember that Trade killed Chivalry and now sits in the throne."[65]

The sense of intellectual inferiority was only enhanced by a defiant provincialism, which enjoyed being the poor relation of European cultural life. Du Perron's polemics with Zentgraaff, a colonial journalist with the subtlety of a Neanderthal and the mentality of a rustic boor, would provide a good example of the shallowness of the common colonial mind.[66] Indeed, one could say with King that "to be an intellectual ... was to talk to oneself or at best a close group of sympathizers—or to be set upon as an arrant traitor for daring to suggest that intellect might be used for something other than the exigencies of regional self-defense."[67] Such a criticism would have been applauded not only by Multatuli and Du Perron, but also by Van der Tuuk, Walraven, Junghuhn, even Bas Veth—all authors included in the anthology of this series. But although few knew such mental isolation, the quotidian loneliness was as debilitating in the Indies as it was in the Old South. Most people, particularly planters, had to find a way of coping with solitude in an unfeeling if not hostile environment. In *Ups and Downs*, Geber mournfully recalls his existence as a "monotonous and isolated life as if ... exiled from the world, deprived of so much that a great civilized European society had to offer." There is no doubt that this feeling of psychological and spiritual malaise contributes to his decision to commit suicide. Daum is sympathetic to the colonial's plight, one that the home country could not comprehend: "One should not have to point out to [the Dutch in Holland] that many of these [Indies] people have led a tedious and melancholy life in remote places year after year, almost entirely shut off from all European intercourse—because they wouldn't believe it anyway" (7:15). The onerous boredom could be devastating, as James van Tuyll in *From Sugar to Tobacco* comes to realize: "I vegetated like a plant on that tedious plantation, without any diversion except for an occasional hasty visit by a European. Ladies? I would have given ten guilders just to *see* one. And as for Drossaarts, not one European female would ever cross his threshold. Was this life? If I had been an ordinary clerk in Holland, I would have enjoyed more of life than I did here, in this miserable hick town" (1:83).

But the ones who suffered the most were the women. "Life went on as usual: monotonous, with few pleasures, restricted to a small circle. A traveling show every so often that, while charging expensive admission, had its worn-out actors perform the caricature of an opera in the local theater, or the small group of dilettantes who could offer little more than avocation and good will. Life's diapason had fallen so low that one became either indifferent or began to complain. Corrie van den Broek was terribly bored. Something had to happen to stop that deadly

depression" (2:101). One remedy for this intellectual and emotional quarantine was what amounted to an almost pathological
interest in the lives of other people. Its physical expression was
gossip, the infamous *kabar angin* or "news wind." One will
find countless examples of this grapevine in nearly all of Daum's
fiction because this sometimes deadly plant grew as abundantly
and tenaciously as tropical nature. In *From Sugar to Tobacco*,
Daum mentions that gossip traveled far more efficiently than
any other form of communication available at the time (1:130),
and presents in the same novel an example of colonial scan-
dalmongering (1:8–10) that is quite as malevolent as the one
provided in the seventeenth chapter of the present text. In
Guna-Guna, Betsy confesses that gossiping is her favorite pas-
time, particularly if it is about sex. Women visited each other
in the morning to review the day's news. Sometimes it was
serious but more often it was comical. They informed each other
"if a new scandal had happened somewhere, or retold an old
one accompanied by 'you remember how,' like an umpteenth
printing of a book newly revised by the author and provided
with fine illustrations" (6:136–67).

Nor was this pervasive malversation restricted to gender.
Every club had its *kletstafel*, the table where one wiled away
the evening hours yacking with other men. Swapping stories
in an entertaining fashion was a highly prized ability, and it
has been repeatedly asserted that colonial literature grew out
of the Indies' genius for conversation.[68] The colonial Indies was
an oral society, partly due, as Allen Tate noted about the South,
to the fact that it was "an extraverted mind not much given to
introspection"; "consummate story-tellers and rhetoricians,
ante-bellum Southerners had been incapable of 'critical de-
tachment.' "[69] Cash listed rhetoric as one of the most significant
patterns of Southern life: "a passion and a primary standard of
judgment." He defined rhetoric as "a gorgeous, primitive art,
addressed to the autonomic system and not to the encephalon
... dear to the heart of the simple man everywhere."[70] Cash
obviously knew that talk is cheap, that it can disguise a lack of
will and energy and can foreclose on action. It is the perfect
screen for weakness. Not surprisingly, the generally infirm
males of Daum's world are good talkers. *Engineer H. van Brakel*
presents Geerling, a young man with little character, a prissy
fop who dresses outrageously, a pedantic fellow with "radical

ideas," whose "conversation was worthwhile" (5:31). Geerling's prototype, in *From Sugar to Tobacco*, is Charltje, an utterly useless parasite but a great drinker and an even better talker, similarly full of "progressive" ideas: "the words flowed over his lips like water through a pipe" (1:225). In *Number Eleven*, George Vermey, who abandons his *njai* Yps in order to acquire a proper wife, is admired by his drinking buddies for his ability to tell a juicy story.

> But when their friend began to talk about what he called "the scenes with Yps," their interest perked up. At first he hadn't planned to fantasize or lie, which is why he began simply enough with the story about the letter, and he described how she had looked at him "with eyes like fiery coals" and then "had run away." But this met with so much success that he, to maintain his reputation and also being the hero of the adventure, couldn't leave it at that. Well, the subject had occupied him for a long time already, even before it finally happened, and, furthermore, his rich and varied experience was at his disposal. And in this manner it became a piquant story, spiced and souped up according to the Indies recipe. One couldn't get a taste of what had really happened between Yps and him, just as you can't really taste rice while eating *rijsttafel*. His friends looked at him admiringly. (8:23)

And, finally, the insalubrious Charles Herwijnen referred to before is a windbag of the worst kind. He conceals his mean character, base motives, and self-indulgent weakness behind a fume of words: "he became angry; he complained about a lack of cooperation and support; he began to orate and even managed to become tragic" (2:25).

Daum himself was known as a great talker and teller of tales. His daughter recalled how he would come home from his newspaper around five, take a bath, relax on his veranda, and tell his family stories from his day at work. She adds that "while talking and narrating, various possibilities for his books would emerge; many ideas and details are due to these domestic chats."[71] Besides, journalism is conversation printed, and, like the verbal company one keeps, it too can vary from babbling to eloquence. Journalism in the colonies was far livelier and less formal than in Holland and allowed an individual to develop a personal style.[72] Daum simply transferred this literary self-determination to his fictional narratives, thereby providing additional proof of what I've argued elsewhere to be the unorthodox excellence of Dutch colonial literature.

Because he was conversant with colonial society, the greater part of Daum's novels is taken up by dialogue. His fictional discourse has remained remarkably fresh and ingenious, perhaps due to his unaffected style and natural ease. His style complemented his demand for realism, by which he generally meant lack of artifice, presentation of the truth about social intercourse, and the recording of the reality of life without dissembling its true motives.[73] Daum was praised by a contemporary as a "Dutch Daudet"[74] but it seems more accurate to dub him the Thackeray of Dutch colonial literature. By this I mean that he was primarily interested in people and in the stories they could tell (as is the journalist), and had little patience for intellectual woolgathering, decorative romanticism, or a bloodless morality. As a result, the integrity of his art makes him still eminently readable and the picture he drew of late nineteenth-century colonial society has been attested to time and again for its honesty and accuracy.

The colonial world of the Indies that has been adumbrated in terms of Daum's fiction and with reference to the old American South harbored paradox at its core: indulgence and immoderation were only achieved at the cost of loneliness, exile, and emotional as well as intellectual deprivation. In economic terms, a planter's life was subject to the insecurity of overseas markets, while the life of a colonial official was never without the presentiment of rebellion and the fear that his usurpation would be declared illegal. The colonial yearned for the sophistication of Europe only to find it disdainful of his provincialism, hypocritical about stealing his wealth, and claustrophobic in a physical and psychological sense. Daum's colonial had not heard about historical necessity or about the instructive parallel of the imperial entrepeneur's demise in other regions of the world. Nonetheless, he knew on a personal level that colonial success was surrounded by failure and was potentially always subject to disintegration.

Daum was neither a historian nor a philosopher, but he was a keen observer and an astute psychologist. It has been said that he was "obsessed" with the decline and decay of Indies society.[75] Brom, the most important critic of colonial literature prior to Du Perron and Nieuwenhuys, assailed Daum for his unrelieved pessimism.[76] The latter is incorrect because of its excessiveness—which was a curiously Indies affliction—and it shows that Brom had no sense of humor, could not appreciate irony, and did not recognize Daum's sympathetic, albeit critical, understanding of his characters. He had not sensed Daum's intuitive knowledge that societies like the colonial one and the Old South were subject to decay.[77] "Decline was an integral part of the Southern family romance," King writes quite plainly, adding the incontrovertible fact that much of Southern fiction—Faulkner's for instance—concerns itself with "the gradual decline in energy and will."[78]

This surrender of the will and the blunting of energy was a nightmare the colonials feared they would one day wake up to as reality. It would mean relinquishing occidental control, submitting to lassitude and elemental matter, yielding, as already noticed, to the irrational element often associated with native life and the feminine archetype. It is also a theme central to much modern fiction and a condition of some importance to modern philosophy. Ennui, revulsion, and despair have become the shibboleths of modern literature, but one will find them to be of no less interest in colonial literature. In the present novel, for instance, the disintegration of Geber bears some resemblance to the existential dread experienced by Roquentin in Sartre's *Nausea*.

Before his penultimate novel, Daum had presented his readers with other versions of this decline. He wrote earlier of the engaging erosion of *Engineer H. Van Brakel*, the debacle of the decadent aristocrat Van Leeuwendaal in *The Van der Lindens* and *Indies People in Holland*, the moral bankruptcy of Kees van den Broek in *How He Became a Councillor of the Indies*, the indolence (at least from a European viewpoint) of Drossaarts, the sugar planter who is the only "intellectual" in Daum's fiction, and the degradation, in the same novel, of Mrs. Van Heert. But one should never forget that Daum was chiefly a teller of tales and that he refrained from loading his fiction with extraneous intellectual baggage. The following scene from *Engineer H. Van Brakel*, describing the end of a binge shared by the engineer and his father-in-law, is not only compositionally perfect, but it also foreshadows the final stage of Van Brakel's retrogression from successful official to alcoholic flunky of a cobbler and opium smuggler.

> The two men slept in the chaise longues; the old one quiet and peacefully; he'd slept a thousand times in a chair like this when he was still living in the country; the younger one was snoring loudly. Both faces were swollen and red from drinking and shone in the sunlight as if they'd been covered with grease. A small ray from a beam of light created in the brandy carafe's center a beautifully clear, golden star that sparkled and glittered with a gay and lively change of color as the result of even the slightest movement.
>
> A native servant crept up softly on his bare feet; he went onto the small veranda, removed the bottle and glasses, brought them for the moment behind the low wall that separated the front from the back yard, and raised the carafe to his unwashed lips.
>
> It seemed to Van Brakel that he was going blind when he, upon opening his eyes, looked straight into the sun. (5:203)

Or Daum can mark it in purely physical terms as an ironic comment on Herwijnen's grandiose illusions:

> While he slid back deeper into the ample easy chair, with the empty champagne glass in his hand, and while in his imagination loomed up gigantic agricultural projects that produced millions in profits, that had been constructed, designed and run in a scientific manner— while thus occupied, she [Herwijnen's wife] looked at him with pity. He had aged so much. How could she ever have known that the young, handsome man full of life who had asked successfully for her hand could change that much in a relatively short time? Had that been the same person as the one collapsed there in the chair, with the deep lines in his emaciated face, with his few, sparse gray hairs, and his wrinkled, as if withered hands? (2:82)

But Geber, in what is, arguably, Daum's best fiction, is the most memorable embodiment of colonial declension. Geber's fate is more significant than that of Van Brakel because Daum insinuated a dimension that encompasses far more than purely colonial causes. One should note, for instance, that the reasons for Geber's depression are contradictory, if not absurd. He is a wealthy planter of distinction, handsome, congenial, and not without intelligence. "Please understand," he said, "that the usual reasons don't apply to me. I've not been hit by disasters, have no worries, no debts or grief." Yet he is a man who is weary of life. When he becomes overtired his nerves go awry but his mind becomes sharper. The notion of suicide represents itself during an enchanting tropical night at sea. His wife, Rose, is repulsive to him, and he rekindles an old affair by making love to his wife's aunt in his own house during a two-day party that has brought all his wife's family to his plantation for a celebration. He is riddled with doubt amidst the affluence of his life; he has a feeling that his existence is replete, Sartre's *de trop*, "a horror of boring redundancies," and that he is "shackled by life and his circumstances." Life has lost meaning for him and he no longer feels essential either to himself or to others, including Clara, his recaptured love. While in despair he finds himself alone and vulnerable, "facing the world like an unarmed combatant." His nihilism is best expressed by his observation that life is like a house where one lives, but where one does not remain when it no longer pleases. Though in some ways kin to Daum's typically weak males, Geber is unlike them when he acts upon this insight with courage and consistency. In fact, by committing suicide Geber exercises the notion of modern man's final and ultimate nobility: the existential freedom to voice a nay.

What Geber rejects is the pointlessness of humanity's antlike labor, a tedious effort without meaning. What he experiences is remarkably close to Sartre's nausea. "And for what [all his money]? What was the use? At home a mechanical life of indifference; a wife who would always remain a stranger to him, even if she had twenty of his children. He could trudge through life like just another kind of coolie, civilized and well off!" He also knows the futility of alternate courses, realizing, for instance, that exchanging Clara for Rose would not make any fundamental difference. Daum's suggestion of an inherited pathology seems like a red herring, as if he recoiled from his own creation that implied more than his nineteenth-century audience would find acceptable.

Geber's decline has greater implications than Van Brakel's. The latter is due entirely to his weak personality and the two nemeses of colonial life: alcohol and gambling. But Geber's tragedy is only more absurd because of its colonial setting. The pungent tropics have become fusty; the extravagant hedonism is proven to be trivial materiality; the rhetoric has been silenced by the "cold little 'o' " of the barrel of a gun; and the salubrious physicality of the tropics has become the cause for existential revulsion. The anguish Geber experiences is not particular to the colonial tropics, although it may have been exacerbated by the hyperbolic attributes present. It is profoundly disturbing because, when this man finally comes to terms with himself, the only meaning he derives from the encounter is the consolation of death. Perhaps this is also the reason why the (omitted) second half of the present novel is glaringly inferior to the first. The trenchant fate of this lone individual is so uncompromising in its honesty that the almost perfunctory ups and downs of the second volume pale by comparison. Geber's death is too irrevocably an end, anything after that can only seem like an anticlimax.

The critical reputation of Daum's work has had its own irony. Popular in Java during the last ten years of his life, Daum was quickly forgotten after 1900. When he published his first novels he was favorably reviewed in Holland by an influential critic, Lodewijk van Deyssel, who later turned against him because he felt that Daum was too realistic. After the turn of the century there were some attempts to revive interest in Daum's work, for example by Henri Borel, Jan Prins, and Brom (with his back-handed compliments), and especially by the two most influential critics of the twenties and thirties, Du Perron and Ter Braak. They had a high opinion of Daum's work and they praised it not only for its narrative excellence but also, if not primarily, for its authenticity and realism. In the sixties Rob Nieuwenhuys wrote a long essay about Daum, calling him one of the finest novelists of *tempo dulu*. Daum's work had run the gamut from being considered too realistic to being seen as a storehouse for nostalgic recollection.[79]

Tempo dulu, the Malay phrase for time past, is in Holland a metonymy for its colonial past and for the literature it produced about what Tennyson called "days that are no more." The irony is that Daum's work does not look back to a past nor does it look forward to a future. The ten novels are firmly planted in the present. Daum was never a writer of cultural melancholia or a "passatist," as Couperus liked to call himself. To enlist Daum into the ranks of the memorialists one has to enlarge his undeniable affection for colonial society and reduce his robust criticism and redirect his irony. Yet we also found some attitudes in his work that, though they were for Daum a present danger, could be used against the forces of progress and historical necessity, which, after all, were the demise of the colonial Indies.

The literature of *tempo dulu*, that is to say not the texts that chronicle an era but those that recollect with elegiac yearning, bears a family resemblance to that written about the American South.[80] It too looked from the inconstant present back to the grace of a past that was a better and heroic time summed up in the phrase "something great was accomplished there" ("daar werd wat groots verricht").[81] When the colonials were faced with the evil days of postwar Europe they too, like many Southerners, were "filled with an immense regret and nostalgia; yearning backward toward its past with passionate longing."[82] Like Isadora Duncan they saw "only the ideal," but also like her they knew that "no ideals have ever been fully successful on this earth."[83]

The notion of the colonial Indies in this kind of writing was, as was also perceived about the South, "a sensuous image, a fantasy construct, grasped by feeling not by thought."[84] The sensibility one encounters is naive rather than hypocritical; it feels rather than thinks. Akin to Cash's Southern mind, it is an "impulsive force" that prefers sensuality, concreteness, hedonism, and violence. Mesmerized by memory, it would like to overcome time by stilling it, as if the repetition of desire can deny reality to privation.

Allen Tate admitted that the characteristic attitude of the Southern authors derived from "an extraverted mind not much given to introspection."[85] That temperament was reactionary and regressive in the sense that it preferred to tend the grave of the past in the house of the present. It searched the lost horizons of mind and soul for a restorative. It is in fact, as I have argued elsewhere, very much like modern romanticism, an imagination that ruefully endures a "separation between thought and feeling, intellect and emotion, tradition and energy."[86] The writers of *tempo dulu* would have recognized as kin the group of Southern writers from the twenties and thirties known as "the Agrarians" or "Regionalists."[87] Like them, they were fugitives from another era at bay in a world they never made. They too would have reasserted the legend of the fabled Indies, to admit once more to "the old certainties" of an arcadian aristocracy, to insist on individualism over democracy, and to defend a defiant parochialism against the egalitarian domination of international modernism. And one will find that in the final analysis the apologists of *tempo dulu* believed in the same virtues Cash considered the best of the Old South: "honor, courage, generosity, amiability, and courtesy."[88]

A Note on This Text

Ups and Downs of Life in the Indies was chosen for inclusion in this series not only because it might be Daum's best work, but also for some practical reasons. An author like Daum who had a genius for the peculiar rhythms of an oral culture is very difficult to translate and will inevitably lose a great deal. Furthermore, of his ten novels, two (*Abu Bakar* and *Indies People in Holland*) are too specialized for our present purposes, while the two novels about the Van der Lindens are his least satisfactory, though they also contain some fine passages. His first two efforts, *From Sugar to Tobacco* and *How He Became a Councillor of the Indies*, would do very nicely except that they are so completely the products of Indies speech that the necessary explication would ruin their originality. Daum's best books—*Engineer H. van Brakel, Guna-Guna, Number Eleven,* and *Ups and Downs*—present their own problems. *Guna-Guna* was rejected because it would overlap with Couperus's *Hidden Force*, already published in this series. *Number Eleven* primarily explores the world of the Indo and was therefore judged too narrow an interpretation of the colonial world. *Engineer H. Van Brakel,* however, was seriously considered. It is a fine novel and answers to most of the demands of this project. Unfortunately, the symbolic impact of Van Brakel's deterioration is contained in the final two pages by juxtaposing a Dutch working song with one in Malay. Satisfactory equivalents could not be found, and the ending therefore loses all its power and beauty. On the other hand, the first half of *Ups and Downs* is the most accessible of Daum's fiction, is tightly written, and, though colonial society is present in full force, is distinguished by Geber's story, which lifts the book to a more universal level, thereby overcoming historical limitations and regional peculiarities.

After all, presenting literary excellence is one of the criteria this series of Dutch colonial literature also hopes to fulfill.

E. M. Beekman

Notes to the Introduction

1   There is no standard edition of Daum's work. Because I am using an assortment of editions, I have listed them here chronologically. Numbered references in the text correspond to this list.

1. *From Sugar to Tobacco (Uit de Suiker in de Tabak)*: feuilleton, 1883–84; first printing, 1885; reprint ed., 's-Gravenhage: Thomas & Eras, 1977.

2. *How He Became a Councillor of the Indies (Hoe hij Raad van Indië werd)*: feuilleton, 1884–85; first printing, 1888; reprint ed., 's-Gravenhage: Thomas & Eras, 1978.

3. *The Van der Lindens (De Van der Linden's c.s.)*: feuilleton, 1885; first printing, 1889; reprint ed., 's-Gravenhage: Thomas & Eras, 1978.

4. *L. Van Velton-Van der Linden (L. van Velton-van der Linden)*: feuilleton, 1885–86; first printing, 1886; reprint ed. in the same volume as 3, but with separate pagination.

5. *Engineer H. Van Brakel (H. van Brakel, Ing. B.O.W.)*: feuilleton, 1886; first printing, 1890; reprint ed., Amsterdam: Querido, 1982.

6. *Guna-Guna (Goena-Goena)*: feuilleton, 1887; first printing, 1889; reprint ed., Amsterdam: Querido, 1980.

7. *Indies People in Holland (Indische mensen in Holland)*: feuilleton, 1888; first printing, 1890; reprint ed., Amsterdam: Querido, 1963.

8. *Number Eleven (Nummer Elf)*: feuilleton, 1889; first printing, 1893; reprint ed., 's-Gravenhage: Thomas & Eras, 1981.

9. *Ups and Downs of Life in the Indies (Ups en downs in het Indische leven)*: feuilleton, 1890; first printing, 1892; reprint ed. (of only the first volume), 's-Gravenhage: Thomas & Eras, 1977.

10. *Abu Bakar (Aboe Bakar)*: feuilleton, 1893; first printing, 1894; reprint ed., 's-Gravenhage: Thomas & Eras, 1980. This work was originally in two volumes, now reprinted in one volume with separate pagination. My references in the text list both 10 and the separate volume number.

Biographical information is based on the introduction to the various editions of Daum's work, by Gerard Termorshuizen and Rob Nieuwenhuys. Other sources are Termorshuizen, "P. A. Daum, journalist van Tempo Doeloe," in *Engelbewaarder Winterboek* (Amsterdam: De Engelbewaarder, 1978), pp. 81–91, which is followed by Daum's fine description of a public hanging (pp. 93–97); Corine Spoor, "Hoe journalist Paatje Daum romanschrijver Maurits op de vingers keek," *De Tijd*, 2 January 1981, pp. 24–28; Nieuwenhuys, "Maurits, romanschrijver van tempo doeloe," in *Tussen twee vaderlanden* (Amsterdam: Van Oorschot, 1967), pp. 67–100. Gerard Termorshuizen, who is writing a doctoral dissertation on Daum's work, recently published an article on *From Sugar to Tobacco* ("Daum contra de dubbele moraal. Maatschappijkritiek in *Uit de suiker in de tabak*," *Indische Letteren* 1, no. 1 [March 1986]: 13–28). Termorshuizen makes some remarks similar to my discussion of the role of women in Daum's fiction.

2   Nieuwenhuys, *Tussen twee vaderlanden*, p. 10.

3   6:vi.

4   Quoted by Termorshuizen in *Engelbewaarder Winterboek*, p. 85. As is understandable of a man who had to write so much in so short a time, Daum's style sometimes leaves something to be desired. But I have not "edited" it. This, and, with the exception of the present novel, all subsequent translations are mine.

5   This illness was most likely a form of dysentery that often caused a liver abscess. See E. H. Hermans, *Gezondheidsleer voor Nederlandsch-Indië* (Amsterdam: Meulenhoff, 1925), pp. 146–47.

6   2:3–4. Nieuwenhuys, *Tussen twee vaderlanden*, pp. 87–89; E. Du Perron, *Verzameld Werk*, 7 vols. (Amsterdam: Van Oorschot, 1955–59), 7:135–38.

7   Nieuwenhuys, *Tussen twee vaderlanden*, p. 89.

8   Du Perron, *Werk*, 7:135.

9   Termorshuizen quoted by Spoor, "Hoe journalist Paatje Daum," p. 26.

10   In writing of the American South, I am primarily relying on two works: W. J. Cash, *The Mind of the South* (1941; reprint ed., New York: Random House, Vintage Books, 1960); Richard H. King, *The Cultural Awakening of the American South, 1930–1955* (1980; reprint ed., New York: Oxford University Press, 1982). Other sources are mentioned where applicable.

11   Samuel Eliot Morison, *The Oxford History of the American People* (New York: Oxford University Press, 1965), p. 502. Some other observations by Morison on this page can be applied to the Indies colonials: the description of the Southern aristocrat, and his view of the planters as self-made, hard-working men who lived simple lives. Morison's description of the hard life of the planter's wife would match that of an Indies woman, and his sketch of the "crackers" somewhat resembles the Indos (502–3, 504).

12   Bertram Wyatt-Brown, *Southern Honor: Ethics and Behavior in the Old South* (New York: Oxford University Press, 1983).

13   Multatuli, *Volledig Werk*, ed. Garmt Stuiveling, 13 vols. (Amsterdam: Van Oorschot, 1973–81), 9:148 and 172. See also *Brieven van Multatuli, Bijdragen tot de kennis van zijn leven*, ed. Mevr. Douwes Dekker, 10 vols. (Amsterdam: W. Versluys, 1891–96), 10:216.

14   See Multatuli, *Max Havelaar* (1860), trans. Roy Edwards (Amherst: University of Massachusetts Press, 1982), pp. 185–86. For Scott, see Hendrik Vissink, *Scott and His Influence on Dutch Literature* (Zwolle: W.J. Berends, 1922).

15   See E. M. Beekman, "Dutch Colonial Literature: Romanticism in the Tropics," *Indonesia*, no. 34 (October 1982): 34–35.

16   Cash, *Mind of the South*, p. 32.

17   Nieuwenhuys, *Tussen twee vaderlanden*, p. 49.

18   Harry J. Benda, "The Pattern of Administrative Reforms in the Closing Years of Dutch Rule in Indonesia," *Journal of Asian Studies* 25, no. 4 (August 1966): 592, 591.

19   Nieuwenhuys, *Tussen twee vaderlanden*, pp. 8–9.

20   Cash, *Mind of the South*, p. 113.

21   Nieuwenhuys, *Tussen twee vaderlanden*, p. 49.

22   Cash, *Mind of the South*, p. 35.

23   Quoted by Benda, "Pattern of Administrative Reforms," p. 592.

24   Quoted by Nieuwenhuys, *Tussen twee vaderlanden*, p. 14; see also pp. 13–15.

25   W. F. Wertheim, *Indonesian Society in Transition* (The Hague and Bandung: W. van Hoeve Ltd., 1956), pp. 101, 98, 99.

26   Cash, *Mind of the South*, p. 163.

27   C. Vann Woodward, *Origins of the New South* (Baton Rouge: Louisiana State University Press, 1951), p. 314 (his chapter entitled "The Colonial Economy" is on pp. 291–320). See also King, *Cultural Awakening*, p. 298 n. 12.

28   In an interview published in the *New York Times Book Review*, January 9, 1977, p. 22.

29   King, *Cultural Awakening*, p. 26.

30   Tate quoted in ibid., p. 100.

31   Cash, *Mind of the South*, pp. 439–40.

32   Nieuwenhuys, *Tussen twee vaderlanden*, p. 64.

33   King, *Cultural Awakening*, pp. 34–35.

34   Ibid., p. 34.

35   Ibid., p. 27.

36   Cash, *Mind of the South*, p. 51.

37   How true this was can be ascertained by a quote from a little book about servants, a text that would be quite offensive to modern sensibilities. The child born in the Indies of European parents "is not the one who came but the one who was born here. . . . And he won't be a stranger in the servant quarters where he is entering an alien, forbidden world . . . but he'll be welcome and feel that he is part of it. . . . He will learn words there that his parents will never know, eat and drink things that his parents will never taste. . . . The servants will have far fewer secrets for him than is the case with their master and lady, they will explain and tell him things about themselves and their thoughts the way they explain or tell them to their own children. Part of his day is spent among them, and when he has become an adult, the main building, the yard, and the servant quarters will be as one to him: his home in the Indies" (M. H. Székely-Lulofs, *Onze bedienden in Indië* [Deventer: W. van Hoeve, n.d.], pp. 79–80).

38   G.J. Resink, "Baboe Han," in *Maatstaf* 9, no. 3 (June 1961): 192.

39   Rob Nieuwenhuys, *Komen en blijven. Tempo doeloe—een verzonken wereld. Fotografische documenten uit het oude Indië 1870–1920* (Amsterdam: Querido, 1982), p. 129.

40   Rob Nieuwenhuys, "Het Indische kind dat ik was en ben," in *Rob Nieuwenhuys: Leven tussen twee vaderlanden* (Amsterdam: De Engelbewaarder, 1982), pp. 18–19. I have kept the peculiarities of the original text which does not use our customary typography. *Sirih* refers to the betel chaw which, together with all the other ingredients mentioned, was chewed by both women and men. *Selematan* is a religious offering that includes food. The very particular way in which true Indies people fondled each other is described in Lin Scholte, *Takdiran en andere verhalen* (Amsterdam: Querido, 1977), pp. 21–23. A kiss was not like one in the Western sense; called a "kiss jawa," it was more of a sniffing, an inhaling of the other person's odor. There was also a great deal of tactile contact, including special ways of kneading and pinching the loved one's flesh or skin. Hence meeting a loved one was a very sensual affair, at least for women, but one without sexual overtones, as would have been assumed in Europe.

41   See Nieuwenhuys, *Komen en blijven*, p. 134.

42   Du Perron, *Werk*, 7:137.

43   Nieuwenhuys, *Tussen twee vaderlanden*, pp. 18–19.

44   R. Nieuwenhuys, *Trade World and Worldtrade* (Rotterdam: Internatio, 1963), pp. 80–81.

45   See, for instance, Fraser Harrison, *The Dark Angel: Aspects of Victorian Sexuality* (New York: Universe Books, 1977), pp. 7–8.

46   Scholte, *Takdiran*, pp. 22–23.

47   Wertheim, *Indonesian Society in Transition*, p. 136. Javanese aristocracy was also patriarchal, but for the common population, allegiance was most closely to the mother. The father represented *bangsa*, which means something like "kind," "sort," "rank," but the mother stood for affinity. This general sentiment is expressed in the Malay proverb: "When you marry off a woman you gain a child, when you marry off a man, you lose a child." Quoted in J. Th. Koks, *De Indo* (Amsterdam: H. J. Paris, 1931), p. 41.

48   Michael Ondaatje, *Running in the Family* (New York: W. W. Norton, 1982), p. 53. This is a very fine and beautifully written memoir by the son of the Ceylonese equivalent of the "Indisch" society in colonial Java. There was quite a lot of Dutch influence in Ceylon, as is seen in the names of Ceylonese upper society: Van Langenbergs, De Mels, Batholomeusz (p. 40), and De Vos (119). See also p. 64 and witness Ondaatje's own name.

49   King, *Cultural Awakening*, pp. 35, 187–88, 37.

50   Daum uses here the untranslatable Dutch expression *zuurbier*, literally "sour beer," to indicate a "sour" or sad future. Once it also referred to a daughter who was older than twenty-five and not likely to get married; the correct expression for such a woman was "een vaatje zuur bier," or a barrel of sour beer. This was incorporated in the Dutch proverb: "een huis vol dochters is een kelder vol zuur bier," or, a house filled with daughters is like a cellar filled with sour beer.

51   In the original "buiten bezwaar." In Daum's time *bezwaar* often referred to a financial burden, hence the current expression in the Indies: "buiten bezwaar van den Lande" which, literally translated, means "outside of the nation's

obligation," that is to say, a profit made that the government couldn't touch. This is just one example of how much ones loses when translating Daum.

52 Ondaatje, *Running in the Family*, p. 41.

53 Myra Jehlen, *Class and Character in Faulkner's South* (New York: Columbia University Press, 1976), p. 85.

54 King, *Cultural Awakening*, p. 282.

55 Victor Ido was the pseudonym of Hans van de Wall (1869–1948), who was an Indo himself. His main work (*De Paupers* [1915; reprint ed. 's-Gravenhage: Thomas & Eras, 1978]) was based on personal experience. Tjalie Robinson was the pseudonym of Jan Boon (1911–74), who also used the pseudonym of Vincent Mahieu. He too was an Indo. He wrote some very fine stories about Indo life in Jakarta which are utterly untranslatable because of the particular Indo dialect he used. The best collection is *Piekerans van een straatslijper* ('s-Gravenhage: Moesson, 1965). A good study of the Indo question can be found in Koks, *De Indo*.

56 See, for instance, Louis Couperus's novel *The Hidden Force*, published in this series. See also Couperus, *Oostwaarts*, in *Verzameld Werk*, 12 vols. (Amsterdam: Van Oorschot, 1953–57), 12:262–63, 275, 285, 344–45, 347, 360, 387.

57 Cash, *Mind of the South*, p. 39. There was no real aristocracy in the colonial Indies, nor was there one in the Old South (pp. 63–65). Some genuine Dutch aristocrats did go to the Indies, but they were exceptions to the rule. And yet, within the history of the Dutch colonial Indies that was, after all, three and a half centuries long, one can speak of something approaching it, perhaps a "bourgeois aristocracy" as Carl Bridenbaugh described the planters of the Chesapeake Bay area in eighteenth-century colonial America. Certainly Jan Pieterszoon Coen (1587–1629), the founder of the Dutch colonial empire in Indonesia, was anything but an aristocrat. Yet what one could describe as a "colonial aristocracy" did exist. It was a landed gentry with agrarian fortunes established primarily in the eighteenth century. Their history is too long and complicated to be discussed, but it is a fascinating one. Most of this gentry were true individualists, some were genuinely odd, all were rich. But this was a small group and, as if to underscore my contentions in this essay, most of the families on Java intermarried or became kin in some manner or other, and there were a surprising number of mixed-blood children who were legitimized and shared the wealth. An oblique way of gaining insight in that world is by considering their houses or estates in or around Batavia when it was still a small and pastoral community. Four such houses are described in V.I. van de Wall, *Indische Landhuizen en hun Geschiedenis* ("Koninklijk Bataviaasch Genootschap van Kunsten en Wetenschappen") (Batavia: G. Kolff, 1932). One will find descriptions of such families as Van Riemsdijk, Ament, De Klerk, Siberg, Poelman, and others. The book includes a biography of the legendary "Major Jantje" whose real name was Augustijn Michiels, a self-made man as rich as Croesus of mixed-blood parentage (he was a Mardijker) and perhaps the epitome of the eighteenth-century Dutch colonial nabob. Through his daughter, the Menu family became associated with his name. A descendant was E. Du Perron, one of the foremost colonial writers, who is represented in this series by his novel *Country of Origin*. Bridenbaugh's study—*Myths & Realities: Societies of the Colonial South* (1952;

reprint ed., New York: Atheneum, 1965)—demonstrates that the colonial planters' mode of life persisted for the greater part of the nineteenth century in the South. His findings are remarkably similar to the ones presented in this essay about the Dutch colonials in Java during the same century.

Another rich mine of information on these early figures is the major study by the great historian of Java: F. de Haan, *Priangan. De Preanger Regentschappen onder het Nederlandsch Bestuur tot 1811*, 4 vols. (Batavia: Bataviaasch Genootschap van Kunsten en Wetenschappen, 1922–23), especially the "Personalia" section in the first volume.

In the latter half of the nineteenth century a new cadre of "aristocrats" arose: the "tea squires," "sugar lords," "rubber barons" (in Sumatra and Borneo), and other planters of coffee and tobacco. Again, they were a relatively small group, but one as remarkable as their eighteenth-century predecessors. Several of them were exceptional men who, because of their isolation, became immersed in native culture and lived like native aristocracy. One such was Karel Holle who was a tea planter in the Sundanese highlands and who died known as "mitra nu tani," the friend of the farmer. Another figure like the legendary Holle was Kerkhoven, also a tea planter. And there are others. These families also married among each other, creating a distinct society unto their own, forming settlements in the Javanese highlands similar to American settlements in the West. See Rob Nieuwenhuys, *Komen en blijven*, pp. 13–60, and C. W. Wormser, *Ontginners van Java* (Deventer: W. van Hoeve, n.d.).

58 Betsy, in *Guna-Guna*, confesses a similar revulsion for children (6:97).

59 "House sparrow" is a literal translation of the original *huismus*. House sparrow is the English name for the weaverbird (*Passer domesticus*), but in Dutch "huismus" invokes the common connotation of a homebody.

60 King, *Cultural Awakening*, p. 189.

61 There is a picture of a *leestrommel* in Nieuwenhuys, *Komen en blijven*, p. 46.

62 Cash, *Mind of the South*, p. 97.

63 Gerard Brom, *Java in onze Kunst* (Rotterdam: W. L. & J. Brusse, 1931), pp. 115, 130, 131.

64 Chailley-Bert, quoted in Nieuwenhuys, *Tussen twee vaderlanden*, p. 56.

65 Lanier, quoted by Edmund Wilson, *Patriotic Gore: Studies in the Literature of the American Civil War* (New York: Oxford University Press, 1962), pp. 460–61.

66 See E. M. Beekman, "Dutch Colonial Literature," p. 37. See also J. H. W. Veenstra, *D'Artagnan tegen Jan Fuselier* (Amsterdam: Van Oorschot, 1962).

67 King, *Cultural Awakening*, p. 11.

68 Here too there is a parallel in Ceylonese colonial society. "She belonged to a type of Ceylonese family whose women would take the minutest reaction from another and blow it up into a tremendously exciting tale, then later use it as an example of someone's strain of character. If anything kept their generation alive it was this recording by exaggeration. Ordinary tennis matches would be mythologized to the extent that one player was so drunk that he almost died on the court. An individual would be eternally remembered for

one small act that in five years had become so magnified he was just a footnote below it. The silence of the tea estates and no doubt my mother's sense of theatre and romance (fed by vociferous readings of J. M. Barrie and Michael Arlen) combined the edited delicacies of fiction with the last era of a colonial Ceylon" (Ondaatje, *Running in the Family*, p. 169).

69 Tate, quoted by King, *Cultural Awakening*, pp. 100–101.

70 Cash, *Mind of the South*, p. 53.

71 Rob Nieuwenhuys, *Baren en oudgasten. Tempo doeloe—een verzonken wereld. Fotografische documenten uit het oude Indië 1870–1920* (Amsterdam: Querido, 1981), p. 84.

72 3:vi.

73 Nieuwenhuys, *Tussen twee vaderlanden*, p. 89; see also 8:1–2.

74 1:1.

75 Nieuwenhuys, *Tussen twee vaderlanden*, p. 94.

76 Brom, *Java in onze Kunst*, pp. 116–19, 126–30.

77 Cash, *Mind of the South*, p. 153.

78 King, *Cultural Awakening*, pp. 35, 92.

79 For Nieuwenhuys, see *Tussen twee vaderlanden*, pp. 67–100; for Van Deyssel, pp. 68–69, and for Borel and Prins, p. 70. For Brom, see *Java in onze kunst*, pp. 115–30. For Du Perron, see *Werk*, 2:627–29 and 7:135–38. For Ter Braak, see Menno ter Braak, *Verzameld Werk*, 7 vols. (Amsterdam: Van Oorschot, 1950–51), 6:184–90. Compare Justus M. van der Kroef, "The Colonial Novel in Indonesia," *Comparative Literature* 10, no. 3 (Summer 1958): 215–31.

80 For an examination of Southern literature in these terms, see Richard Gray, *The Literature of Memory: Modern Writers of the American South* (Baltimore: Johns Hopkins University Press, 1977). Compare also Daniel Joseph Singal, *The Man Within: From Victorian to Modernist Thought in the South, 1919–1945* (Chapel Hill: University of North Carolina Press, 1983).

81 This phrase was used several times as a title and became known as a slogan for diehard colonials. It was used, for instance, for a collection of texts from a symposium on the Indies: *Daar werd wat groots verricht: Nederlandsch-Indië in de XX eeuw*, ed. W. H. van Helsdingen and H. Hoogenberk (Amsterdam, 1941).

82 Cash, *Mind of the South*, p. 127.

83 Isadora Duncan, *My Life* (New York: Liveright, 1942), p. 320.

84 King, *Cultural Awakening*, p. 160.

85 Tate quoted in ibid., p. 100.

86 King, *Cultural Awakening*, p. 101.

87 This erstwhile famous group of writers and critics included J. C. Ransom, R. P. Warren, and Allen Tate. They published in the journal *The Fugitive* (1922–25) and defended their opinions in *I'll Take My Stand* (1930). See also Cash, *Mind of the South*, pp. 389–94.

88 Cash, *Mind of the South*, pp. 391, 392.

Ups and Downs of Life in the Indies

1 *"It's Yours for Half a Million"*

Because no visitors were expected and no visits were to be made that evening, Mrs. Uhlstra and her daughters had gone for a ride in the bright moonlight.

They were lately so used to socializing that it seemed as if a family member were ill if they quietly spent an entire evening alone together. Mr. Uhlstra didn't go for the ride because he had to keep his guest company, although the two didn't say much to each other. After all, they'd known each other for many years.

Their plantations were separated by a narrow river; at one time they had built a bridge across it to make it easier for them to see each other, either for a chat or a game of cards. They had lived like good country neighbors for many years, a relationship that was occasionally marred by ferocious fights about trivialities, which were soon followed by passionate reconciliations and an inevitable big party. But Uhlstra finally gave up. Though still energetic, strong, and quite healthy, he said on his fiftieth birthday that he had had enough. He'd spent half of his life on his plantation, and his oldest son was of age and could easily replace him. There was enough money, and the girls, who were quite grown up now, also thought that it would be much nicer to live in the city.

That's when he had the beautiful house built that he was living in now, an open house in every sense of the word because not only did he let his friends stay, but also *their* friends, and he often cheerfully extended his hospitality to young people he had never met, simply because they had a note from an old *sobat* in either Europe or Java's interior; a "meal ticket," as he called it, laughing loudly.

He had just received a long letter from his son Henri, who managed his plantation, a letter dealing with business from beginning to end; about the *padi* harvest which was just in, the prices and amounts of coffee, horses, cows, and the condition of the warehouses and buildings.

He had to get his glasses for it, and he was now peering through them at the sheets of paper covered with large handwriting. He had a feeling of quiet satisfaction and the conviction that everything was in good hands as if he were still at the helm.

Henri wrote briefly about the land that belonged to Geber, the house guest, who was now sitting in pajama pants and *kabaja* in a chaise longue at the other end of the table leafing through a magazine, casually looking at the pictures. First Uhlstra carefully put the letter away under lock and key in his office. When he returned he put his arms on the table, leaned his upper body on the marble top and rubbed his graying stubble with stubby fingers. He looked at Geber somewhat seriously, like someone who wants to say something, but hesitates to bring it out into the open.

"Why are you looking at me like that?" asked the other man while he slapped the magazine on the table.

"I have a letter from Henri."

"So," Geber said without interest, while fishing another magazine out of the full reading box* that was beside him on a chair.

"How's it going?"

Uhlstra nodded and waited a moment as if in doubt.

"Good," he said, "it's going very well."

"Has he been over to see *my* place?"

Uhlstra took a cigar from the open box that was on the table. He lit it slowly to gain time, thinking before saying anything that might not be very pleasant. He got up and walked several times across the marble floor of the rear veranda with the long steps of a man who is accustomed to covering distances as quickly as possible. He pulled heavily on his cigar, removing it each time from his mouth with a sweeping gesture of his arm.

"Well?" Geber asked wonderingly, though his tone was scoffing while he looked over the magazine he was holding in his hand. "Nothing has hit the fan, has it?"

"I won't say that, but I do think that it's time you took a look for yourself."

Geber lowered the magazine onto his knees and leaned his

---

* The phrase "*reading box*" is used to translate *leestrommel*. This was a metal box that contained mostly magazines and some books which were circulated among the European population. It was very common and was something of a godsend for those who lived in isolated places.

head against the back of the chair with an expression of boredom and weariness on his face.

It didn't occur to him for a moment that he might be one too many as Uhlstra's guest. A few months ago, when he was still living on his plantation, his health began to decline. He was feverish all the time and experienced the unpleasant feeling of being unwell that Europeans so often can have in the Indies. That's why he had gone to the city, moved in with Uhlstra, and put himself under a doctor's care. They had "fixed him up" right away, and the lively goings-on at the house, the frequent parties, and the pleasant company of many old and new friends had completely "seduced" him, with the result that he dreaded going back to his country house. It was beautiful and comfortable, and he could buy whatever he wanted, but as a single man he was very lonely there. Nor did he get along very well with the younger edition of the Uhlstras, his closest neighbors. The bridge over the *kali* had been swept away by a *bandjir*, and nobody had said anything about building a new one. "Well now," said Uhlstra, putting his broad figure in front of his old *sobat's* chair. "You understand, I hope, that it has nothing to do with trying to get you to leave...."

Geber shrugged his shoulders as if to indicate that that would be a bit much. "In that case," Uhlstra continued, "I have to tell you that I don't like at all what Henri has written me. That Jozef...."

But Geber interrupted him. "Yes, well," he said, "you don't have to tell me anything about that! Henri can't stand him, it bothers him that Jozef plays the boss over there and that he is about the same as an administrator. *Voilà!* He's a good kid, your son Henri, no doubt about it, but when he gets going about Jozef...."

"That's possible," Uhlstra said. "He doesn't write anything about him really, at least not directly. But he has heard that the people are dissatisfied and I felt that I had to warn you about that."

"Satisfied, satisfied! That bunch is never satisfied. Oh well, I'll take a look one of these days. They never complain when I'm around, though."

"I know that, that's just why it's such a bad thing.... Once the lid is off...."

Geber laughed a little angrily.

"There you go! As far as that is concerned you're exactly like your son. Even though Jozef isn't a European he knows the business thoroughly and stays on top of everything as well as anybody. The lid isn't off at all."

"*Sudah*," Uhlstra said, "it's your business."

While he made them each a drink he broke off the conversation. Changing to something else, he asked casually:

"Anything new in the reading box?"

They looked at the illustrations together and talked about irrelevant things, depictions of buildings, pictures of statesmen, reproductions of paintings, and whatever else they encountered.

When the women returned a loud and cheerful conversation developed about all sorts of things that had gone on in town, and the talk continued until after dinner when it dissipated into trivialities, just as would have happened with other normal people who have no particular preferences or cultural inclinations, but who are well off and go through life without material worry. Meanwhile Geber was glad that dinner ended rather quickly and that the women went to bed early. He thought he had noticed that lately mother Uhlstra and her oldest daughter, Rose, had been treating him differently from before, differently than he, an old friend, was accustomed to.

It seemed that they had discovered a new trait in him, and he was far from pleased with that discovery. As if struck by a mutual flash of insight, they had suddenly started with all kinds of remarks, questions, and jokes that always pertained to the same subject: marriage. He could not say that it was entirely out of the question, but that he would try to die as unmarried as possible was very clear to him. But whether he let this be known openly or hinted at it ad nauseum, the women were unperturbed and stuck to their notion. It became clearer every day that they saw him as a candidate for their dark, oldest daughter. No matter how unpleasant, he gallantly joked along with them at the table, his face more mocking than ever. His dull blue eyes would rest on Rose from time to time, and he thought that *if* he wanted one that dark, he could find one far easier and cheaper among the native population.

While he and Uhlstra were taking a little walk that evening, going back and forth in front of the yard in order to help digestion, they both thought about the same thing: their short conversation earlier that evening. It always progressed in the same way, with neither one abandoning his initial position.

"You know what," Geber said finally, "I long for Europe. I wish I was rid of the whole business!"

"I don't think that'd be very difficult."

"You mean, I could sell the property."

"Sure you could."

Geber stopped suddenly, like someone who's been struck by a new idea.

"What would you give for it," he asked.

But Uhlstra shook his head and rubbed his stubble harder than ever.

"I've got enough to do with my own business, too much in fact."

"Well, think it over. It might not be such a bad idea for one of your boys. They can't all manage Tji-Ori."

Again Geber said this in that same mocking voice people had gotten used to. It was true that the young Uhlstras weren't making much progress in Europe. According to their own letters, as well as those from others, they were very happy, healthy, and enjoying life, doing all kinds of things that cost a lot of time and money. But studying, the only thing they had gone for, wasn't to their liking.

And Uhlstra, who sensed the mockery, but also the unmistakable truth, answered frankly:

"Yeah, you could be right about that. I'll think about it."

Chomping on their lit cigars, they walked silently back to the house, Uhlstra's short stocky body with its thick gray hair, in step with the slender, somewhat sunken figure of Geber, whose skull concentrated and reflected in a shiny little spot the illumination from the lamp light on the front veranda. Geber stopped once again, just in front of the steps to the veranda.

"It's yours for half a million," he said, extending his hand like a cattleman who is selling a cow at auction.

Uhlstra deliberated for a moment; he really seemed to be thinking about an offer, but then he shook his head as adamantly as before.

"No," he said. "I have to think about it first."

"Not too long though, because I want to get it over with as soon as possible and get out of here!"

He had noticed that Uhlstra didn't object to buying his plantation Kuningan; hence while they were drinking their grog, he came back to the topic:

"I'll talk to a few people about it, but if by any chance you'd want first refusal for a while.... "

"Hm!" Uhlstra said, "two days is enough."

It was such an important business for both of them that they sat together for quite a while without saying anything, each occupied with his own thoughts.

It was also something they couldn't fool each other about. Uhlstra had a pretty good idea of how much Kuningan brought in and knew, therefore, to what extent it was worth half a million, while Geber understood very well that his old friend only wanted the time to think it over because he distrusted the present situation and wanted to consult Henri first. In fact he was sorry now that he had allowed that privilege. It was crazy. If anything, Kuningan had improved during the last few years and was certainly worth half a million. But now that he had given his word, he couldn't go back on it.

"You understand," he went on, "that we should keep this between the two of us, because if you decide not to buy, it would put me at a disadvantage."

They agreed on that, and now that the real significance of the purchase and sale was getting through to them and occupying their thoughts completely, the interest in small talk faded. They were on the point of going to bed when a carriage drove into the yard.

"Who the devil can that be," said Uhlstra, "it's ten thirty already."

A tall, thin man, who looked to be in his fifties, wearing white pants and jacket with a large black vest underneath, stepped cautiously out of the carriage like a man who doesn't trust his legs and is afraid of stumbling.

He remained standing by the carriage, put on a pince-nez, bent forward, and looked inquiringly at the house.

"Hey, Twissels!" Uhlstra shouted in his loud, cheerful voice. "Come on in." But the man didn't move, laughed softly in reply, and extended his long arm toward Uhlstra's outstretched hand.

"If you could use a third man for a little game," he said in a delicate effeminate voice, "then you're looking at him. If not, I'll leave again."

The two men thought that he was both unique and nice. That Twissels was a real gambler! Though he worked all day long very hard in his office, and though his long thin body appeared to be weak and he always had a somewhat sickly appearance, he never was ill. And yet he played cards at least two evenings a week until half past two or three in the morning.

Geber and Uhlstra dragged him inside, cheerful and happy about this unexpected diversion; in reality they had only been planning to go to bed because the Kuningan business had been bothering them. They too weren't used to such a quiet evening lately. Twissels, knowing perfectly well how welcome he was, rubbed his narrow, thin hands in anticipation.

"I have a feeling," he said when they sat down at the card table and Uhlstra was dividing the chips, "that I'm going to make a killing tonight."

2 Jozef and His Enemies

At Kuningan the rice harvest was already in, and the now withered and stubbled fields that stretched into the distance on every side looked somber and monotonous in the diminishing light of the day's end. Only over by the big meadows, where a herd of fine Bengal cattle was eating its evening meal in the luxuriant grass, was the view fresh and diverse: the paleness of oncoming twilight was broken by the reddish-brown or black-and-white spotted robes of the slowly moving cattle against the green background of sloping wooded terrain.

Geber's factotum, chief *mandur* Jozef, was walking along one of the small paths that crossed the length of the plantation. His hands dangled over both ends of a stout coffee pole that rested on his shoulders while he peacefully smoked a cigarette. He had gone far. No one knew who he really was or where he came from before he entered Geber's service a number of years ago. His European first name (which also served as his last name) might make one think that he was a Christian, but nothing ever confirmed this notion.

His robust, square figure, his confident bearing, his handsome face with the jet-black mustache and short-trimmed whiskers indicated that he was neither Malay nor Javanese, or of any native origin at all. But that was all; he could just as well have been an Arab or a Bengali.

Now that Geber was gone, the management of the estate was completely in his hands and he showed, at least on paper, an administrative ability that was quite extraordinary for someone who, as far as his job was concerned, was in all respects a self-made man.

Yes, he *had* come far; no one was more convinced of that than Jozef. Every so often he stopped and let his big, black, glistening eyes roam over the land with the air of a lord and master. He would go even further, he thought, and felt that he was on the right track.

Even when Geber was still managing the estate himself and Jozef was really no more than a *mandur*, he had known how to make something on the side. He never did so at Mr. Geber's expense—he wouldn't have dared, and his employer always got his due—but at the expense of the natives who feared him more than the plantation owner. His wallet had become very fat indeed during the last few months now that he enjoyed nearly unlimited freedom of action. He had put on the screws in his own way with utter contempt for the welfare of the native population, without the least concern for the gentle way Geber had always treated the natives, or even for what the law demanded, as far as that was concerned. Now that the lid was indeed off, he played havoc with the Javanese and shrank from nothing in his fervent desire to get enough money to buy a small estate for himself and become a *tuan tanah*.

He secretly disdained Geber and Uhlstra for their amicable attitude toward the people, and the goodness and generosity that prevented them from levying as much as they were strictly entitled to and that even caused them to be foolish enough to be interested in those lying and fawning slaves and help them with money and cattle, if not with free medical care when they fell ill.

Even though the people of Kuningan hated Jozef like the plague because he fleeced them, shamelessly stealing their goods, labor, and money, that wasn't the worst. After all, they had been exploited by either native or foreign parasites for several centuries already, and though a little more or less did make a big difference, they bore their fate in silence. And if there were some who grumbled and resisted, Jozef's big stick very quickly got to know their shoulders, and they felt for days that it was better to keep their own counsel.

But there was one thing they wouldn't tolerate, and it had transformed their hatred into a desire for revenge. Because now Jozef could play the boss on the plantation whenever he felt like it, he had given his lust free rein. He used to do it surreptitiously and pulled off some questionable stunts, but he was always cautious and secretive because he was afraid of Geber. Lately, however, he quite literally couldn't leave any woman alone, be it in the *kampongs* or in the fields. He openly permitted himself all sorts of liberties and would try any trick, even force, to have women submit. In this manner he almost always got what he wanted, while his appealing oriental looks did the rest. It was this that constituted an unforgivable crime for many of the native young men when they discovered whose hands their women had passed through, and for the fathers as well when their budding young daughters returned home in a most shameful manner.

There had been trouble brewing for weeks. In the evenings the men secretly met in various places far from the main house, ostensibly to smoke and talk, but in reality to incite each other to do something about the brown tyrant who spared nothing and nobody. And Jozef, who otherwise knew so much about what happened on the plantation, remained completely ignorant of the meetings. His vanity as a spoiled servant and his deep contempt for the "slaves" made it impossible for him to imagine anything resembling resistance to him.

He walked back home, watching the herdsmen drive the cattle from the pastures back to the corrals. When darkness had fallen and the native who served under him as *djuragan* had reported that everything was in order, he locked the front of his house, a small separate wooden building partly covered with vines that had big clusters of bridal tears hanging among them. It was a scene so picturesque and sweet that when the sun shone during the day, it resembled a bucolic idyll.

Inside, by the light from the brass lamp that was of a very old-fashioned design that could be traced to landowners from *tempo dulu*, Jozef was quietly doing some administrative work. He paid attention to each letter he wrote and to each figure he put down, doing his employer's books first, following them with his own modest notebook. When he was done and wanted to get the metal box from a small safe in order to count his money, he sent his boy to the *kampong* and locked the rear of his house, not out of fear but from distrust.

With great satisfaction he carefully counted everything once more, sorting the money with care and affection into the compartments of the box until, after lengthy contemplation and silent calculation, he locked it away again. He ate his simple meal of rice and fish, washed it down with a glass of water, blew out his lamp, and stretched out contentedly just as he was on his not very fresh or clean bed.

There was no moon. The watchman stationed between the landowner's house and Jozef's dwelling rang the large bell by the warehouse approximately every hour and half hour.

Shivering in the cold night air and trembling under the *sarong* he had thrown around his naked shoulders, the watchman had just stepped from the *baleh-baleh* he had been dozing on to the pole where the bell hung from a cross-beam, when he suddenly landed full length on the ground. Bound and gagged in a second, he never saw or heard anything else than the dull thud of his own body, though he felt it all the more. He was an old man. They had left him ignorant of everything. He didn't know about a thing first hand and didn't concern himself with anything, and yet he understood perfectly well what was going to happen. Afraid, eyes open wide, he stared into the dark night. He saw faint shadows moving back and forth in the inky darkness, and heard the soft tread of bare feet on the ground and moving bodies brush against each other. And though this indicated very little, he could still guess who they were and where they came from. In a tight group they crept on, without a sound almost, until they reached Jozef's house.

For several minutes everything was deadly quiet except for the usual night sounds: frogs croaking in muddy pools, a night owl calling in the tall trees, and the soughing whisper of the crickets in the grass.

Suddenly Jozef leaped out of bed and stumbled against a chair which fell over on the wooden floor with a loud noise. Startled, still half asleep, he was unable to account for what was happening or the meaning of the dull banging that shook his entire house. Suddenly he knew and understood, or at least could imagine what was going on: the heavy door made of *djati* wood that was locked from the inside with two bolts and a *palang pintu* was being rammed with a tree trunk. Faced by the mortal danger he was now fully aware was threatening him, Jozef stood wondering what to do. His hand was around the loaded shotgun he had groped for on the wall.

In a burst of rage and anger he wanted to open the door and start shooting, but when he peered through the cracks of the shutter he saw only pitch darkness that was without a sound to indicate anything. And that very darkness, the uncertainty, and the silence diminished his anger, replacing it with fear. He had matches handy but didn't dare to light one. Under the dull, regular blows of the tree trunk, the door screaked on its hinges, just about to give away. He turned to the other side, felt for and gripped the *palang pintu* on the rear door, pushed it silently away, pulled the bolts back, suddenly yanked the door wide open and leapt outside, his finger on the trigger of the gun.

The shot went off harmlessly into the air and Jozef went down like a pole-axed ox, without a cry, almost without any sound. Dozens of hoarse and savage voices screamed and yelled furiously like wild animals, roaring over the fields and up along the trees.

The dull blows of the tree trunk stopped. One *obor* after another lit up in the hands of half-naked natives, their faces made unrecognizable by black and white stripes. They all gathered silently around Jozef's body for a moment. He was lying flat on his back among the bushes in the backyard. The light brown hilt of a *kris,* shining splendidly in the glimmer of the torches, protruded from his *baadje* and was surrounded by a broadening blood stain. It had been plunged right through his heart.

The one who had done it pointed with his finger triumphantly at the *kris* and was dancing with pleasure, but the others, who had also sought revenge, were disappointed. Each man wanted a share in Jozef's death, and each one had had his own idea about striking a blow. Now he had died instantly from the skillful thrust of the *kris* that had been executed in the dark with the same certainty and steady hand as that of a toreador planting his sword between the horns of a bull, forcing the animal down to its knees. Once aroused, the repressed and abject people's desire for blood wasn't so easily satisfied. They struck with their lances and hacked with their *ariets* and *parangs* wherever they could get at the dead body. For at least half an hour they cut off pieces and limbs in the most gruesome manner until they were *bosèn* of it and tossed the shapeless body over the fence. Both the natives who lived in the neighborhood and the servants from the main house had been awakened by the noise and the barking dogs. They came outside and peered into the darkness, but when they saw (or at least understood) what was happening and that a *ketjo* was underway, they all withdrew as quickly as possible, locked their little houses, and, trembling with fear, barricaded themselves as best they could.

Jozef's house was plundered and *rampassed* for hours. It took a great deal of trouble and many broken weapons to force the small safe open because they couldn't find the key which Jozef always hid in a special place. When they had forced the box, everybody grabbed whatever money he could lay his hands on. They jumped around like madmen shouting loudly and incoherently, and smashed everything in their rage until there was nothing left to destroy.

High flames shot up through a thick cloud of smoke that rose quickly like a gray pillar, lighting the underside of the nearby trees with a bright pink and the tops with a beautiful reddish gold. The *obors* were extinguished and the perpetrators of the gruesome deed vanished left and right down the dark narrow paths and into the fields. As if by agreement, one of the servants from the main house suddenly found the courage to come outside and sound the fire alarm on the *tong-tong*, which echoed loudly and dismally in the night.

Because the card game at Uhlstra's had started late didn't mean that it would be any shorter, and Twissels had kept his word as if it were gospel. He took big chances, both high and low, and pulled them off, no matter what. When it struck three in the morning Geber, somewhat disgruntled by his continuous bad luck, said that they could make the last game "sans prendre."*

"Have you ever seen such rotten luck?" he shouted, banging his fist angrily on the card table. "That's the second time in half an hour."

"True, you're not having much luck," consoled Uhlstra, "but it can change."

And Twissels, with his delicate lady's laugh, said mockingly while he raked in the chips:

"All great things come in threes."

No sooner had he said this than Uhlstra's servant, who usually

---

* "Sans prendre" is a term once used by people playing omber, and refers to a player's not upping the ante. The omber game was extemely popular in the colonial Indies during the nineteenth century. It originated in the seventeenth century and was commonly played by three people with forty cards, i.e., with the eight, nine, and ten of each suit removed. Every player received nine cards, and the person called the "omber" was the one the other two tried to prevent from getting the required number of tricks. In the original, Daum used a variety of French terms associated with this card game. They were omitted in the translation.

sat at the entrance to the front yard, came in and stood with a frightened expression on his face near a corner of the card table between Geber and Uhlstra.

"What is it?" Uhlstra asked in Malay a little roughly; he was annoyed by the man's unusual liberty.

The houseboy pointed with his thumb over the shoulder of his red-collared service *baadje* toward the yard.

"There is a man from Kuningan."

"What's he want?" Geber asked, putting down the new hand that Twissels had dealt.

"He says that there is *tjilaka*."

"What's the matter!" both Uhlstra and Geber shouted impatiently.

"He says," the Malay continued very calmly, "that there's been a *ketjo* at Mr. Geber's, that the house is on fire, and that *tuan* Jozef is dead already."

Dumbfounded, the three men looked at each other, Geber very pale and alarmed, Uhlstra with a red glow on his brown face. Geber jumped up in fury and yelled to the man who had stayed out in the yard to come inside. The poor native approached the broad marble veranda, half crawling on his sore feet and gray up to his knees from the dusty road. He squatted on the lowest step. He had no more to say than what he had already told the houseboy; he didn't know anything else.

The sound of the loud talk, shouting and cursing of the men traveled confusedly via the inside veranda into the house and awakened Mrs. Uhlstra. Twisting her hair into a *kondé*, her heavy figure covered by a large, loose *kabaja*, she walked hurriedly from her room to the front of the house. When she learned what had happened, she became frightened and afraid of her children's fate on their own plantation which bordered Geber's. With a loud torrent of words she tried to get more out of the messenger, shaking the poor devil as if she could shake loose what she thought was still in him. But it made him so *bingung* that he finally did not know anything at all anymore. By then Rose and the other girls had appeared too, all of them overcome by fear. Pale, with tears in their eyes, they wailed in confusion about the fateful message. It got worse when Uhlstra ordered the coachman awakened so that the carriage with his best horses could be brought immediately to the front. Afraid for his safety, they wanted to hold him back by force, because in the dark of the night the idea of murder and arson took on enormous proportions. Only Twissels, who had poured himself an extra grog to celebrate his winnings and was now leaning against a pillar with his large black vest sticking out like a colossal ink spot, only Twissels hadn't succumbed to the confusion at the course of events. He laughed softly and ironically, though nobody looked at him in the nervous confusion, and in a sweet falsetto voice he said to himself: "Those women, women!"

No matter how good-hearted he was, Uhlstra couldn't be moved from his decision. He knew the natives, and his own conscience was perfectly clear. Whatever was happening, he had to be there, come what may.

"I'll go with you," Geber said hesitantly, like someone who out of decency has to say something, but it sounded indecisive and lacked enthusiasm. Though still persisting to keep up appearances, he was glad that Uhlstra refused him firmly. It was better he stayed behind. What was done was done and couldn't be helped anymore.

The horses flew down the road, but they were still far too slow for Uhlstra. He arrived at the borders of his plantation just as day was breaking. Everything was quiet and peaceful as usual, something he found almost unbelievable in his excitement. In the gray dawn half an hour later, as he turned into the driveway of his old mansion and saw that some people were already up, bringing grass to the cattle in his stables, a deep sigh of relief escaped him. There at least nothing had happened, he would dare swear on that.

His son Henri, exactly his younger self, met him in the yard with an amazed but happy face.

"Hallo Dad, that's damned quick!"

"Is it true?" Uhlstra asked, jumping out of the carriage, happy and visibly moved when he shook hands with his son, who was standing in front of him unharmed and in one piece.

Henri nodded, with a grave and serious look on his face.

"Sad but true," he confirmed with barely disguised glee. "It's a nasty business for Geber."

"And is Jozef dead?"

"From what I hear, dead as a door nail. They must have really butchered him! Oh well, it's Mr. Geber's own fault. Why did he leave such a swine in charge of his place?"

The father didn't answer. What good would it do?

"How about changing them?" he said, looking at his steaming horses while they were rubbed down.

But Henri didn't want to hear of it and neither did his young wife. They made the father understand that the whole thing was really of little importance. The murdered man got exactly what he deserved. If Europeans didn't mind having their business managed by such mean and base folk, then it was beneath the dignity of a decent landowner or administrator to concern himself with the consequences.

Uhlstra, reassured for the time being and hungry after the sleepless night and the long ride in the cool morning air, let them talk and accompanied them into the house. He longed for a cup of strong coffee and got one immediately from his daughter-in-law. Now that it had proven to be no worse than the messenger had told him, he wasn't in such a great hurry anymore and wanted to question Henri and Lize first.

That was easy enough. He only had to listen to the stories about the tyranny of Kuningan's murdered chief *mandur*. Henri returned to the same point over and over again: it was all Geber's fault. He repeated for the umpteenth time that a European landowner should employ decent young Europeans and not such strange riffraff.

An hour later Uhlstra wanted to have his horses hitched up again. He had promised Geber that he would investigate everything; a promise is a promise. Although Henri now claimed that it was dangerous, if not unnecessary, because the assistant resident had been informed, Uhlstra drove to Kuningan anyway. And his son, curious to see how they had *tjientjanged* that swine, went with him.

3   After the Riot

The Uhlstra women had calmed down when, around noon, a man on horseback brought a short note from Uhlstra. They could now speak at great length and with a certain pleasure about the fear they had experienced that morning.

Mrs. Uhlstra never tired of talking about the trials of that day, which she told repeatedly in fluent though faulty Dutch, first very demonstratively with her hands folded, then again with the right hand pressed against her heart or the left against her forehead. Geber was glad that nothing had happened on Tji-Ori because he wished the Uhlstras no harm, not even the son, though he didn't like him all that much.

The case was far from closed, as far as he was concerned. The more he thought about it the more he was overcome once again by the feverishness that had originally driven him to town, but which hadn't been bothering him lately.

"It's a simple matter," Uhlstra said when he returned that evening, "but it's a nasty business for you."

"What about the books?"

"That's the least of it. Among his burnt belongings I found part of an account book that was still in pretty good shape. Also a smaller one. I brought them with me and had them put in your room."

"What about the rest?"

Uhlstra had to tell the story in great detail: how the body had been abused and about the state of the plundered and burned house.

"Did you notice anything about the people?" Geber asked.

"Oh no, Kuningan was as quiet as my rear veranda. Imagine, the government got word of a general revolt. Troops have been sent in and soldiers are bivouacked on the plantation!"

Geber shook his head indignantly. He knew that they'd done that.

Acquaintances had kept on stopping by throughout the day to hear what had happened, and he learned then that soldiers had been sent to his plantation. Impressed by that rather unique fact, everybody fell silent. They understood what it meant, even the girls. The murder of an overseer, not even a European, and some looting, in short, a disturbance during the landowner's absence, that sort of thing was of little importance. The reputation of a plantation wasn't badly damaged by that, and its value remained nearly intact. But serious rumors about a revolt of the native population and the sending of troops by the government, that was a severe blow for the owner and he would need years to recover from it.

"It's a shame," Rose was the first to say. "It's just as if they did it on purpose."

Surprised, Geber looked at her in agreement; that idea had occurred to him too. He had experienced a number of not very pleasant run-ins with the authorities, and when there was a difference of opinion, he lacked the tact of the seemingly much gruffer Uhlstra, who could pride himself that he always got whatever he wanted from a succession of government officials. All of them were secretly convinced that Rose was right, but no one mentioned it anymore. They nodded silently at each other until Mrs. Uhlstra got up with a long drawn-out sigh and said softly that it was "terrible, just terrible," and went to her room to get dressed.

They barely had time for that. By the beginning of the evening the big front veranda was full of visitors, as if there was a public reception. Driven by curiosity, everybody stopped by. They had seen the troops march, they had heard something about murder and revolt on Geber's plantation, and they would surely be able to learn all the details from the Uhlstras.

Geber had taken Markens aside and complained bitterly to this senior official who along with the others had come to see him to express his "condolences" and who was a good friend and a frequent card partner. And the former government official, who was against the military, agreed with him completely and promised to do his best to have the soldiers recalled as soon as possible and to see that the report in the official bulletin would be as favorable as possible. While insisting on the latter, Geber made much of the humane treatment he extended to the people who worked on his plantation, and of his uncommon mildness in exercising his rights and demanding his due.

But later in the evening, after he had taken a long look at the big account book from Kuningan and at Jozef's small book, and with great difficulty had deciphered the secret of this book-keeping and understood the connection between the two, he became profoundly depressed.

He realized now that it was all his own fault, that a certain amount of carelessness and a stubborn trust in untrustworthy people was the cause of his partial ruination. While he, despite his oddities, had striven all his life to be honest and decent, a great deal of shameless stealing and cheating had gone on for months in his name and with his alleged authority. Disconsolately, he looked for Uhlstra and told him about it. Working himself up to an unusual state of anger, he cursed and slammed his fist on the table, but in spite of everything that had happened, he never maligned the memory of the murdered man, admitting only: "It's my own damned fault."

And now Uhlstra told him the rest. He learned that there'd been women *perkaras* and that they were the real cause for the murder and what followed.

When he knew everything, down to the last detail, it seemed as if all hope failed him.

"It's a hopeless mess," he sighed.

"Yes, that's probably true. We don't need to kid each other. At the moment Kuningan's practically unsalable. Yesterday you talked about half a million and I really thought seriously about that, but right now, now that the whole *perkara* developed as it did, I wouldn't want to put a hundred thousand into it. But be a man. Go back, keep to yourself, and keep on working quietly until, in a few years, the whole mess is forgotten."

It was good advice, and just about the only course available, Geber was fully convinced of that. Nevertheless he shook his head and pulled a face as if something disgusting had been offered to him.

"I can't make up my mind about that. When I think about being out there all alone again for four or five years, then, by God, I'd rather end it all with pill number eleven."*

* "Pill number eleven" was a colonial expression to indicate that someone had been poisoned. The curious phrase derives from the fact that during colonial times military hospitals had ten standard kinds of pills for any variety of illness. When a patient's condition was hopeless he was given one other, a lethal drug, to help him out of his misery. Hence it originally referred to a kind of mercy killing.

It kept him awake all night. Every time he sank down in a chair and closed his eyes hoping he would doze off after restlessly and nervously pacing back and forth in his room, he could clearly see Uhlstra's unperturbed figure sitting opposite him, and again he heard the terrible words: "Today I wouldn't want to put a hundred thousand into it." Not a hundred thousand for that beautiful, fertile, and well-populated land of over eight thousand acres, completely unencumbered. Not even a hundred thousand!

Then he thought about how much he himself had paid for it twenty years ago, and about the isolated and monotonous life he had, as if he were exiled from the world, deprived of so much that a great civilized European society had to offer. That had all been lost to him during that long succession of his best years. And now that he was at the point of turning all that work on the estate into money. . . .

Geber got up again with tears in his eyes, tears of pity for himself and for his circumstances. He was more fully awake than he had been when he sat down but also more agitated and nervous. When the big old-fashioned clock on the rear veranda struck five, tolling slowly and heavily like a death-knell, he went to sit outside hoping to be diverted by the break of dawn and by the quiet comings and goings of the servants in the yard who were washing at the well, drinking their coffee, and eating their rice before the awakened family would put them all into motion.

Rose was the first of the Uhlstras to appear. In order to reach the *mandi* room she had to pass Geber. Astonished when she saw him sitting there, she asked:

"Up already?"

"I haven't slept all night," he sighed pitifully, and the girl, who could understand that very well, sighed with him.

"Yes, it's terrible," she sympathized. "There'll be a lot of *susah* before it's all over. So much is lost, so much!"

Now that the initial sorrow had taken its course that night, and Geber had finally been able to complain to a human being, he became his old self again, and for the first time in twenty-four hours that mocking look so typical of him reappeared on his face. He got up, leaned a hand against a pillar, crossed one leg over the other and said:

"Yes, Rose. In fact I'm a poor man now. What your father said is true. If I wanted to sell Kuningan right now or even in the near future, I wouldn't even get a hundred thousand for it. Nice, huh?"

"*Kasian*," she said wholeheartedly because, though from childhood she had heard about prices of great estates in terms of half or whole millions, she had only a very vague notion what such amounts meant. Even so, she thought a hundred thousand ridiculously low, mainly because her father and Geber had spoken contemptuously about that kind of money. "*Kasian*," she said again. "But you know what, you go back to Kuningan and work *terus* again for a few years."

"That's what your father said too, Rose, but it's not all that great to be all alone like that again."

Geber was surprised when she suddenly walked away to the *mandi* room. She and her mother had been teasing him continually about being a bachelor for so long, supposedly in fun, and he had expected that she was going to advise him to get married. That would have been only natural.

He leaned back against the pillar and crossed his arms, thinking and seeing connections quicker and more decisively than was usually the case. He automatically shouted "yes!" when Mrs. Uhlstra called out that his coffee was waiting. She had also gotten up and was sitting in the semidarkness of the rear veranda in a red *kabaja* with black velvet trim. But he didn't come right away. The pros and the cons were becoming clear to him.

"Your coffee's getting cold!" the lady of the house called out once more, and again he answered, "I'm coming," but he didn't move a muscle.

Well, it was certainly the best solution, from every point of view, and when Rose returned from the *mandi* room, he turned around while she walked past him, took her by the arm and, attempting to be funny, laughed and said:

"Hey Rose, want to be my administrator?"

"Come on," she said, also laughing. She pulled her heavy arm out of his thin hand and skipped lightly up the steps. For a moment Geber still felt a sensation in his hand, but one that wasn't exactly poetic. It was a cold feeling, as if he had held a fish. But he paid little attention to it, still preoccupied with the big decision he had just made quite unexpectedly.

They didn't make it difficult for him. Rose, who had understood perfectly well that there was more to the plan than appointing her administrator, immediately told her mother that "he bit." It was obvious that morning that Geber had dressed with more than his usual care, that he had shaved carefully and curled his mustache. It was obvious too that he looked in a special way at Rose, who pretended not to notice, and that it was he now who spoke about marriage again and again, while the women carefully avoided the subject.

After breakfast while Uhlstra was writing letters, Geber suddenly found himself alone with Rose. Playing the young lover was beyond him; besides, given the circumstances and the nature of their relationship, he found it ridiculous.

Casually, Geber sat down beside her while she embroidered intently, took her hand and simply asked if she wanted to marry him and accompany him to Kuningan. She did breathe a little deeper than usual for a moment, something that could be clearly seen by the movement of her well-developed chest, but she answered just as simply and calmly as he had put the question, saying that she consented and that he ought to speak to her father. He thought it natural to give her a kiss, but was surprised when he got one in return, not only without coyness but like the good European kind that he could remember having had only once during the twenty years he had spent in the interior. There he had restricted himself to a native housekeeper who, in his opinion, had to be kept at a distance without caress or affection except in the strictest sense that pertained to her inevitable service.

Now that the die was cast Geber could only say that it wasn't all that bad. What disappointed him was the face of his old *sobat*, who had been completely ignorant of the goings on and didn't suspect anything when Geber came to him with the proposal.

Uhlstra saw that there was speculation in it on both sides, and though extremely practical himself, he disliked it in such matters. He pressed his lips together in a very unfriendly way, looked down on his desk and said abruptly that it struck him as strange and that he couldn't immediately decide. He would give Geber an answer one way or the other within twenty-four hours.

When Geber, rather taken aback, returned to his room, Uhlstra, *betul* angry, went to see his wife in order to call her to account. She wasn't at all afraid, and Rose, who had been called and had seen to her amazement that her father didn't approve of it immediately, strongly supported her mother. In fact, there wasn't anything to be said against the marriage except that Geber was twenty years older than his future bride. Whether this was an advantage or not belonged to those unresolvable issues and would probably remain that way for as long as there was a difference of opinion.

During the discussion the feelings that Uhlstra had felt at first gradually softened, and reason and calculation came more strongly to the fore. He finally had to admit to what Geber had figured out from his point of view early that morning: that it was still the best solution. The only thing that amazed him now was that he hadn't realized this immediately. He went to see Geber without delay and with a laugh slapped him forcefully on the shoulder.

"I don't have to wait twenty-four hours," he bellowed in his loud voice. "As far as I'm concerned, marry Rose. I really hope that it works out for the two of you."

"Why shouldn't it? Didn't we always get along, both in and out of business?"

"That's true," Uhlstra agreed and winked at him with his sly, sharp eyes. Then he added: "We both know the score."

The general opinion was that it was a good deal for both sides. Kuningan was suddenly redeemed by this marriage. The news of the murder had caused quite a sensation in town. For the first few days everyone talked about "the rebels." Everywhere the locks on doors and windows were improved and there was a brisk demand for revolvers. But the "civilian and military authorities" who accompanied the soldiers to the plantation found to their great surprise that everything was completely peaceful at the "scene of revolt."

Now that this force had been called out, they couldn't just send the soldiers back again, even though everyone understood how unnecessary they were. The judicial investigation resulted in the arrest of half a dozen natives. But Uhlstra and his son had provided such damning information about the murdered man, and so much criminal evidence came to light about the late Jozef, that people quickly formed an opinion that was favorable to the suspects.

4 Mama Tjang

It was most unusual that the engagement had been announced without celebration. Geber had returned to his plantation to straighten things out. Everyone agreed that everything about that ugly *perkara* had to be taken care of first. Besides, things became very hectic at the Uhlstras. Rose's mother's, her sisters', and her own time was completely occupied with preparing her trousseau. There was a great deal of foreign correspondence because so much had to be shipped from Paris. *Tokos* were visited every day, extra seamstresses were hired, and the spacious rear veranda sometimes looked like a *toko* too because it was filled with blue and white cardboard boxes, piles of table linen, and all kinds of colored and white goods thought to be indispensable for the future Mrs. Geber when she went to live out in the country with just her husband. In the midst of all this bustle, which Uhlstra hated with a passion, a note arrived that startled everyone and occasioned a close huddle of the women's dark-haired heads.

"What is it?" Uhlstra asked, who had been taking care of his plants in the back yard and was walking barefoot on the marble veranda.

"*Kasian,*" his wife said, "it's a note from Clara; we have to go there immediately.

"What is it this time?" was the second and not very friendly question. "*Kasian,* man, the old woman's in a bad way." He mumbled something, shrugged his shoulders and went to his room.

"You're coming too, aren't you?" his wife shouted after him.

"No thanks!" he yelled back. "I'll hear if it was worth the trouble when you get back."

"Come," Mrs. Uhlstra said to her daughters, "we'll take the landau. Hurry up and put on a clean *kabaja.*"

They rode into the yard of a house that was bigger and more beautiful than their own. It was built high above the ground, elegantly furnished with European furniture, and very well kept. They didn't enter the main building, however, but drove straight to the back, where a slender and handsome, though no longer young, Indies woman met them, apparently expecting the visitors.

They kissed each other with a great display of affection, but there was a tinge of sadness on their faces.

"How is she?" Mrs. Uhlstra asked softly, as if they had to whisper even outside in order not to disturb the sleep of someone who was gravely ill.

"Come and see for yourself. The doctor said that it won't be long now."

Whispering among each other, they walked down the long veranda that connected the outbuildings and entered a room that gave off a strong smell of Javanese oils and ointments. The windows were closed, and in the semidarkness the shapes of many different Indies and European objects stood out against the white wall. It was an odd collection of cheap and native things made out of bamboo and rattan for everyday use, contrasting strangely with marble teapoys, beautiful gilded vases, and other luxury articles. And at the rear of the spacious room, on an ordinary *baleh-baleh* enclosed by beautiful lace mosquito netting that was tied back with red ribbons, lay an old native woman on a *tikar*. It was Mama Tjang: thin and wrinkled, quiet, with eyes closed, hands folded on her chest like a mummy that has been lying there for centuries and has completely dried out. When she heard the voices her big eyes opened wide and her clear and steady gaze suddenly returned the full expression of life to the mask. Mrs. Uhlstra went up to her immediately, sat down in a leather armchair beside the improvised bed, and inquired with great interest in Malay about the health of Mama Tjang, who proved immediately that not only had she good eyes, but that she hadn't lost her power of speech either. In a soft whining voice she began to complain bitterly, speaking quickly even though she was interrupted time and again by deep breaths as if it cost her a lot of trouble and she could barely go on. They neglected her, no one bothered about her anymore, a poor old woman in the *kampong* was better off than she was, she wished she were dead, she probably would die soon, then she wouldn't be in the way any longer, then no one would be troubled by her anymore, then they could bury her in the ground, then they would be rid of her. Mrs Uhlstra knew that old song and she knew how well her sister Clara, in spite of the furious protests of her husband, Lugtens, took care of Mama Tjang and had her looked after. Yet she didn't contradict her, only now and then did she interrupt her with a few soft and encouraging words. Rose and her sisters also came to the bed and spoke in the same way, all in Malay and all at the same time, with tears in their eyes caused by the lamenting of the old woman whose temples they refreshed with eau de cologne. All the while two *babus* were sitting on the floor like stone statues, not moving a muscle unless ordered to. After about half an hour the women went outside again and breathed in deeply after the stuffiness of the sick room.

"Come in for a minute," Mrs. Lugtens said, pointing toward the main building with her fan, "Jacques is home."

Mrs. Uhlstra had to greet her brother-in-law for the sake of appearances. She didn't like to do it and would rather have gone home. Followed by the girls she climbed the high stairs with heavy tread and followed her sister through the beautiful hall that formed the middle part of the house and into one of the rooms where Lugtens sat writing at his polished rolltop desk. She entered with something in her bearing that suggested an affected outward display of decisiveness.

"So!" Lugtens greeted her gruffly and haughtily, "How are you?"

"Oh fine. We're very busy now that Rose is getting married."

"When is that going to happen?"

"A date hasn't been set yet, but it'll be within six weeks or so...."

He turned his head toward Rose. When she and the girls entered the room he had greeted them with a single nod. His "so" was meant for all of them at once.

"You're making a good marriage there, Rose!"

His sharp gray eyes looked straight into hers and there was something about his features that made her shy and nervous, just like it affected her mother, but like her she braced herself, doing her best not to appear *bingung* toward Uncle Lugtens.

"You think so?" she asked, smiling and friendly.

"Sure, sure.... It's a good plantation and Geber'a good man."

"Yes," Mrs. Uhlstra interrupted with forced cheerfulness, "men who play cards together always back each other up."

The only response to her remark was a nasty sideward glance. As if she hadn't said anything, Lugtens continued to Rose:

"You know what life is like in the country, and you know the language well. Those are two very important things."

"Yes, Uncle Jacques."

Rose really didn't know what else to say. She only heard her impending marriage referred to from a business point of view.

"Well," Mrs. Uhlstra said, "we just came to say hello because we have to go home soon."

"And I have my hands full too. Goodbye then, and say hello to your husband for me."

Again he nodded briefly, a curt general greeting, and the women left. Mrs. Uhlstra uttered a brief "Bye," happy that she was out of the office again. At the foot of the veranda stairs she put one hand over her heart, turned up her big dark eyes in exasperation, took her sister's wrist with her other hand, and said in a whisper as if afraid to be overheard by the others:

"What an awful man, Clara! How can you live with him? I couldn't even stand it for twenty-four hours!"

"And I've been taking it for twelve years already," her sister said with a painful expression on her face, "but it's never been as hard as it has been lately, now that the old woman is sick."

"Is he still harping on that!"

"Oh, Lena, stop it. He sours my life with that every day."

Mrs. Uhlstra looked at her sister with sincere pity.

"I thought it better not to begin about that. Mine doesn't want to talk about it either, but such a bully as Jacques...."

The girls had already kissed their aunt goodbye, and called their mother from the landau.

"Well," she said, saying goodbye to Mrs. Lugtens, "if there is anything, just let me know, all right?"

Lugtens had calmly continued with his correspondence. His handwriting was neat and regular, and he paid full attention to his work. He wrote with a permanently grim expression on his face, a typical calm despot. And he was known as such throughout the Indies. For many years he had been in charge of a big company that he had founded himself. He ruled it with an iron hand. His word was law there and he had made it very prosperous through his ability, tact, and devotion. No one liked him. His broad head, as if hewn with short forceful strokes from one piece, expressed the greatest obstinacy, and though he had neither beard nor mustache and was always clean shaven, the strong lines along his nose and mouth made his face masculine and energetic like that of a Roman emperor. Whether he was at home or at work in the service of his company made little difference to him. His wife, his childern, and his subordinates at the office all had only one thing to do: obey him. And he was feared as much here as there. When he had finished his correspondence he went to the back ot the house, looking around as if he were making an inspection and hoped to find something to criticize. But Clara had been well trained in the service of her marriage. As always, it was quiet in the house, and neat and clean to the point of absurdity, with everything in its place.

"All of them were in the back before, weren't they?" he said to her.

"Yes, the old woman is very bad."

"So, she's very bad again, is she? The usual tricks, of course! You really saddled me with this one, but this is the last time. As soon as she's better, it's over."

Clara let him speak. She resisted him in this one respect, and even though no day passed without hearing the most unpleasant things about it, she had persevered and was determined to continue taking care of her old native mother in her own house.

While he continued with his nasty remarks and reproaches in a gruff commanding voice, a small coach drove through the gate into the backyard. Before it came to a complete stop two boys and two girls jumped out. They were the Lugtens children coming home from school. They ran up the stairs happily and noisily, but when they saw their father was home, they seemed to experience a shock. They suddenly became silent, walked on quietly, with a worried look at the schoolbooks they held in one hand while they straightened their caps and smoothed their hair with the other. Only the youngest girl continued as before. She didn't seem to be intimidated to the same degree as the others by the sight of her father. She was also the only one he really greeted in return, obviously doing his best to change his brusque tone to one more mild and friendlier.

Yet there was nothing special about this child. She was fair and blond like the others, a complete Lugtens type without any trace of the native origin on the mother's side.

What Mrs. Uhlstra, Aunt Lena, hadn't dared, little Lena did immediately: she asked about Mama Tjang. When her mother, hesitant and fearing new outbursts from her husband, said that she was very ill, the child didn't hesitate for a moment. Without bothering about her father, she went to the outbuildings with the firm step and straight bearing characteristic of Lugtens himself. The other children had immediately crept to their rooms, preferring to get away from his direct and disagreeable presence.

Mama Tjang lay waiting with her eyes wide open and fixed on the door. She had heard the children come home, and when one approached and opened the door of her room she knew it was little Lena. Her old brown, parchmentlike face relaxed and gained some liveliness. When the child sat down on the edge of the *baleh-baleh*, she took the small white hand into her brown one. And she didn't complain now that no one bothered about her and that they neglected her.

Chattering rapidly in Malay and employing many gestures, the child talked about her school, the other girls, and the stories in her books, continuing for at least a quarter of an hour. Now and then Mama Tjang got a word in or made an exclamation, but she kept on looking at the child's face, caressing the small hand she wouldn't let go of, and stroking the blond curly hair. No one knew that this ordinary native woman kept on swallowing the charity of that house simply because of this grandchild. She would have preferred to live in a small house in the *kampong*. In her old age she could only remember her early youth, and the *kampong* was part of her memories. She felt a great longing for a quiet little yard where the chickens rummaged amoung the *pisang* and *manga* trees, for a small bamboo house that was built right on the ground in a shady spot, with an *atap* roof. She would have gotten it too, and readily. She knew very well that her living in Lugtens's house was an aggravation, and she was very angry about it. She was indignant in her own way, but when she thought about that one grandchild she would have to leave behind, everything else faded.

Her daughter took care of her. When they thought they could make the old woman happy with something, they brought it with them. The room resembled a second-hand shop of beautiful, colorful things that were all over the place in variegated confusion. They left her cold; she didn't care about them. But the least little thing she got from her grandchild she treated like a treasure, be it an old ribbon, a picture, or something else without any value. She locked them away carefully, neatly bundled up in a drawer of her own dresser.

It now came back to her that Lugtens made it very difficult for Clara, and almost simultaneously that she so often longed to return to the *kampong* she had come from.

"Why do I stay here?" she said as if to herself.

"Why?" little Lena asked, and answered immediately: "Well, because you live here, like we do."

But Mama Tjang shook her head.

"I don't live here, dear, your father does, and he is angry with me."

"I think so too," Lena said very wisely, "but why is he angry with Mama Tjang?"

The old woman couldn't answer that. She knew, but she didn't think that the child would understand it. But she was wrong, because Lena had her own opinion about it and was pretty close to the truth. She went to see her father who was working again in his office. When he looked up for a moment she asked emphatically:

"Daddy, *why* are you so mad at Mama Tjang?"

He straightened up with amazement. No one else in the house would have had the courage except for this little thing. Although he was often at the point of snapping at Lena in his usual gruff and superior way, he could never bring himself to do it. Besides, he was amused by her boldness, as if his character needed to be pushed around at least in some way. He thought it was funny that this little blond curly-head was not afraid of him at all and dared to stand up to him quite naturally.

"I'm not mad," he said, and wanted to resume his work. But he couldn't get off that easily. She stood right next to him and put her arm casually on his shoulder.

"Oh yes. You are mad, Daddy. You don't want her to live here in the outbuildings."

"Come," he said, and frowned, "you shouldn't be a nuisance."

For him that was quite amiable, just as if he had spoken to an adult, and he added: "You know that Daddy doesn't like natives."

"She can't help that, Dad, she's still Mama's own mother."

"Yes, yes," he grumbled, driven into a corner, "but I just don't like them."

"But Mama has to take care of her, right? You'd take care of your own mother too, wouldn't you?"

Lugtens put his pen down on the big silver inkwell and turned pale. His lips were pressed tightly together and he looked straight in front of him without seeing anything. No, he hadn't taken care of his own mother. She had been dead for years and had died in abject poverty as a member of the lower class in a big city.

Fighting as hard as possible to improve himself in colonial society by making money, he had detached himself from everything when he was still on his way up. But now that he was older and couldn't go any further, now that his fortune was made and increased automatically, he sometimes had trouble repressing thoughts that were tied to memories and were full of reproach, although he never mentioned them to anybody. It wasn't hard for his ego, toughened by thirty years of working and worrying about all sorts of business interests, to dismiss what he liked to call cobwebs. And that's precisely what he did time and again. Yet he was stunned when he heard his short-comings so unexpectedly put into words by the only one of his children he was very attached to. He looked at Lena distrust-fully, wondering whether she had come up with this herself or if someone had put her up to it. And what was really perfectly normal now seemed extraordinary to him: she had the same eyes as his mother. As if he had suddenly become superstitious he was overcome by a feeling that his mother, who had been dead a long time, was looking at him through the child's eyes. His distrust vanished immediately. Yet he still asked:

"Did Mama tell you to say that to me?"

"Mama!" Lena said, amazed. "Not at all, I just asked for myself."

Lugtens took a deep breath.

"Well," he said, "run along then. The old woman can stay. Daddy won't get mad about it anymore and will never say anything about it again."

The child skipped out of the room, completely unaware that she had accomplished something extraordinary. She was simply satisfied that Mama Tjang didn't have to leave and that her mother, as she called it, wouldn't get "scolded" anymore. And she said it loud enough for Lugtens to hear, much to the shock and consternation of Clara, who almost dropped her crocheting from her lap and whispered:

"Be quiet, Lena. What did you do this time?"

"Well," the child answered as fearlessly as always, "I asked Daddy not to be mad anymore because...."

Mrs. Lugtens got up in a hurry.

"Come, we'll go to the *gudang*," she said quickly, interrupting the child, "then you can get some *padi* for the *perkututs*. They haven't had anything to eat yet today."

But she did so only to have the little one repeat word by word what she had been *brani* enough to say to her father.

5 "Well, Aunt Clara!"

Clara didn't understand it entirely either. Her comprehension was generally restricted to the awareness that this little devil had put one over on her domestic tyrant, and had fooled him completely. That is what she told her sister and was also what the Uhlstra girls heard. Geber learned the same thing when he came to town that Saturday night in order to spend Sunday there. He was told by his prospective bride, between two busy stints of work on the trousseau. Better raised and educated, he felt that there was more to it than simply besting Lugtens, but he kept it to himself.

He also preferred to say as little as possible about the Lugtens family. Once in a while he visited them and he was always invited when they gave a dinner or a party. But he kept his voluntary visits as short as possible, and during the special occasions he went to the card table as soon as politeness allowed.

The contrast between Lugtens's powerful despotic character and Geber's lazy indifference didn't stop the two men from liking each other. On the contrary, Lugtens was rather fond of Geber and often said that he would be pleased if Geber would stay at his house when he was in town or, at least, drop by for a pot-luck dinner in the evening. But it never happened. Geber's impromptu visits were rare. When they now told him at his fiancée's house about what everyone saw as little Lena's recklessness, his thoughts went back to days long past, years ago in fact, to a time that explained his reticence. And now he was to marry Rose, and become related to Lugtens and his wife! It was absurd, he thought, and while he continued to muse about that absurdity with a mocking smile on his face, Rose suddenly made a remark that struck him.

"You know," she said, "it's very strange, but Aunt Clara is the only one who didn't congratulate me on my engagement."

"She did congratulate me, though," Mrs. Uhlstra said in a tone of voice that sounded as if she resented the remark. But she didn't look up and continued diligently to embroider the *kabaja* edges she could do so well and which were her fame and pride.

"She could have congratulated me too. I don't think it's very nice. What do you think, Willem?"

But Mrs. Uhlstra didn't seem to want Geber to get a word in on the matter.

"Why do you keep nagging like that, Rose? She immediately wrote me a very nice letter. You know that."

"I didn't read it."

Meanwhile Geber, quietly smoking his cigar, had his own opinion. He and Mrs. Uhlstra knew all about it; they knew the heart of the matter, he better than she. It was the only time such a thing had ever happened to him. Lugtens had been presiding over his company for only a short time and still traveled extensively throughout the entire Indies archipelago in order to see everything about the business he now managed all by himself.

One day, when Geber left his plantation to go to town in order to shop, get some money, and pay his bills, he had gone to Clara and brought her the plants and flowers she had asked for in a letter. Mrs. Uhlstra, who was staying with her sister, had left for the *tokos*. Geber was a different man then, twelve years younger, and by comparison even younger than that. He and Clara had known each other for a long time. They laughed together and called each other by their first names. He teased her, she teased him back, all without any ulterior motive. What had gotten into him that day and what put her into that kind of mood they never knew, but when Mrs. Uhlstra returned from her *toko* visits, they were sitting across from each other on the rear veranda, astonished and burdened. They were both unhappy and discontent, and felt strange and shy.

The good Lena hadn't noticed anything. She was so preoccupied with her purchases and her stories about the prices the Chinese had dared to ask and about her own talent for haggling, that she thought of nothing else and couldn't keep quiet for a moment. She didn't even see anything strange in the fact that Geber didn't return to Kuningan that day, but postponed his departure repeatedly. Each day he could be found in Lugtens's house, always coming when Mrs. Uhlstra was with her friends or shopping. Of course it was her personal maid who told her everything, and, infuriated and with a great show of anger and indignation, she spared neither her sister nor Geber. Dismayed and ashamed, he immediately beat a retreat. In fact, he really wanted nothing better. Though the event had repeated itself time and again and was agreeable in itself, it nevertheless filled him with melancholy thoughts for most of the day. Not the least in love with Clara, he felt terribly annoyed about making an irreparable mistake, one that could put him into the greatest difficulties. At the time he had heavy financial obligations to the company managed by Lugtens. Uhlstra, his best *sobat* and neighbor, was no easy man where the moral reputation of his family members was concerned. Geber was glad that the short affair with Clara, which had filled him more with worry and alarm than with pleasure and joy, had come to an abrupt end in such a convenient way. It also seemed that she herself didn't see much point in a future where so terribly much was at stake. He didn't hear from her anymore, and he continued to live as usual in the country with his native housekeeper, who represented no risk at all.

He didn't show up for months, but when at last he could no longer willingly avoid coming to town for business, and was therefore obliged to accept an invitation from Lugtens, he and Clara behaved normally toward each other. To strangers it must have seemed as if nothing special had ever happened between them: he was most polite, and she was gruff and cool.

Thus it ended, though with this one difference: when little Lena was born, Mrs. Uhlstra, Geber, and Clara had their own notion about it. And Lugtens, if he ever paid attention, could have remarked that the nice blond child had the same violet-blue eyes of his own late mother and like those of one of his friends.

Rose's fiancé was thinking about all of this, while the girls were bickering with his future mother-in-law about the familiar question of whether it was nice or malicious of Aunt Clara not to have congratulated Rose personally but only in a letter to Mama, as Mrs. Uhlstra had assured them at least ten times.

To the great regret of the Uhlstra women, both mother and daughters, Geber was annoyingly busy during these premarital days. Usually, when he was in town he could spend his free time as he pleased, but just now they thought it was very unfortunate that he and Papa Uhlstra had to do some very important business, about which they kept a mysterious silence. The women could only find out that a lot of money had to be made, something that they, who hardly knew the value of money, were less interested in than the regrettable fact that the bride couldn't show off her beautiful clothes every evening. There was nothing to be done about it, however. It seemed to be a law that the "conferences" concerning that important business could only be held at night at Lugtens's house. And it even seemed necessary that the business discussions had to start with a good dinner and finish with a good card game.

They were meeting like that once again this evening, at seven o'clock, sitting in a separate room of the big house where Twissels, the merchant, had joined them. Under the light of a big crystal lamp they put their heads together over some pages of writing: Uhlstra's big pepper-and-salt head, Lugtens's thick blond curls, Twissels's tufted little chicken head, and the bridegroom's shiny pate. They didn't say anything for a long time, concentrating on the sheets of paper and the lists and statements from which each took his own figures to support his own calculations. It concerned a big contract for the transportation and delivery of government goods, in a manner that was still feasible in those days of plenty. They had agreed to form a *kongsi* for it.

Now they were almost ready and they compared and checked each other's figures. Finally, Twissels recapitulated everything, reading softly to them in his sweet girl's voice that rose higher with each new sentence like a child reading a story from a school book. In the meantime the other men stared down at the tablecloth. While puffing at their cigars, they nodded approval in silence when one or the other heard the figure concerning his own share in the plan. After mentioning the final figure, Twissels looked around the table through the big lenses of his pince-nez. He looked at them one after the other with a friendly, questioning face as though he expected a compliment because he had just completed the preliminary work so accurately. Lugtens raised his heavy head with a satisfied smile on his broad, smooth face.

"Well," he said, "now at least we know where we stand more or less."

"If there's no mishap," Uhlstra commented. Participating in something like this for the first time, he didn't have full confidence in it yet. And Geber, who had had a run of bad luck lately, sighed.

"Yes," he said, "something might still happen that we hadn't counted on."

Lugtens looked at him both pityingly and amiably and then looked at Twissels, who laughed shrilly and reassured them that they should trust in his unfailing luck.

"When I'm part of it," he continued, "and Lugtens is in it too, it would be surprising if there wasn't something extra left in addition to the share we're due for."

Now the three of them were laughing out loud. Twissels was really one of a kind, Uhlstra thought again, and he brought his big planter's hand confidently down on the narrow shoulder of the merchant, who cried out in his falsetto voice: "Hey, take it easy, you big oaf!"

Content and satisfied with their work, they got up and, while talking loudly about unimportant matters, they walked back and forth on the big marble front veranda until about eight o'clock, when a carriage pulled by a pair of big horses drove into the yard. It was Markens, who had come to dinner and who had to drink a glass of fine Burgundy first before they thought he was in the requisite mood. He had to help them get the contract.

Of course he knew why he was there. Uhlstra had already worked it all out with him privately. There were other people interested in this matter, so they had to have someone who could neutralize the competition. After dinner, which was attended only by the men, they had a friendly discussion about it. Not a word, not even a hint, was mentioned about any financial interest that Markens might have in awarding the contract to their *kongsi*. It looked very much as if it was solely a question of simple logic, expounded in arguments that were advanced by all four of them, one at a time. Now and then Markens raised an objection or mentioned a problem, but it was immediately solved. And he nodded approvingly when he was convinced, agreed with them, and finally declared that he would do his best. It was really no more than a formality, but it had to happen that way. They all understood that this was necessary, yet they all longed for their beloved card game.

When at two o'clock in the morning Markens got up to leave, he put some considerable winnings in his pocket. It was remarkable that Lugtens, Uhlstra, and Twissels got terrible hands all evening long! Geber could play as usual; he always lost more than all of them, anyway. When Markens had gone, the four of them still talked for a moment.

"It's a nice piece of business, believe me," Twissels, who had drunk one grog too many again, assured them.

With a gleam of satisfaction on his face, Lugtens stretched himself and leaned back in his chair. As usual he hadn't drunk anything but a glass of water and hadn't even smoked a cigar.

"Unless something totally unexpected happens," he said seriously, "we should be able to make a million on this deal!"

The contract was awarded to the kongsi the day before Rose and Geber were married. The bridegroom was in extremely high spirits on his wedding day, but so were the witnesses from the kongsi.

Though Rose had a rather dark complexion she was still a lovely bride in her wedding gown of heavy Lyon silk with a real lace train, and if Geber didn't look youthful, he did look like a gentleman. It was so crowded at the reception that one could faint from the heat, and even one of the largest rooms in the house was too small to store all the beautiful gifts.

For Rose it meant an hour and a half of endless kisses from congratulatory women, something that annoyed Geber very much. He, on the other hand, had to put up with dozens of handshakes until his fingers hurt from all the cordiality and his almost continuously outstretched arm felt stiff. What a liberation when the last well-wishers got into their carriages around eight thirty and the newlyweds had one final ordeal to endure: dinner! One felt sorry for them. Geber was at the end of his rope, miserable with having to wear a black suit and from being on his feet during the entire afternoon and evening despite the heat. Now and then he yawned quietly behind his hand; he felt that the whole affair was boring and tiresome. It mesmerized him. When they were finally riding toward Kuningan after a nervous goodbye to Mama and the sisters that included tears, trembling lips, encouragements like "Take care," and kisses on the young woman's much-kissed cheeks that resounded like gun shots throughout the veranda, Geber collapsed against the cushions in the carriage with the horrible temptation to take off his black pants and frock coat. There wasn't a dry stitch under his waistcoat! "Good God," he thought, "what a trial getting married is."

Rattling along the graveled road, they sat for the first ten minutes without talking while recuperating from the fatigue and, refreshed by the cool evening air that streamed in through the windows, slowly recovering from what Geber had called a "trial." He held her hand in his, convinced by his male conceit that she was thinking about something and that he knew exactly what it was. It amused him. It roused him, and he almost broke into laughter when he gave her a kiss, the umpteenth that day! What else could he have thought she was thinking?

"Did you notice?" Rose asked suddenly.

"What's that?" he returned the question, still in that same jolly mood.

"Well, Aunt Clara!"

"Come on," he said, "what about Clara?"

Inwardly he was angry that at precisely *this* moment she seemed to think of that topic and had to start talking about it. It was the last thing he wanted to have mentioned and now, of all times, the conversation threatened to turn in that direction! His ego was not at all flattered. For the first time it struck him as highly unpleasant that her marriage, as far as the real motive was concerned, didn't seem to arouse even the same amount of interest in her as she would have for a successful pudding or a plate of well-mixed *rudjak*.

"*Sungu mati*, Wim, it really is true; she didn't congratulate me again, nor you either."

"As far as I'm concerned, I didn't pay any attention to it, and I couldn't care less."

He let go of her hand and once again leaned back against the gray upholstery of the carriage.

"Something must have happened, she must be annoyed about something," Rose continued without paying any attention to him, totally preoccupied with this new wrinkle in her family's history.

"Could be. What do we care?"

"I've never quarreled with her, and I've always loved her very much. She was so nice, you know, and she loved me very much, very very much."

And when Geber didn't answer, being the only way to get

out of this annoying conversation, Rose repeated it most assertively:

"Never, you know. I never quarreled with her."

"Well, so much the better. Then you don't have to reproach yourself for anything, and I wouldn't worry or think about it anymore."

"I *have* to think about it, Wim," she persisted with the stubbornness of an Uhlstra. "You see, she is Mama's only sister.... I don't care about Uncle Lugtens's beautiful gift.... not at all. ... but that she's so nasty and unkind...."

"Now the fat's in the fire," Geber thought. After that "trial" all day long, we're now also going to get a crying fit in the carriage on the way to Kuningan, and for the most miserable of reasons! By the dim light of the two lanterns he saw that she was really crying and holding her handkerchief to her eyes. He gently tried to get her away from the matter and turn the conversation toward a more cheerful subject, using his initial mood as a point of departure. But in spite of his good intentions and gentle attempts, her first sad exclamation after the tears had been dried was: "What can she have against me?"

"Nothing, of course," he repeated, a little impatient now. "Maybe she has something against *me*."

That silenced Rose for a moment. She hadn't looked at the matter from that point of view.

"Can she have something against *you*?" she asked with great interest.

That was really too much! He couldn't treat the young wife he was bringing home for the first time to that crazy story about his old love affair with her aunt.

"I don't know," he said evasively, "women are so strange."

But she wasn't that easily placated. She took his hand and leaned against him cozily, trying everything to satisfy the curiosity that had been provoked by the idea that the wind could be blowing from another direction. It was extremely annoying, he thought, and it irritated him immensely, but he did not want to frighten her off with a gaucherie so, in the hope to end it, he said:

"Oh well, she *does* have something against me. At one time I had some differences with her that she never seems to have forgiven me for. I really can't say more about it."

It had been said. Nothing could change that now, but it was suddenly clear to him that he was irretrievably lost; he had thrown oil on the fire and the only choice left was to come up with lies or tell the plain truth. He had disliked the former his entire life. He couldn't lie. It didn't suit him and went against everything he stood for. But to tell the truth. . . . no, he couldn't do that either.

They were quarreling when the carriage stopped in front of his house. Rose was overwrought and in a very bad mood.

"That just isn't right!" she said. If something serious existed between her husband and one of her closest relatives, so serious that it had necessarily led to a rift, then it was unheard of and mean to keep the reason from her. First of all she had already experienced the consequences and, furthermore, she refused to be treated like a child. She wanted nothing to do with Geber until he had told her the honest truth.

But Geber had no intention of doing that, although he otherwise tried everything to get her in a better mood, asserting that it was just ridiculous to argue that much about such a relatively small thing, calling it childish, exaggerated, and foolish. All to no avail. The end of the matter was that an hour later Rose was crying angrily by herself in the big, beautiful, neatly made bridal bed, while Geber, dressed in pajama pants and *kabaja*, was lying on a long rattan chair on the back veranda, smoking a cigar. At first he too was in a bad mood, but he finally saw the comical side of this odd spectacle and made fun of the foolish figure he was cutting on his wedding night.

When he had finished his cigar, he went quietly to the bedroom. Rose was enviably sound asleep, probably overcome by the fatigue of that day. For a moment he stood there, hesitant and undecided. Then he went to the guest room, grumbling to himself, and yet with a sense of the ridiculousness of it all and with an urge to laugh at himself. He did the only thing he could do: he also went to sleep.

When Geber awoke refreshed and rested at five o'clock sharp the next morning, he saw the incident in a much different light. It was much more serious and humiliating. He thought about writing a note to his mother-in-law to ask for her help. Yet before he would do that and before he would open the house to let the servants in, he really ought to see if his young wife's mood had blown over. As always the night seemed to have brought counsel and the incipient dawn put the world in a different light.

An hour later he tore up the note he had already written to Mrs. Uhlstra in the guest room, tore it into the smallest possible pieces....

And now life at Kuningan became more pleasant and comfortable than he had ever known. He hired a respectable European as a supervisor. His housekeeping, which had been neglected for so many years, perked up, as it were, and everything took on a neat and well-kept appearance under the busy hands of the young woman who, brought up in the country by a competent mother, was completely in her element. In that first month Geber's plans to sell his estate and go to Europe receded into the background and totally different ideas took their place. As if inspired by his wife's practical activity, the indifference that had come about more from habit than as part of his nature diminished, and his active role in the delivery of products needed for the *kongsi* stimulated him.

He formed all kinds of plans for buildings and waterworks and for the construction of roads and new acreage in order to increase the productive capacity of his estate, until ... one morning a note arrived from Lugtens inviting Rose and him to a ball.

It was one of Lugtens's habits: when an undertaking had partially succeeded he would give a party, the way a native would give a *sedekah*, though it was done by instinct rather than superstition. And at these times nothing was too good. The finest wine, the most beautiful pastries, the most expensive dinners, all of it in abundance for the guests. All the "notables" the town could muster loved to come to the luxurious parties at Lugtens's beautiful house, where he, in his black frock coat and white tie looking as if he had just walked out of an old-fashioned oil painting, received them with his stern but dignified face. Always polite and aloof from the crowd, he was yet mysteriously familiar with people in high places.

Markens came with his wife. She was received with particular deference which she accepted as a matter of course. Markens, who by now had done very well in government service, was as much oppressed by her importance as he had been when he still belonged to the lesser gods. He was simple in his ways, priding himself on the fact that he had started at the bottom, even boasting about it, though not when Etienne was present because he feared her ever-increasing haughtiness. She was indeed from a good family, though it was one where some off-shoots had deteriorated, and she sprouted from one of these. In Holland she had suffered from this, but in the Indies, married to Markens, away from the miserable surroundings of impoverished, demoralized, and alcoholic relatives unknown to Indies society, she had successfully used her fine old sonorous maiden name until, forgetting everything in her obsession, she fell victim to her own importance, which was increased by Markens's good position.

She remained a beautiful and slim woman in spite of the imminent threat of old age. She was a woman who still spent time on her appearance, who still wore low-cut dresses, and who could and did dare to invite comparison with much younger women in terms of skin tone, and the curve of her shoulders, bosom, and arms. It wasn't because of that reason, that is to say, jealousy, that people generally detested her; it was solely because of her haughtiness, which everyone considered a voluntary vice and which no one saw as a disease. Her entrance would probably not have been bad for a ball at the court of Henry IV. Here, among the prosperous middle class and well-placed officials, it resembled a farce that was only enhanced by the figure of Markens who walked after her, slipping somewhat on the marble. He was always in a bad mood at such occasions and democratized himself, as it were, to provide a counterbalance, though he achieved nothing more than presenting a silly contradiction.

Lugtens rather liked her, and she thought him the only distinguished man present. With an even sterner face than usual, he bowed, offered her his arm, and brought her to a chair.

Clara laughed to herself.

"Those two are well suited for each other," she said to Mrs. Uhlstra after both Markens had greeted her.

Mrs. Uhlstra turned up her nose behind her fan.

"It's a pity that *he* doesn't have such a crazy wife."

"Why didn't Rose come?"

"*You* don't need to ask that, Clara. Someone who acts as unwisely as you...."

"*Sudah*, Lena.... Don't scold. Maybe you're right.... We'll talk about it some time."

6 Sly Digs

Rose and Geber squabbled about the ball at Lugtens's. She still wanted to know what that old mysterious dispute was all about. She prodded him about it all the time and kept track of his weakest moments, times when he showed the least resistance. Finally, when his head was resting on her arm and she was caressing him, he relaxed to the point of indifference and told her in a manner as if it didn't mean anything, because, in the final analysis, he didn't care at all anymore. Little black devils danced and flickered under her long, curled-up eyelashes. So that's what they had kept secret from her! In and by itself, it left her totally indifferent. What did she care how Geber had spent part of his youth many years ago. No, it wasn't that, but the fact that now, even now, Aunt Clara was still jealous of her, Rose. Even now. That meant that she was still capable of, even now, when the occasion presented itself. . . . The short, fat, dark hand with the dimples on the knuckles became a nice fist, threatening Mrs. Lugtens in silence.

Ever since Mrs. Uhlstra had received a letter from Rose with hints that left nothing to the imagination, the sisters had talked about it endlessly, quietly, with pent-up rage, but without intending to have a quarrel. Yet it was almost the only topic of conversation whenever they saw each other. It was as if they were not able to talk about anything else, even though they had been silent about it all those years. This bit of ancient history had been dug up and was not to be forgotten again.

"It would have been the first big party after her wedding."

Clara's "*Sudah, Lena*" didn't prevent Mrs. Uhlstra from carrying on. As she freely admitted, she was furious that her only married daughter was not present at this splendid feast and couldn't show off any of her beautiful clothes and jewelry.

"Why didn't she come. *I* wouldn't have devoured her!"

"Because she couldn't; her sense of honor. . . . "

"She's jealous!"

"Of you?"

It was more of a sneer than a question; everything was implied by the tone. Red flared in Clara's eyes. All their eyes were like the eyes of Mama Tjang (who meanwhile had recovered but had not gone to the *kampong*). Mrs. Uhlstra saw it and it scared her. She closed her big fan, thereby finishing the short angry conversation that had been carried on behind it without anyone noticing it.

Clara spoke to Mrs. Markens, who had just sat down on the other side of her. With her open fan covering half of her chest, her head held royally high, Mrs. Markens received the respectful homage of the officials who were a step below her husband and who were spoken to by others with a trace of irony, something she didn't notice at all, fully absorbed by her own superiority.

The small talk of the men coming to pay their respects kept Clara and Mrs. Uhlstra busy as well. The young men talked about the heat, not yet knowing how to converse with women above a certain age, while the older ones, who did know how but were gradually beginning to forget, thought that they complimented the women by saying that they carried their years so well. But everyone spoke to Mrs. Uhlstra about Rose's absence, because it was so noticeable! She had been a part of all the parties given during the last number of years, dancing regularly until the end of each program, including the "encores." The Uhlstra girls were always mentioned as being the regulars at each festivity in town. Rose, the oldest, had been married numerous times when the men talked about her. There wasn't one young man of any importance in town who hadn't been told by his friends or acquaintances that she would be just the right wife for him. And the various young bloods did think about it during deliberations when poor Rose was often tested financially, socially, and personally but always found wanting. Anyway, they never got any further than imagining it until, very practically, Geber had asked her and married her. Now they all thought that their abstinence had been really dumb.

"How's Mrs. Geber, your niece?" Mrs. Markens also asked.

"My niece Rose? Oh, very well, thank you."

"Please don't mention that name. I think it's an awful name."

"Oh really? I think it's very sweet."

"How is that possible? In Holland that name would be un-

95

thinkable among people of standing. One still finds it, I believe, among the lower Jewish classes."

The red glow hadn't left Clara's eyes yet. She still felt a great need to seek revenge for Lena's insulting remark. Without hesitating she came back with a parting shot.

"I wouldn't know," she said with her eyes down and her face an impassive and inscrutable Indies mask. "I'm not familiar with those neighborhoods."

Mrs. Markens paled and was tempted to get up and leave. They dared make such nasty remarks to her! And she had to bear it, coming from such a *nonna*! But she controlled herself, acting as if she hadn't heard it. Drawing herself up, she said over Clara's head to Mrs. Uhlstra:

"Do you like being here in town this long?"

"Oh yes, it's nicer for the children. Are you thinking of going to Europe?"

It was her nightmare. Here Europe meant Holland, and Holland was where the whole degenerated branch of her good family would assault her immediately like a flock of hungry and lowly crows whom she wouldn't be able to ward off. They wouldn't let her go. They would pull her back down from the heights she had reached in the Indies, down to the low level of their own personal vices and social miseries.

"Perhaps," she said, softly modulating her voice and moving her head slightly to and fro, "we also would do it for the children."

"Yes, the boys are beginning to shoot up."

Mrs. Markens shuddered. What a terrible expression that was, "shoot up," but that was to be expected from such farmers and country folk. They talked about people as if they were plants.

"They are getting bigger, certainly. It is absolutely essential for their further upbringing. The education here in the Indies...."

Now Mrs. Uhlstra, who also hadn't recovered yet from her conversation with Clara, got angry again. And besides, didn't she have a son who had received a very successful education in the Indies?

"Oh, I don't think that the education is to blame. One child has a quicker mind and is more studious than another."

"That could be. But here in the Indies there prevails such a nouveau-riche atmosphere...."

"That is something entirely different. That can't be the reason that there are boys who can't get through their exams."

"But it is.... One can be more sensitive than the other."

"Well, I know youngsters who are so sensitive that they do the vilest things in the *kampong*. Then the parents have to use all their money and influence to *tutup* the matter. And in school those boys are laziness and stupidity itself...."

Again Mrs. Markens paled and again her lower lip trembled. Good heavens, how nasty these people were! She understood exactly what Mrs. Uhlstra meant. It was as if she'd been stabbed through the heart when she had to endure here once more what had already cost her so many tears and so much sorrow. It was the second insult and again she thought bitterly: "such a *nonna!*"

"Yes," she said, as if such cases didn't concern her. "It's terrible. But we are still thinking of going to Europe. An Indies upbringing has a highly detrimental influence on young people of good family. It's possible that a colony of criminals can perfect themselves here, but it is deadly for people of our standing."

"If I remember though, some respectable people came here about twenty-odd years ago, your husband, for example, and when I see how they're doing now, I don't think that it takes criminals to succeed here."

"Oh, I don't want to say that. There are a great many exceptions, of course. Mr. Geber, for instance, Mr. Lugtens, and there's your husband, Mr. Uhlstra...."

"Excuse me, but Uhlstra doesn't fit. He was born here, just as I was. But he certainly would have gone under if he'd had an unhappy family life, because that is really the worst thing that can happen to a man."

"Yes.... that's true," Mrs. Markens agreed hesitantly and painfully.

"One has to admire some men for their inexhaustible patience. If, as respectable people, they don't become criminals it certainly isn't due to their happy environment."

It caught Mrs. Markens by the throat. She had to swallow it and it went down hard.

Stiffly, as if moving on a hinge, Markens bowed to the lady of the house. Lugtens, with a forced friendly laugh, his eyes opened wide, moved his head with feigned gravity and, with his white-gloved hand outstretched, asked Mrs. Markens to open the ball with him.

She was released. She recovered immediately, drawing herself up from the depths into which she had been plunged so mercilessly, and looked out proudly over the hall. What did she care about the cackling of such a pair of insignificant beings, so far beneath her?

Clara had loved it. How Lena had beaten that foolish woman who always took on such airs and who had, as everyone knew, ruined her husband and neglected her children! She forgot all her grievances because of it. She would immediately have taken her sister's side in spite of that deeply cutting "Of you?" a minute ago. Though it certainly hadn't been necessary. But *if* Lena had been bested by Mrs. Markens, she would have given her sister a hand, even though as the hostess she was obliged to keep a pleasant atmosphere. Sure, they were quarreling together about that old mess, but they were *family*, and that's all there was to it. All those strange men. Well, one could marry them and they served more or less as a necessary evil, but the *family* took precedence! Mrs. Lugtens would like nothing better than to reconcile with Rose amidst tears and kisses. She understood that this wouldn't happen for some time yet because Geber was at this point still too important and the novelty of the marriage hadn't worn off. But when there was a child at Kuningan—and she was certain that there would be one—the family would again claim their old rights on Rose's heart. Then the nest would be finished, with the "young one" in it, and the *laki* would become from that moment on a big or a little bother, depending on his mood and habits.

The ball had been opened. The older men were playing cards: Lugtens with Uhlstra, Markens, and a general. They had assigned Twissels to another table. After all, it was a bit annoying that he was always so lucky.

"Your son-in-law didn't come," Lugtens said with some irony and a lot of dissatisfaction.

"He wrote me that Rose wasn't well and that he didn't want to leave her alone."

"Hm! Has he delivered yet?"

That last remark referred to the delivery for the *kongsi*.

"We're all through."

"Good. Me too. Have you heard anything about it yet?" That question concerned Markens.

"The inspection committee was very satisfied."

"That pleases me. Your deal, General."

It was one of his special amusements. He liked to pronounce the word "General." When it came from his mouth and was heard by his own ears, he thought that it sounded like a command. A beautiful word! They talked now and then between games. To their right was another foursome that included Twissels. One could see them put their heads together all the time. There was a person there who, from time to time, told a joke. He had a whole collection of them. Whenever he heard one on his official inspection trips he would write it down as part of his business notes. When he returned, he'd work them out even before his official reports. One could hear the high-pitched laugh of Twissels, who was sitting at that table, above everyone else.

"He's at it again," Uhlstra said with a nod and an amused glance in that direction. He liked it and would have loved to laugh with them over the famous jokes. But Lugtens detested it.

"I don't understand how anybody his age can still be so childish," he said.

"He's not that old yet," said the general soothingly. He would like to have listened too.

"Is it true that you'll be going on furlough?" Markens asked.

"You know already? That's quick. Yes, I think. . . . at the beginning of next year."

"That's too bad," Lugtens said.

He thought it was unconscionable that someone still healthy and strong would leave such a wonderful position to loaf around in retirement.

"If I were a general, I would stay in the service," he continued. "I think that's the only beautiful thing about the military."

The general looked at him with a strange little laugh, twirled up his gray mustache, and narrowed his eyes between the sharply edged lines.

"I'd rather be a second lieutenant," he said.

Markens nodded, understanding like the wise person for whom one word is enough. He knew about the service with its joys and sorrows, especially its sorrows. And life! He would also much rather be a lowly young clerk who has to make do in a poor section of town, but who feels the rich surging of life coursing within him with force, if not recklessness. To be such a young fellow with great physical faculties and to be free, free from ties and obligations!

Lugtens didn't understand that. Money and position were the only factors that governed his life. Money and power were all that had ever fascinated him. He thought it was childish that those two men still longed for their lost youth. Disdainfully he shrugged briefly and said, dryly and curtly:

"Hadn't we better go on playing?"

What did *he* care that he was getting older, that time pressed its *tjap* on his face, and that the past glistened among his blond curls? There was only one thing in the world that mattered to him: the social standing by which one could live. If that was good, then everything was good; if it was bad then everything was bad.

Markens stopped playing very early. His wife had let him know that she wished to leave. It mattered little to him because he was losing. It was her regular custom at parties to arrive last and leave first. It was part of her idée fixe that she was cut from better cloth than the rest. Her leaving wasn't regarded as a sign for the others; they hardly paid attention to it. Wherever she passed on her host's arm with her head tilted backward, the men bowed and the women greeted impassively. Markens, walking behind them, got friendly nods and handshakes. People liked him; he was such a good man.

After a few more hands the other three men stopped playing too.

"I'm going to have a word with the women," Lugtens said. "Afterward I would like to talk to you and Twissels. Go to my office. I'll be there in a minute."

They did so. They obeyed the commanding despot without hesitation, not even noticing it themselves. He hadn't the slightest intention of giving orders to his friends. Even though he sometimes spoke to them as if they were his subordinates, it was done entirely out of habit, unintentionally.

"What could he want?" Uhlstra wondered, leaning back in a green leather armchair, sticking his increasing paunch out with artificial dignity, while the tall thin Twissels, who had taken a

Havana cigar from a box on the desk, was lighting it above the glass of the lamp.

"Who knows? He's an extraordinary man. It must be something important."

The guests were walking past the open door, from the front of the house to the back: young people excited from the dancing and intoxicated with their own youth, with the beautiful sparkle in the girls' eyes, with the heady scent of flowers and perfume and the immediate proximity of uncovered curves, shapes, and shades that were normally hidden from view. They talked and laughed loudly, doing their best to be pleasant and gallant and to give themselves an air of *savoir vivre*, with an artificiality in their voices and with drastic changes in volume they wouldn't do otherwise. The young women seemed to glide over the marble with delicate steps, engaged in busy but soft conversations and rapid movements of their fans. They flirted with sudden sparkling little laughs, slight nods, pouting lips, and unexpected glances. Among the young men along the wall were some loners who concealed their awkwardness behind old men's attitudes, doing their best to look down on everything with angry expressions as if it were all far beneath them. But they too were overjoyed and externally grateful for a passing young lady's glance or greeting, bowing deeply in return two or three times.

Lugtens came into the office with hard, angry steps, as always stamping somewhat as if to make the floor aware of the weight of his personality.

He closed the double door behind the portiere. He wanted to lock out the sound of all that happy excitement and of the dance music that blared from the brass instruments into the rooms, but it didn't work. The whole building was filled with it and it penetrated everywhere.

"I've got a little something for us," he said.

He probably meant to say it cheerfully, but a stranger, judging by the sound of his voice, would suspect that he was informing them of unpleasant news.

"It must be something good, if you care so much about it."

"It is indeed! I don't want to do it alone as a matter of principle. It concerns contracts in the outer possessions. . . . "

"Yes," Twissels said. "I heard about it. You mean those spices from...."

"Quiet," Lugtens interrupted him angrily. "How the hell did you know about it already? And you talk openly about it, as if it's nothing...."

"You're allowed to hear it."

"One should never do that. Well, if you all participate.... It is quite a fortune! We'll need a lot of cash and a lot of credit. I want to buy everything that's available along the coast. Three million dollars."

Uhlstra grew pale.

"I'll play my part," Twissels laughed, like someone who's used to any kind of transaction.

"Me too," Uhlstra said, but his mouth was dry from nervousness due to the large scope of the business. They began to expand on it, quietly, coolly, in a whisper. Once Uhlstra mentioned Geber's name for a partner, but Lugtens rejected it with a curt gesture and a word or two. The other two knew why. Petty as it was, Lugtens was angry that Geber and his wife hadn't come to the party. That's why he was not allowed to participate. The sound of the festivities floated around them, harmonious at one point and then a murmuring background pierced by a few shrill notes.

Dancing, drinking, joking. Music and laughter! With serious faces they were standing close together in the office, frowning from concentration and thought as they roughly outlined the plan that Lugtens had described in a few words. It began to dawn on Uhlstra. He understood now why they had included him: his knowledge of the population, his ease in dealing with the native chiefs, his fluency in Malay, those were his strengths, more so than the money he would have to raise for his share.

7 Such Good Boys!

When the carriage rode into her yard, Mrs. Markens saw an unusual commotion of natives walking back and forth. She hadn't exchanged a word with her husband; they had nothing to say to one another.

"What could that be?" she asked fearfully, her hand already on the door handle of the carriage.

"Stay calm, Etienne. We'll hear about it in a minute."

But nervous and already trembling with fear, she opened the door before the carriage had come to a halt.

Markens stopped her.

"Be careful now, you'll have an accident yourself."

She pulled herself loose and jumped onto the path. The gravel gave way under her dancing shoes and she fell backward, though not very hard, and then sideways onto the lawn. It made her even more nervous. Quickly getting up, her beautiful evening cape left behind on the grass, she walked on, with Markens grumbling behind her, although he too was worried about the commotion where he was used to finding always perfect silence and peace.

The servants stopped talking and ceased walking back and forth. They were standing on the rear veranda in front of the door. Inside a dim light was on.

"Eddy! Freddy!" Mrs. Markens called out loudly, almost stumbling over her own feet in her nervous fear, convinced that the children had had an accident.

"Here, Mom," one of the boys said.

"What happened? Did something happen to you?"

"Oh yes, Mom," the oldest one shouted, "you were robbed and now they say we did it."

The boys in their pants and *kabajas* looked healthy and well built, yet there was something old and drawn about their faces.

"Robbed!" their mother repeated, amazed but calm again since no bodily harm had occurred. "We were robbed?"

As they had done in the beginning, both boys talked at the same time, walking along with their mother to her bedroom. Loud and yelling, they brought their parents to a mirrored mahogany wardrobe that was open and had had its lock forced. Again talking at the same time, they said that they had heard a thief and yelled for help and *malieng-malieng*. Then the servants had come, and they believed that they had done it. . . .

"Done what?" Markens asked suddenly.

"Stolen the money," the boys said.

"Was money stolen? How do you know that money has been taken?"

For a moment the boys hesitated, stammering from having to swallow the verbal barrage they hadn't finished yet.

"My purse with thirty silver guilders is gone," Mrs. Markens said rather indifferently. "The children may well have known that it was in my closet. They must have seen it there when they were in the room."

"Yes, it's Mom's purse," the boys yelled at the same time, "and there were thirty guilders in it in *rijksdaalders*."*

"I'll have the police called immediately," Mrs. Markens declared indignantly, "I'll have all the servants rounded up and their rooms searched." Walking quickly to the back of the house where the servants were still waiting, not knowing whether they should leave or stay, she exploded furiously, calling them thieves and burglars, and threatening them with the police, prison, and forced labor. All the while Markens stood behind her, not at all convinced but with doubt and fear in his heart. But he pulled an angry and aloof face, as if to threaten in harmony with his wife's angry words.

When she had finished speaking, an old houseboy stepped forward. His face bore the determination that characterizes a native who has finally decided to stand up for his rights.

"We've done nothing," he said. "Not them and not me. I myself kept watch here while the master and mistress were out. The others were sitting in front of their rooms. I could see them by their little lamps in the distance. The *sinjos* screamed and

---

* A *rijksdaalder*, sometimes translated as "rixdollar," was a silver coin worth two and a half guilders. It was at the time probably the most common coin of considerable value.

I went inside immediately, the others followed. There was nothing. The wardrobe was open and the *sinjos* said that money was gone. We don't know about anything."

The boys, who had crept up closer on their bare feet, jumped with angry faces from behind their parents.

"He's lying, Mom. He was already in the room. And he also must have taken it!"

Mrs. Markens got more and more excited.

"Do you hear?" she asked her husband who, with a somber face and holding his chin in his hand, was staring straight ahead. "Do you hear? The children caught those thieves themselves, and that one still dares to deny it. But they'll know about it, I'll promise them that. It's lucky that the children discovered it."

The old native, who understood Dutch well, pulled at the edges of his *kabaja*. Now also nervous, he was forcing himself not to lose the proper tone and become insolent.

"I would like to speak to the master alone."

"You don't speak to the master alone! You can say what you have to say while I'm here."

That "impertinence" almost put her beside herself with anger. That *she* would be ignored and not reckoned as number one in the house by such a despicable object as a native servant! And Markens, sensing what terrible scenes were about to happen if he gave in to the native, nodded in agreement when she spoke.

"What you have to say should be heard by Mrs. Markens as well as by me," he said to the servant.

The man cleared his throat. It wasn't easy for him, yet he spoke in a firm voice.

"The *sinjos* took the money. They hid it in their bed. They often hide things there that they've taken. I've known about it for a long time and the others know it too."

They were all defeated for a moment. Markens had seen it coming. His old inspector's sense had noticed immediately who the guilty ones were. Now he knew for sure. Along with the great sorrow that overwhelmed him, a feeling of imperative duty also ran through him, a duty that had to be performed no matter what the cost.

"We'll investigate it immediately."

His wife had stood there stunned for a moment, though there

had been an instinctive movement as if to protect her boys who, with white lips, angry yet sneaky, were looking around and kicking sideways at the servants with their hard heels. When she heard *this* she suddenly became herself again, recovering her haughtiness and pride. Calmly and in a disdainful voice she asked:

"Would you really do that?"

"Absolutely."

"Would you dare insult me and my children so shamefully?"

"It *has* to be investigated."

"And I tell you that it will *not* happen."

He shrugged his shoulders like someone who is dealing with a fool and looked sternly and severely at the boys.

"Ed, Fred, *ajo*, come on."

But she held them back, trembling from head to toe and almost screaming in her nervous agitation. Imperious in the way she stood there with her arm outstretched and finger pointed, she said:

"Markens, you won't. I forbid you to humiliate me so shamefully in front of my lying servants or I'll leave this house immediately."

They were "her" children and "her" servants and, according to her, apparently not his. She always put it that way, and it had always bothered him. Especially now he was struck by her hostile attitude toward him while all he wanted to do was his duty. He had always been good, complaisant, and mild tempered, influenced by her superior origins which she continually brought to the fore as if it were her personal accomplishment. He had always treated her with indulgence and deference and had asserted himself so rarely as the head of the family that he had ceased being that for a long time. Now that it had gone this far, in other words, now that it was too late, he couldn't take it anymore. He forgot his usual nice manner which, though forced, he had always kept in mind when they had differences. His face turned red and the veins on his forehead swelled with anger.

"Then get the hell out! Ed, Fred, *ajo*, come on!"

And reaching with his right leg, he gave Freddy a good kick. The boys were frightened the most. They didn't know their father like this. With hearts pounding they walked fearfully to their room. For a moment Mrs. Markens, teetering on her legs, leaned with her hand against the wall. She felt that everything was lost and that nothing could help her in defending her children, no matter what. But she was also shaking because of her memories. That was the same crudeness she had known thirty years or more ago coming from her drunken father, who beat her every day, and from her sordid brothers. It was the same terrible tone of voice that she had tried to forget for so long, that she thought she would never hear again, and that now suddenly loomed up again from a terrible past with the harsh "Then get the hell out!" from her otherwise so good-natured and docile husband! But it didn't last long. She went after him. She had to know what was going to happen. She had to be there to defend her children.

When she came in, the bed's mosquito netting had been pulled apart and the straw mattress was turned over. The boys were standing fearfully beside it, biting the nails of their trembling fingers. By the light of the night lamp that the old servant held high, she saw the silver coins shine in Markens's hands and she also heard other things rattling around. More than just money appeared: half empty cans, objects she thought she had lost or which had disappeared, sweets from the bakery, an unopened bottle of port, and nearly empty bottles of other liquor—a small *gudang*.

Markens looked desperately at the boys. His terrible sorrow evoked a mad rage, a desire to kill them with one blow.

"Oh God," his wife said, clasping her hands together in a theatrical pose, and standing directly in front of him. "How shameful, how vile! Those people hid that on purpose to ruin my dear children!"

But she didn't speak about the police, prison, or forced labor anymore.

"I'll get you tomorrow," was all Markens could say to the boys, and at that moment he didn't know himself *what* he would do the next day. He only said it in order to say something, glad that for the moment the scandal was over. Eddy and Freddy were just as glad, and began immediately to fool around and secretly swear at their father and the servants whom they "were going to get." They didn't feel any regret for their behavior, totally imbued as they were with the characteristics of the degenerated branch of the family from which their mother came, and which had been transmitted into their minds and souls almost as if photographically.

Markens hadn't been able to sleep. He was sitting in his study trying to think, but influenced by what had happened he was unable to do so. Now and then tears rolled down his face. What would happen when he died? Now he had a good income which he managed to increase considerably without directly injuring anyone, though nevertheless in a way that could not bear the light of day. And yet they were in debt nevertheless, even though they were only a small family. He would have cared less about it if those two boys had only been a pleasure to him. But that had never happened, and now—now they were guilty of theft, and not for the first time, either. Perhaps he could put a stop to it right now if he really tried. But what was the use? His wife would act as a counterbalance for the worse, all his efforts would be fruitless, and his children would, as it were, end on the gallows anyway!

8 Mrs. Uhlstra Goes to Kuningan

While the Uhlstras were riding home from the party, Uhlstra was particularly quiet and withdrawn. As long as the girls were with them, Mrs. Uhlstra had company enough, but when they were alone in their bedroom at night she asked:

"Don't you feel well, dear?"

"Oh sure. I'm fine."

"You're so quiet. I thought that something was the matter. Did you lose a lot?"

He shrugged his broad shoulders with a violent gesture of indignation. What a foolish female idea!

"Where did you get that notion!"

She was sitting on a low couch with her legs crossed under her, her arms hanging limply across her knees. Her stiff coiffure was undone and her hair fell down her back. Dressed in a sarong and bodice she looked just like a native woman of indeterminable age, only more robust, with her health and strength preserved because she was protected against the miserable life of an Islamic woman. Her husband also looked dark, but completely different, more like a southern European with his short gray-black beard and his broad, compact, stout body. It was a type all by itself, descended from Gascony farmers. Sitting on a chair opposite her, Uhlstra was struggling with his shoes and grumbling about the lack of a bootjack because he had barely been able to get the shoes on before, and now they didn't want to come off his swollen feet.

"But there is something."

"Well, yes, there really *is* something. We've set up a big deal again."

"Are Lugtens and Twissels in on it too?"

"Of course."

She was glad. She knew that her husband was a good planter and a decent administrator, but she didn't consider him capable of dealing with such extensive business matters all by himself.

"Of course," he continued, kicking a loose half boot away with a sigh. "It's such a beautiful little deal again. I'll have to travel to the outer possessions for it."

"How many of you are in on it?"

"The three of us, no one else."

"Not Geber?"

"That's just it. I would have really liked to see him join us too. Once you're in such a business with a small group, you're well off. You only have to play the game. Geber knows Lugtens's weakness: you have to come to his parties. And now, the first one after their marriage and, I think, partly in their honor, he's dumb enough to stay home."

"But Rose...."

"Yes, I said that she was sick, but you can't fool him with that. He was angry about it."

"Did he say so?"

"He didn't have to. I saw it. I put out a feeler about letting Willem in, but he shook his head and acted as if he was swatting a mosquito."

"So Geber's out of it completely?"

"Of course."

"Is it much rugie?"

"It sure is! It's a big affair. That other thing was child's play by comparison."

Mrs. Uhlstra sighed. There you are! After so many years Geber's chickens were finally coming home to roost. It couldn't stay that way. She had to put an end to it.

"Come," she said, "let's go to sleep. *Sajang.* But if nothing can be done anyway, *sudah-lah!*"

She had reached a decision and fell asleep instantly, while Uhlstra was still worrying about the new enterprise that kept running through his mind and that he still couldn't quite grasp entirely. When she woke up the next morning he was sound asleep. Without waking him she left the room quietly and, rushing nervously, she took a bath and put on a beautiful *kabaja.* She wanted to prevent any attempt by her husband to stop her from going to Kuningan, and she also didn't want him to come along. She was glad once she sat in the light carriage and the beautiful horses were flying over the road at a full gallop.

Her arrival at Kuningan came like a bomb. Geber had just

come back from the fields and was eating a sandwich while Rose was sitting at the table with him eating *nassi* from a *pisang* leaf with her fingers. They were talking quietly and amicably about his new seedlings and how nicely they were beginning to come up already. The shoots were still very tiny peeping out of the soil, but they were so beautiful and healthy. She listened to it pleasantly and attentively. It was familiar territory for her because she had always heard a lot about it. She was knowledgeable about it, about that and training horses, dairy farming, making coconut oil, putting up fruit, baking *kwee-kwee*, and preparing *sambal*—it excited her, made her enthusiastic.

"Hey!" she shouted, pointing outside with a finger moist from the rice: "There's Ma!"

They abandoned their second breakfast. Rose, who boasted about her growing "condition," went to meet her mother with some needless showing off in her gait and posture, as if she was quite far along already. She forgot about it though when she saw the set and angry face, and the display of determination with which Mrs. Uhlstra got out of the carriage.

"You two pulled off a good one," she said to her daughter, walking up the steps to the front veranda with great authority. She went past Geber without noticing him.

"I guess you mean because we didn't go to that party last night!" Geber helped his wife.

"After all, we can stay at home when we don't want to go out."

"Oh sure! You don't have to pay attention to anything! You think that's enough to just sit here, right? And when you have a large household later on, it won't matter if you own more than just Kuningan."

"I don't understand any of this," Rose said angrily.

"I'm glad Papa didn't act that way, and I too was never too lazy to keep up with the world."

"Ma, please don't talk so foolishly.... You know very well why I don't want to go to Aunt Clara's!"

"Did Geber.... did you....?"

She was at a loss for words. It was too much for her. A man who told his wife such things!

"Yes, he told me everything, and that was good of him, Ma, very good!"

111

She shook her head, defeated for a moment. But not for long. If that's the way it was she wasn't going to worry about it, even if she didn't understand it. She hadn't come for that old nonsense.

"And are you so terribly angry about it, Rose? Such an old story that no one thinks about anymore!"

"That's just it, Ma! She does think about it. She showed that at my wedding."

"But what if she hadn't shown it and you had known about it anyway."

"Yes, then I wouldn't have cared about it very much."

Geber felt uncomfortable. Rose was standing there with her ample figure in the bright light with a calm and quiet determination. She spoke with her mother and not with him. And though their conversation was in fact about him, it seemed once again as if he had nothing to do with it.

It wasn't the old trespass that bothered Rose, but the new one. His former relationship with Aunt Clara didn't bother her, only the present one did.

"She regrets it now," her mother said. "It's just crazy, Rose. Wasn't she always nice to you? She still wants it that way, just like before."

For a moment the young woman hesitated. Her Indies weakness for one's family came, saw, and conquered.

"Well," she said, "if she wants to!"

Though on the one hand Geber was annoyed about playing second fiddle in family affairs, on the other he was glad about the forthcoming peace. He didn't want to say so though, afraid that Rose would find his approval suspicious.

After talking it over some more, she herself asked what he thought of it.

"It's all the same to me. I'm like a blank sheet of paper. You can be friendly again or not, I don't care at all."

Distrustful, his wife and mother-in-law looked at him searchingly. He had tried to be too smart. If he had said outright that he was for or against it they would have been reassured. His superficial western slyness was child's play for them. Even though he put on his most innocent face they still didn't believe him.

Mrs. Uhlstra passed lightly over her doubt. That shouldn't deter her from her goal.

"We have to see how we can work it so that Lugtens isn't angry with you anymore. What an awful man!"

"Not at all," Geber said. "Leave it to me. I always got along well with him."

They didn't want to hear it. What was he saying: that he knew that nasty Lugtens? It didn't look like it. They knew him and knew what he was. Lugtens never forgave anyone anything. He was vengeful. He would never allow Geber to "be in on anything" again, not if he could prevent it. That is, unless they did a real job on him now.

"I'll talk to Twissels about it," Mrs. Uhlstra said at last, "he's the only one who has any influence with him." Caught up in her continuing involvement and instinctively happy to be able to act independently now and then, she said that she would go to see Twissels that very day.

"Where?" Rose asked.

"Well, at his house."

"But, Ma!"

Geber thought it was crazy too. Everyone knew that Twissels, who was not married, had a young Indo-European girl as a "housekeeper." That by itself wasn't so bad, but he wasn't bothered about having the girl sit with him on the front veranda, where she served him his tea in the afternoon. Yes, it was even known that he permitted himself to invite Louisa for a chat with the men at night while they were playing cards at his house. But, of course, he had to have had one too many then.

People had warned him in private. If he had been without means or influence, the matter wouldn't have ended with warnings. He would have been ostracized. But one couldn't do that to a wealthy and well-connected merchant whom everybody would need at some time in the future. Thus he placed himself squarely above the law of social behavior.

"If you don't want to see her, ha ha," he said, "just close your eyes." Lugtens had angrily and emphatically pointed out to him the immorality of it, and had given him the kind of scolding he would have given his employees in the office or his wife at home. It had made Twissels angry and he had grown pale a little, but he didn't let it show.

"First of all you shouldn't meddle in my affairs," he said in a thinner and more sing-song voice than ever. "Secondly, Louisa has no reason to complain about me. She's very well off, and if I die she'll be even better off. She's happy with her lot. She's never had it so good in her life. Many a married woman is worse off in every respect."

Lugtens could have thrown him over his own railing, but despite his autocratic tendencies, he had enough sense never to let business interests suffer from private differences. He lightly passed over the allusion he had understood perfectly well.

"Marry her, then," he said.

"Thanks a lot! I'm not crazy, thank God. She's perfect as a housekeeper and subordinate, but as lady of the house she would be intolerable. I'm too old and not dumb enough to be sweet-talked into that kind of foolishness."

There was nothing to be done. No argument derived from public, general, or individual morality made enough of an impression on Twissels. And there was no one who found the moral question important enough to become embroiled with a man like Twissels about it. Yet married and unmarried "ladies" shouldn't frequent the house of someone who, as it were, displayed his mistress on his front veranda every day.

Mrs. Uhlstra hesitated a moment. No, it was indeed *terlalu*. She *couldn't* do it.

"Forget it, Ma!" Rose said. "I'll go to Aunt Clara's tomorrow, and I'll ask everybody in town to come to a big party here at Kuningan. We haven't done anything here yet, and we would have to do something soon anyway."

"Wouldn't it be too tiring for you," Geber asked concernedly, and looked meaningfully at her stomach.

"Not now. If we wait till later, then *that* will get in the way again."

It was true. Nothing could be said against it. *That* would get in the way with the whole kit and caboodle! They agreed immediately, happy and cheerful now that there were no pressing worries or misery. They immediately set diligently to work making numerous plans and talking excitedly about the still-to-be-determined day, the preparations, the table arrangement, the invitations. In the afternoon Mama rode home, all excited by the activity. In her handbag she had a long shopping list and in her mind was a series of unwritten plans and orders.

9 Aunt Jansen

When she came home it started to get a little cooler. The setting sun barely warmed anymore and the freshening breeze made her sigh with pleasure after the exhausting day.

Riding into the yard she saw with astonishment that many people were sitting on the front veranda. She saw her husband and an old Indies woman with snow-white hair wearing a wide black merino dress that in terms of style was not reminiscent of any particular fashion. She saw Notary Stern and, of course, Lugtens and Twissels, who were always there when something important was to be discussed among the small group to which they belonged.

What now? Her first thought concerned the planned garden party: if only nothing had happened to have it fall through.

Everyone looked up when Mrs. Uhlstra's carriage stopped in front of the steps. The old woman came wailing to meet her. She threw her outstretched arms around her neck and, crying, dropped her gray head on her shoulder.

"Lena, dear child, now Aunt Jansen is completely poor!"

Mrs. Uhlstra looked with surprise at the men, who were staring straight ahead of them silently and seriously, their faces resembling undertakers. Only the notary smiled, his face lined with irony that had left its mark from seeing and hearing so much human foolishness.

"What happened, Aunt Jansen?" Mrs. Uhlstra asked compassionately, lifting the old woman up and leading her back to her chair while supporting her arm.

"We've told Mrs. Jansen that her expenses are running too high," Lugtens said, his hard, uncompromising voice ringing gloomily through the veranda as if he was reading a death sentence. "Her estate doesn't yield that much anymore. Henceforth she can't have a penny more at her disposal than three thousand guilders a month."

Aunt Jansen had sunk down in her chair, her dull eyes, surrounded by wrinkles, staring straight ahead. The loose skin of her old cheeks hung sadly over her lower jaw.

"Poor as a church mouse," she groaned, deeply unhappy. "Poor, Lena, in my old age."

They really felt sorry for the old woman. They did think it strange that she spoke about being poor with such an income, but that wasn't the point. She had always been able to do as she pleased with her money, as if an inexhaustible gold mine was at her service. Now she saw herself limited to a fixed amount that she wasn't allowed to exceed, though inevitably she would do so anyway. Mrs. Jansen had a very real sorrow and it didn't matter what anyone else thought about it: whether they thought it sensible or foolish, explicable or absurd, she had it and she felt it.

"Poor as a church mouse!" she repeated time and again, and it didn't help when Mrs. Uhlstra consoled her. She cried now and then as she followed her own train of thought, and wiped her handkerchief over her eyes with a sallow, bony hand that trembled with emotion. "If Jansen had lived to see this!" she sighed. "It's lucky! Lord, Lord!" And then her dull, staring gaze was unexpectedly directed at the men, as if a thought she hadn't yet understood had suddenly crossed her mind and developed into a clear image. They looked down, inwardly ashamed but without knowing why. They had done their duty.

"You're doing this to me," the old woman said. "You! I can still see you as if it were yesterday. I can still see all three of you as lowly employees of my husband." Even Lugtens couldn't avoid it, although he was the only one who showed signs of impatience, saying curtly:

"That has nothing to do with it, Mrs. Jansen. We had no choice. The capital...."

"I can still see you," she continued, interrupting him dreamily, but more to herself.

"How humble you were when you came to do an errand or to get orders from my husband. And now that he is dead, you act like this."

It was very unpleasant for the three "big" men. Uhlstra beckoned a tall and fat young man who was waiting in a corner of the veranda. He was dressed very neatly, though dandyishly, and stood idly by, looking around with sly little eyes.

"Come, Aunt Jansen, shouldn't we go home. Isa was going to come."

"Yes, dear. We'd better go home."

He took her arm, greeted the men very politely, and led the old woman off to her carriage.

"Good day," she said, and to Mrs. Uhlstra: "Bye, Lena." She went to her carriage on her nephew's arm, shaking her head constantly and softly, grumbling to herself: "I can still see them come! They were still such insignificant clerks. Now they bark at me, now that Jansen has been dead for so long."

"She's becoming senile," Lugtens said spitefully when the beautiful, though old-fashioned, carriage rode out of the yard.

"Ha, ha," Twissels laughed, "we'll all get there if we stay alive long enough."

"*Kasian*," Mrs. Uhlstra complained. "It's really hard on her."

Her husband said nothing, although he looked after the carriage with a heavy heart, rubbing his short beard.

Tempo dulu stood out clearly in his mind too, along with the great Jansen whom they had all served under. The king of trade and agriculture. He was annoyed that they had to take measures against the queen of yesteryear. She had reigned over receptions dressed in very simple dresses and without any jewelry, though the female slaves behind her were laden with a fortune in jewelry and precious stones.

Back in the carriage, fat little nephew Jansen found his voice. He bravely scolded "those guys." Now he called it outright scandalous, saying that Aunt Jansen was being robbed, and that "those guys" were living in style on Uncle Jansen's money. The old woman, tired now, listened quietly to César's voice rattling on. He stammered a little as if he couldn't get out of his words. She didn't hear or didn't understand half of it, due to the noise of the carriage wheels on the road and the incoherence of the boy's chatter. But she did understand that little César, as she called her favorite, was of the opinion that these fresh kids, as she called the managers of her fortune, were shortchanging her. And she thought so too. That an old person with so few needs could spend more than the earnings of the fortune left by Jansen was unbelievable. And she didn't believe it. They had often warned her before, but she had considered it a form of childish intimidation and the desire of parvenus to have something to say. Nothing more.

Isa was already waiting. Little César saw her as soon as they rounded the corner and rode into the yard. She had been his wet nurse and he still loved the native woman very much. When he had helped his aunt out of the carriage, Isa kissed his hand and noticed, her eyes beaming with joy, how tall and fat he was. She had brought a bunch of especially nice bananas and some exceptionally big *djeruks*.

The old woman sat down tiredly in a rocking chair on the marble front veranda. Her red shawl slid down from her shoulders and hung over both sides of the arm rests: a bright spot like fire against the light color of floor and walls.

"They're beautiful *djeruks*," Mrs. Jansen said. "Where did you get them, Isa?"

"From my brother's garden."

"How is your brother?" was the immediate and interested question. He had been the coachman for the late Mr. Jansen, who had always been pleased with him.

But now he wasn't doing so well at all. His oldest son could get a job in an office, but he first had to pay off a debt of three hundred guilders to the Chinese who was a cashier in the same office and who would help him get a job as a *mandur*. They were in quite a *susah* about it because the Chinese still had to have his money even if the job didn't work out, and Isa's brother would have to sell his possessions. They talked about the affair.

Isa had counted on the *njonja*. She was so rich and would certainly help the people who had served her and who would always be willing to serve her. Of course she would help her former maid. She never thought of refusing the request or doubted the professed reasons. And she firmly refused the *krabus* and the diamond hairpins that Isa wanted to give her as collateral. She didn't do things that way; she had always been too great a lady for that. It almost insulted her.

Mrs. Jansen got up slowly and, using the marble table top for support, shuffled softly into the house, to the money box that had been a conduit for an incredible amount of paper money, gold and silver.

César went after her.

"Aren't you going to take the *krabus*, Auntie?"

"What do you think, dear?" she said indignantly with a somber face.

"It wouldn't be such a bad idea," he said. "They are very beautiful and always worth the money."

"César, César!" the old woman warned peevishly, rummaging through the box with her stiff, somewhat crooked hands. Separating large and small rumpled bills, she added up the three hundred guilders.

"Really, Auntie, it's better to take the *krabus*. What use are they to these people."

"They're of no use to me, either. I don't want anything to do with them."

"But it's still better, Auntie. Otherwise they'll bring their stuff to the pawnshop."

"I don't care, dear."

"But they won't pick it up again, Auntie, and then they're sold without them ever getting anything back."

"*Sudah!* Leave it be."

"It's still a shame. They have no use for them. And. . . . and. . . . "

Money in hand, she shuffled over the slippery floor till she was outside again. She was followed by César, who cast very worried glances at the banknotes.

Isa had put away the *krabus* and the hair pins. She knew that they only had to serve as a display of honesty and good faith on her part, and that the *njonja besar* would never think of taking valuables as collateral for lending money.

César held his aunt back by the arm before she had even reached the door to the front veranda.

"Believe me, Auntie, you've got to take them. Remember, you don't have so much money yourself anymore."

Startled Mrs. Jansen looked into the boy's small, glistening eyes, eyes that were almost hidden behind the fleshy folds of his fat cheeks. She had forgotten about it for a moment. With a deep sigh she stood still. It was true! She did have little to manage on. She could no longer give whatever she wanted to the hundreds of former male and female slaves, old *babus* and wet nurses, and old coachmen and gardeners. Or to their children and their children's children, who were after her money like a swarm of parasites. For the most part they lived in her yard and were salaried as servants, though they hardly ever had anything to do. And if they lived in the country, it still didn't prevent them from coming regularly under all kinds of pretexts to ask for money. It was supposedly a loan but there was never any intention to give it back.

"I still can't do it," the old woman said, crying again.

"Sit down a minute, Auntie. I just want to propose something to you. Then you won't have to concern yourself with anything anymore."

Weighed down by her sorrow and dead-tired from the *susah*, she let herself be convinced by the boy and sat down quietly on a low European chair. It was a beautiful chair with fine mahogany ornamentation, but very old-fashioned.

"Let me do it, Auntie. I'll make it clear to Isa, and I'll take those things from her."

Will-lessly, she gave César the money. He swiftly slipped one hundred guilders in his pocket and with the two hundred guilders in his hand and an angry face, he walked outside and ordered Isa, who looked up in amazement, to follow him to the back of the house.

"I bet you think that I'll let you people continue to *rampas* my aunt, don't you?" he said. "But you're wrong. This time you'll get two hundred. Now give me the *krabus* and the pins, and fast. I'll keep them and when you bring back the money, you'll get them back."

At first Isa didn't want to. That hadn't been her intention at all, because she really didn't need the money. She had just wanted to use it for a nice party, but how could she do that if she didn't have her jewelry? She intended to resist, until César, who had ruled this creature with unrestrained tyranny throughout his childhood, gave her such a punch that, sighing and whining quietly, she exchanged the security for the money and left very disappointed.

Lying back on a couch in his room to smoke a cigarette, César savored the moment, without paying any further attention to his aunt.

Everything considered, life would stay nice and easy, even if Aunt Jansen didn't receive more than three thousand guilders a month. This way he'd make out even better than before. He'd have these *krabus* and pins brought to the pawnshop immediately. If Isa paid back the money then he would redeem them: *habis perkara!* It mattered less to his aunt, and if he cleverly put this scheme into practice, he would be the only person to profit from Aunt Jansen's money. The idea greatly appealed to him. He had been negotiating for a beautiful riding horse, and he was going to buy it now. He could afford it! He would do something about it this afternoon but right now he was hungry. He would first eat something in the back of the house, and indeed he ate enough rice and meat for two. His fat face shone with oppressive overindulgence. And all that time the old woman sat sadly musing about her predicament. Now and then she softly mumbled a word as if she was chewing on it in her almost toothless mouth, and she forgot about Isa and the money.

But she had no peace. Hardly had the worries left her old and weary head that fell back against the chair, asleep for a moment, or a repeated and plaintive singsong "*Tabé, njonja besar!*" drifted in from the veranda. With the sham timidity of a native who has something to ask, a headcloth appeared around the corner of the door and slowly an aged native came, as it were, out from under it. He came *pindjam sepuluh rupia*, or as he still said it, from the time of paper money: scrip. He had made up quite a story which he recited very glibly. It was about an adopted daughter's child who had died somewhere in the *kampong*. They didn't have the money to bury it, and would the *njonja besar*. . . . Of course Mrs. Jansen went to her money box. If people only knew how high her expenses were, she thought, they wouldn't be such mean penny-pinchers. She didn't need much for herself: a big house, beautiful horses and carriages, closets well stocked with batiked and silk sarongs and a fortune in jewelry. None of that needed to be bought anymore. She owned it all. She had no further needs. She preferred to eat rice from a leaf bought at a *warong* and, except for coffee, clean water was her only beverage.

But all those people who always needed money! And you couldn't send them away without giving it.

"*Njonja besar* can take it out of my pay this month," the old houseboy said obligingly, sliding the ten guilders into his jacket pocket with a bow and a *trimakasi banjak*.

Mrs. Jansen waved her hand quietly as if she wanted to say: you can stop now. She knew what "taking it out of my pay" amounted to. She had already forgotten about giving away ten guilders!

10 Pessimistic Reflections

The big celebration at Kuningan would last two days. At first they had planned it for three, in accordance with the old custom, but Rose's "condition" had to be taken into account. Mama said that it would be much too tiring for her. After the celebration there would be a day of *rameh-rameh* for the *budjangs*, so she would still have plenty to do. Two days and two nights—that was good enough. The whole family was tied up with it for weeks in advance. There was hardly time to think about business. First the reconciliation with Aunt Clara had taken place. Between much crying and nervousness she and Rose had kissed each other left and right. To complete the matter, Geber, looking embarrassed and standing there rather awkwardly, also received a handshake and a kiss. Particularly the latter had struck him as strange. He thought it was crazy. During all the years between his short relationship with Clara and his marriage he had lived in the usual way in the country. He had rarely ever thought about it, and if he did it was with fear and aversion rather than pleasure. But now, lawfully married and with obligations he fully realized and firmly intended to fulfill, it kept running through his mind over and over again. There was the beginning of a desire that he tried to suppress as best he could, but which caused him more trouble than he cared for.

Another busy day before the party was done and over with. There was a steady stream of traffic between Kuningan and town: carriages belonging to the Uhlstras and the Gebers, carts full of shopping servants, and *grobaks* loaded with food, drink, and beds. Two hundred guests would stay for two nights! Anything that could in any way be called a room was pressed into service already, and yet there was still a lack of space because these guests weren't just anybody. They were the most notable people from both the government and the private sector. The young people, who had been asked of course for the fun, could stay in groups—billy goats together and nanny goats together—but there were obviously much higher demands for the married dignitaries. It was impossible to apply a system of "packing them together," so Uhlstra had a big bamboo building put up which he divided into twelve rooms in order to keep the main house as much as possible free for people like the Markens, Lugtens, and others.

Mama had been at Kuningan for eight days. Every morning at four o'clock sharp it seemed as if her nerves were wound up like a clock ready to burst. And this continued throughout the day. Fussing here and taking care of things there, she went from the rooms to the *gudang* and from there to the steadily arriving *grobaks*. She made lists of everything that was needed and pressured everybody and made them so tense with her continuous talking, orders, and commands that the native servants, accustomed to peace and quiet, were completely *bingung*. It made Geber's head spin.

"Good Lord, Rose!" he said over and over. "Your mother, your mother!"

She laughed about it.

"She takes care of everything, you know. It would be impossible for me to get it all done without her."

"That's true. She does take care of everything, getting herself all worked up, but it's sometimes awful to see and hear. It drives me crazy."

Rose thought that was really funny. She had been accustomed to it from childhood, hence didn't know any better. She remained perfectly calm. Increasing in size every day, she walked around the house in a kind of sailor's gait holding her arms away from her body, her hands more or less sticky with dough from the cakes and pastries. She went about her business quietly and amicably all day long.

Until evening. Then Mrs. Uhlstra and Rose could barely wait for dinner, and went to bed as early as possible in order to start the show all over again the next morning.

Geber was alone with his cigar all evening, as alone as one can only be in the interior. He too would worry about the upcoming party and what they needed for it. He worried about his guests and how to divide them and assign them rooms. And finally he thought automatically about Clara, who would be staying with Lugtens in the room next to his. He pushed the idea away, but after ten or fifteen minutes it would come back again, as if by itself.

It scared him. In the faint light of the single lamp on the large veranda, with the black darkness outside of the radiating but fading circle, and in the silence of loneliness, he had a feeling that frightened him, yet it came over him again and again. Could it be punishment? Couldn't you do anything outside conventionally accepted lines without being punished sooner or later? Did people drag along the consequences of every wrong move all of their lives, all consequences to be eventually faced? Was it ordained that he who was so happy now and at peace would again be relentlessly driven in the direction he had promised not to go?

It was laughable! You could make such a blunder once, he thought, but once was enough! He wasn't stupid enough to make the same mistake twice. Yet in truth, it was a pleasant memory! With his usual mocking smile on his face, he continued to smoke at ease, watching the smoke spiral upward. If you were always decent and respectable, life would be terribly boring. A single "joke" like that always remained a nice memory. After all, you usually remember your "naughtiness" with far more sympathy than your "acts of integrity." But no relapses! That was really out of the question. He would look like a fool if there was something still going on with Clara, who was well into her forties, while he had such a young wife, though she was somewhat less than graceful, especially these days.

Mrs. Uhlstra had taken over his place beside her daughter in the bedroom. Geber went cheerlessly and alone to the guest room.

He continued his musings.

For the first time he thought that a marriage could sometimes have negative aspects. When he and Rose were alone at Kuningan they both did their own work, and afterward they talked together and were amused with each other. As soon as there was a third person that was over.

If male family or friends came, then there was some diversion for him and she might find life boring. If a woman stayed with them, then he could consider himself temporarily on the shelf. But now there was in addition the imminent delivery which so pleased the entire Uhlstra family. And first of all, that annoying party. Roughly figured, that joke would cost him ten thousand guilders. Life was expensive, terribly expensive, and what did you get from it? Trouble and expense with a minimum of pleasure. And if you enjoyed something, you usually didn't do it because it was not proper or too much *susah*!

Rose, who had never been to Europe, had to have everything she saw advertised in the newspaper. The price didn't matter. The house was full of nonsense things that cost thousands and that no one noticed anymore. Now that party again, and before long the delivery. He always bought the finest wines and the most expensive cigars, and there were clothes in the latest fashion from the finest tailors, though he only wore them on special occasions. Rose couldn't see a fashion magazine without writing to Paris for a new outfit, and yet she lived month after month in nothing more than a *sarong* and *kabaja*. It was the same with everything. While she hardly ever ate anything except rice with *sambal*, some dried meat, and native fruit, her *gudang* was chockfull with the best quality cans which, stacked up, covered entire walls as if in a *toko*.

In fact, individually they lived on so little that it could have been covered by the normal salary of a modest civil servant. Nevertheless the housekeeping cost a fortune. And it was going to cost more and more, that was a sure bet with the oncoming legion of children. He was no longer young and could forget about his chances of going back to Europe to live there permanently. At the beginning of his marriage he had stopped thinking about it. Now it suddenly returned, accompanied by an intense longing. He only had four or five good years left. In his opinion, formed by many years of bachelorhood, it meant that for a while he could still amuse himself at the Paris balls and so on. After that it was over. He could still return later on, but it wouldn't be the real thing. He would feel obligated to restrict himself to chance pleasures, and then he might as well rent a room by the Rhine near Leyden and practice becoming a drunk. . . .

Geber cursed, tossing his head back and forth on his pillows.

Well, darn it, was he living for these many years in one of the world's worst boondocks just for that, with no other prospect in sight! In four or five years he could be having his fifth or sixth child. He didn't dare to figure out what life would cost then! It certainly could make you desperate! Life? Once again he changed abruptly from this pessimistic view to his more usual indifferent and mocking cynicism.

What did it really matter? Wasn't life as a whole an enormously silly joke anyway, one where he played the fool who took it all seriously? All the pleasure and joy of living pass quickly anyway...so what did it matter if you had enjoyed them or not?

You always remained just as wise or just as dumb, and everything disappeared in the past, leaving nothing but memories to amuse yourself with like a hungry stomach with the image of a sandwich. Well, he would calmly accept "married bliss" and that was that! Having decided, he fell peacefully asleep.

The next morning busy life began again very early. Geber was allowed to make out the shopping lists which his mother-in-law had thought up once again. At least a hundred times he would answer her standard questions: hadn't she forgotten something and couldn't he think of anything else?

What a *susah*!

11　The Party

Kuningan was almost unrecognizable when the party was about to begin. Under the direction of the *mandurs*, the native population had decorated it with luxuriant greenery somewhat in a native fashion, but that was part of it, Geber said and laughed.

"The guests should have the impression that they are completely outside and everything should be done to preserve the local color."

"Why don't you feed them rice with fish too," Rose said spitefully.

"Well," he answered dryly, "I know some people who'd like that much better than canned pheasant."

As far as she was concerned she liked it better too, but now she turned up her nose at it. Being the hostess, she did what most of her guests would be doing in a little while: praising expensive dishes that they didn't like, only because they were expensive!

Geber had hired the carriages for his guests, with the result that no one else in town could rent one during those days. When they began to arrive in the afternoon, Geber received the most important guests personally. He let the young people take care of themselves and that went very well. Their mood was immediately one of gay excitement and very catching, Geber thought. The older men at the table on the front veranda had immediately drawn him into a serious business conversation from which he excused himself as soon as possible, citing his duties as the host.

During the first night the feeling of excited gaiety, which was so intoxicating here in the country, persisted and was enhanced by the pervasive nocturnal smell of the forest and the fantastic light of the colorful Venetian illumination.

Geber had constructed a wooden dance floor next to the house, and during the entire night it was never empty for more than ten minutes. Even Lugtens hadn't been able to maintain his stern dignity. Completely against his teetotaler's habit, he'd had a glass of champagne and smoked a cigar while watching the dance floor. One of the young girls approached and teasingly asked him if he would dance with her. He knew why he never drank anything at parties. He only had one glass and it had gone to his head already. His eyes glistened while he looked longingly at the white shoulders of sweet young flesh. His face shone and he smiled with his thick lips pursed as if he wanted to kiss her. Offering her his arm, he bowed with old-fashioned politeness, rounding himself out, though it wasn't necessary with his heavy figure. It made the others smile mockingly at each other. But not for anything in the world did they want to miss seeing Lugtens indulging himself. That would be one of the best moments. People arranged themselves, as it were, to watch with joyous anticipation.

"I think it's very nice of you," said the cheerful girl who had "asked" him.

"Keep quiet!" he answered casually, feeling that he could permit himself such familiarity with youngsters who he had seen at birth, as it were. "Keep quiet! I'd better be careful!"

"Be careful of what?"

"Well, it's been years. . . . I don't know how many . . . since I've danced."

"It's only a quadrille," she said with the contempt of real dance lovers who consider the waltz the only real dance, just as omber is the only game for card players.

But for Lugtens this was precisely the problem.

"You see," he said, "I'm still from the old school. You young people don't dance a quadrille, you walk it."

They looked around for another couple.

Uhlstra saw it and understood that he could be of service to Lugtens. He said to his wife who was standing next to him:

"Hey, Lena, do you want to?"

His eyes behind his glasses were mischievous and his kind, dark face had a cheerfully mocking expression while he took her arm. She pulled back quickly, pretending to be angry, but deep down she was pleased and loved him silently the way people do who, though married for a long time, are still very fond of each other.

"Come on, you must be crazy," she said.

"Let's go," he said, also laughing because of the fun of it, and went on casually: "Let's go, *ajo*! Let's kick up our heels again!"

She hesitated, but allowed herself to be pulled along without any trouble, shaking her head and smiling at her girlfriends and acquaintances about that "crazy guy." The others nodded their encouragement, unconsciously enjoying the pleasant sight of a healthy, robust, graying couple who had lived with each other for such a long time and who could still have a good time together.

Lugtens was pleased when he saw Uhlstra standing unexpectedly in front of him. He smiled and nodded at him knowingly. He knew perfectly well that Uhlstra was doing him a favor, and while he kept the girl busy with, what was for him, cheerful small talk, and sounding his belly laugh frequently, his other self, the businessman, was already looking for an opportunity to reciprocate. But there wasn't much time for that. The figures were called, the first tunes blared from the brass instruments and pounded on the big drums from the native band that was known as the "ronzebons."*

Everybody was paying attention to Lugtens and Uhlstra, amazed by their agility that no one thought to have been possible due to their corpulence. They danced what in their youth had been called a *carré*, with its ingenious movements and steps in counts of five and three: backward and forward, with bows and curtsies. It was agile, lively and tiring with its *avants*, *chaînés*, and *balancés*.** During the fast parts it seemed as if their bones moved independently at first, to be followed by the mass of flesh that also came to share in the movement. The young girl hardly knew what was happening during that old-fashioned quadrille. She got totally *bingung* from it and firmly resolved never to ask one of those old gentlemen, who were so weird, to dance with her again, not even as a joke.

* *Ronzebons* was kept in the text because it is an untranslatable term that in the colonial Indies specifically referred to a small orchestra of native musicians playing on European instruments. The word originally meant "making a great deal of noise," the cacophony such musicians playing unfamiliar instruments were often thought to produce.
** A quadrille is an eighteenth-century French contredanse. Squares (*carrés*) were formed by four couples who faced each other and performed five parts or movements which were each complete in itself. The French words in the text were some of the commands called out: *avant*, "advance"; *chaîné*, "form a chain"; and *balancé*, which referred to a prescribed step. "Quadrille" is also another term for the omber card game (played in chapter 2) when it is played with four rather than three people.

The young people almost forgot to dance themselves while they watched Uhlstra and Lugtens, all the while bursting with laughter behind their gloves at each caper they cut. But the old people around the floor watched with sad enjoyment, as if a memory from their youth was being awakened. Yes, that's how it had been when they were still young, some thirty or forty years ago!

The two men had pulled it off with great aplomb. Lugtens, with big drops of sweat on his forehead, felt as if his legs were about to buckle under him, and as if his stomach was hanging loose. He did his best to bring the girl, who was somewhat embarrassed by the whole thing, back to her seat with a dignified bearing. Uhlstra walked calmly back with his wife, better able to take physical exertion because of his old habits as an outdoorsman. Everybody congratulated them.

"How about that, they did it! That's the real McCoy! Today's dances are nothing compared to that."

The old way was definitely more graceful! And they besieged Lugtens; the older people because they meant it, the young ones as a joke and trying to kid him. But when the girl was back in her seat again and he was going back to his, Lugtens had regained his sense of dignity. He walked stiffly like an ambulatory candle, with a gruff and forbidding expression on his face while he nodded curtly and disdainfully now and then in response to the talk around him, silently cursing the one glass of champagne that had tricked him.

With her lips pressed tight and her head pulled back, Clara had watched it all with great annoyance. She could tolerate it from Uhlstra and her sister, who was much older than she was, but she thought it was disgusting of Lugtens. She had disliked him for so long. She had married him without ever having loved him, just for the sake of having a husband. The continuous effect of fear and repression had developed her dislike into hatred. But she'd rather experience his usual scowl than see him make a fool of himself doing the old-fashioned dance steps.

Geber was also watching, and the mocking smile on his face was stronger than ever. Clara examined him from head to toe in spite of herself. He seemed very much the gentleman with his calm, simple face watching the others quietly, critically, and ironically. She thought that in his well-cut, though otherwise ugly, black jacket he always looked good among the other men; as if he were the president and they the underlings. What differences there were in the world! How favorably could the one who watched be compared to the one who made a fool of himself by the sweat of his grim face.

Slowly Mrs. Lugtens walked up to Geber.

"Don't you want to join?" she asked sharply, clipping her words, and uttering the curt sounds with a light Indies accent.

He laughed softly without looking at her and without surprise. It was just as he had imagined, just what he expected.

After he had brought her inside from her carriage arm in arm, he had intentionally avoided her company. He just knew that she would come to him. Now it had happened.

"If you will too," he answered.

"Thank you. I may be old, but I'm still too young for that," she said in the same snappy manner, now really a little angry with him.

"Excuse me! If I feel the urge I'll look for another partner, one better suited to my age!"

"I didn't mean that you're old enough for such madness."

"That's what you said. But that's not the point either. And what does it matter? You wanted to say something, something unpleasant if you could. That's all."

For a moment she was silent, startled that he could think that. She didn't know if it were true. As far as she could tell, she hadn't had anything particular in mind. But it could well be that he was right.

"You're a mind reader," she said, now also mockingly.

The word affected him. He was upset. It was said good-naturedly and not at all sharply or harshly, but he couldn't stand it and got angry.

"It's open to question whether that's an accomplishment or not."

"You mean, there are so many dumb people. . . . as dumb as I am for example?"

"I didn't mean that."

She looked at him and said:

"Just say so, Willem. It's true."

Now it was headed in a direction that he would have liked to avoid. It was so strange with women. If they made up their minds to steer a conversation in a certain direction, then all roads led inevitably to Rome!

Silently he watched the quadrille dancers without seeing them, not knowing how to get out of this phase that was much worse than any other. She was good looking. To be sure, she wasn't a girl anymore, hence she lacked much and had too much elsewhere: the inevitable double chin, a gray hair here and there, a looseness of facial skin, all that shouldn't be. But her beautiful supple waist and her fine resilient bust were, because she always dressed with such good taste, a pleasure to behold. The way she was standing there—in a light brown raw silk dress that was very becoming because of the color, that fit her like a glove, and that followed every line of her body—contrasted sharply with her niece, Rose, whose fiery red blouse with a dark blue skirt made a cheap impression.

"You could have come to our last party," she said and looked at him.

"Rose was. . . . "

"I know, I know. You are a very special person, Willem!"

"Because I told her? It's true, I shouldn't have done it. Forgive me, but admit that you were at fault."

"Oh yes, I do."

Geber looked at her in amazement. Far from taking it badly, she said it with a laugh, as if she didn't mind.

"But you should have come to that party. I wouldn't have devoured you, I hope. It's crazy, you know."

She waited a moment and then continued:

"Did I ever make the slightest move during all those years?"

"No. That's just what was so crazy. Why did you act so strange and obvious at our engagement and wedding?"

"I don't know."

Neither did he and yet he did, at least he sensed it. With a kind of pleasure, that he couldn't and wouldn't try to explain, he heard her sigh, when she had to admit that she didn't know.

Yet he said softly to her: "Shall I tell you something, Clara? You didn't like it."

"Perhaps."

"There are people who never use the things they have in abundance, yet they still begrudge them to anyone else."

She nodded silently.

"It's a kind of egotism, not a nice one, I shouldn't flatter you with that."

"And what kind of egotism do you have?" Clara asked laughing merrily. "Certainly a very *charming* one, no? For heaven's sake, let's go for a walk. Those dancing clowns over there make me sick."

"Spoken with all due respect for your husband and brother-in-law."

He laughed along with her because he was sick of it too. He offered her his arm and as they walked up the path to the house, they stepped out of the circle of light formed by the Chinese lanterns around the dance floor.

When they came up the stairs arm in arm and went into the house, where a group of musicians was ruining the great arias from Italian operas, Rose was startled. She felt intuitively that this was a couple that physically belonged together, a couple designated by nature to *tjotjok*.

"Have you been dancing, Aunt?" she asked with rude emphasis on the term indicating kinship as she walked toward Clara.

But Clara, who understood very well, smiled in a friendly manner.

"No, dear. I'm too old for that. I leave that to the young folks."

"You look so young tonight!"

"Then I'm very lucky, this time."

"Oh, no," Geber said guilelessly, "you always look young."

Mrs. Lugtens laughed out loud.

"Come on!," she said, "what a night this is. I'm showered with compliments!"

Other people came between them. Dozens of laughing and joking couples streamed onto the veranda with excited, happy faces and with cheerful voices loudly asked for lemonade and ice water. These requests were met by the men with exclamations of "nonsense" because they compared it to the wine and hard liquor, diluted with water more or less, that they were drinking. Each one of them became involved in a different conversation, and they didn't see one another again. Geber wandered off to the rear veranda and the card tables; Rose didn't have eyes enough to watch over the servants; Clara didn't have words enough to keep up with the small talk she encountered simply because she was . . . the wife of her husband.

The night wore on with dancing and gambling. The card tables were abandoned after three in the morning; the seats of honor for the older women were already empty; the guests who could no longer keep up with the young people had gone to sleep, if possible. There were still some couples dancing on the platform, but not many; the girls were also tired and many had gone to their rooms already. Near the buffets young men were still engaged in slow and faltering conversations. Some were still dressed in black tails, while others had already changed to white jackets. Hungry from staying up late and being in the open air, they ate sandwiches and drank, this one grog, that one champagne—it didn't really matter anymore as long as it was wet and cool.

Alone on the front veranda Geber collapsed in a big rattan chair. He was dead tired, yet as the host he felt obliged to be the last one up, just as he had been the first.

He was wide awake; his feet were burning from twelve hours of continuous sauntering through the yard and the house. He could never sleep whenever he stayed up past his normal bedtime and became overtired. His nerves went awry and his mind became clearer and clearer, though he paid little attention to what was going on around him.

Legs crossed, hands folded over one knee, he sat there motionlessly, worrying silently, staring straight ahead of him into ever fading lights illuminating his yard. It became increasingly quiet. Fatigue had slowly overcome everyone, even the servants. Completely spent, they were sleeping here and there on the floor or on benches. Only the watchman stayed awake, striking the hour regularly.

And when the great silence, that always falls shortly before daybreak, enveloped everything, Geber was gradually overcome by feelings of dejection and discouragement, a quiet hatred against everything and an indifference for the past, present, and future. Almost unconsciously the feeling penetrated deeper and deeper, as if he were wound in a veil that was drawn ever tighter. The feeling held him prisoner, so that there seemed to be no escape in any direction. No matter which way he turned, he thought, sighing, he was shackled by life and his circumstances. For every *this* there was a *that* he found insurmountable.

His face became more despondent and his eyes closed of themselves as if bored by the few things that were visible in the light that faded in the distance. A surge of anger welled up in him, a fierce protest against life such as it was, but it never came to an outburst. It rose up and sank away again, a powerless attempt by his weakened energy, the aftermath of a once powerful vitality, the remainder of a capability to fight and resist, the reverberation of lost hope and trust. He felt it sink away and was fully aware that he was in the midst of a calamity, that he was facing the world like an unarmed combatant.

He could escape.

What was stopping him?

What was there, really, to stop him from ending it? No one else would be hurt; they had no financial worries for the future. It was wisest to treat life as a house where one lives, but where one does not remain when it no longer pleases.

This line of reasoning appealed to him, and the idea didn't scare him. Allowing himself to be led along by his slow-churning thoughts, he saw the act and its immediate results. He quietly dramatized it in his mind, and the way it would happen seemed suddenly and simply certain and destined, as if there couldn't and shouldn't be a question of anything else.

The place was a small wood on his land by the river. The instrument was a pistol. That seemed to be fixed irrevocably beforehand, and that realization made him smile. He tried to imagine suicide by poisoning or drowning, but that seemed so foolish and impossible to him that he couldn't take that road. Not even for one step.

12   The Second Day

Clara got up. She had been one of the first to go to her room, had slept well, and was the first to appear. She shook her head at the sight of the empty halls that, here and there, were still lit by lamps.

She was surprised to see Geber in the big rattan chair. His face was turned up, pale and smiling, as if dreaming.

"Good heavens, Wim," she said, learning over him, "are you sleeping here?"

She had approached so softly on her bare feet that he hadn't heard her coming. Badly startled, he jumped up immediately and looked at her with surprise and alarm.

She looked at him wide-eyed and astonished, not knowing what to make of him.

"What's the matter with you?" she asked concernedly. "You must have gotten a fever. How careless!"

With a big sigh, Geber rubbed his hand across his forehead several times and then laughed softly, even though his heart was still pounding from the sudden fright.

"It's nothing, really. I was dozing, somewhat overcome by all the fuss. I don't know why you startled me so much when I heard your voice that close to me."

"And you're still dressed."

"That's true too. I'll go get more comfortable."

"I'd try and sleep for another hour. You need it. It'll do you good."

"That's for sure. Well, I'll give it a try."

He took his watch out of his vest pocket and held it under the light.

"It's barely four o'clock, Clara," he said, shivering. "It's a very cool morning. What are you going to do?"

"Me? Well, what I do every morning before five. Try and make a good cup of coffee."

"That's an idea. How about me?"

"If you want. . . . But I wouldn't advise it. It's not a good prescription for falling asleep."

"For heaven's sake . . . I need it—even more than sleep."

He undressed slowly in his room, his mind was still busy with that foolish, sudden idea of suicide. It was insane! Someone in his circumstances shouldn't come up with such nonsense.

He thought that a slight disturbance in his blood circulation might have caused it. A bit of malaria perhaps, or a cold. Maybe his gallbladder was working irregularly or something! How could anyone who is physically and mentally fit entertain not only such insane visions, but also regard them as something perfectly normal. It wouldn't happen again, he was sure of that. His thoughts were getting clearer already and Geber lit a cigarette and threw himself on a couch near the open window, dressed only in pajama pants and *kabaja*.

He heard a soft knock on the door. It must be the boy bringing his coffee, he thought, and answered in Malay. But it was Clara with a big china cup in her hand.

"There aren't any servants around."

"I can understand that," he answered.

"Yes, they certainly didn't sit around yesterday or last night."

He took the cup from her and drank the coffee eagerly. It was warm and strong. He didn't return the empty cup to her, although she was waiting for it, but put it on the table. Then he put his arm around her and pulled her gently toward the couch by the window. And again it was just as it had been years ago, no premeditation, no previous intent or plan, just something that happened as a matter of course. And there was once again no resistance on her part, not even an attempt.

When they left Geber's room together, none of the family or guests were awake yet. Clara went toward the rear of the house to look after the coffee, and he went slowly down the stairs of the front veranda. He was in a terrible mood and very dissatisfied with himself, the way he had been that other time too.

He walked down a country road with big steps, but without purpose. He hurried without needing to, purely from an unconscious urge to react against his mood with vigorous motion.

A light pink color appeared on the horizon. He followed the

same path that Jozef had walked on the evening before the *ketju*. The road ran along the fields for almost an hour before turning back to the villa through the *sawahs* on the other side. Daylight, light gray over the fields and red in the sky, broke gently, until the color differences melted into a single shade and gilded the treetops with sunshine.

When he returned home, flushed and hot from the forced march, it was completely light. The veranda was full of people who were besieging the bathrooms.

"You didn't get to bed at all, did you?" Lugtens asked when Geber came up the stairs and greeted his guests with a cheerful good morning.

"No. I did try to sleep in a chair for a while, but it didn't work."

"You already had coffee from Aunt Clara," Rose said when she noticed her husband. She intended to ask if he wanted more. He glanced quickly at Mrs. Lugtens, but she was talking to some other women and ignored him.

"Yes," he replied. "But I'd like some more. I had a good walk all the way down the country road."

"Is that very far?" Markens asked, who was enjoying a smoked salmon sandwich.

"It takes a good hour if you keep up a brisk pace," Geber answered.

"And how did everyone sleep?" he asked, looking around.

The stream of answers differed greatly.

But generally the happy festive mood immediately prevailed again. There were young people who had to be almost forcibly restrained from getting on the dance floor. Then someone suggested that they swim "en masse" in the *kali*, and this was met with great approval, even by those who had bathed already.

Almost everybody went along, many just to watch even though they didn't swim. Lugtens, of course, stayed behind, as did Geber. Lugtens was, for his doing, particularly cheerful and talkative, and expressed his satisfaction with the nice party. Absent-mindedly Geber listened with only one ear to the commanding tone of voice, and didn't hear what Lugtens was saying until he began to understand that there was money involved.

"You know that I like you two very much," Lugtens was saying, "but you shouldn't stay away. That won't do. I have a nice timber contract in mind. Well, we could do it again with the four of us. If we could get the railroad to run through the forest, we'd really have something. There's only one thing, and you know what that is. I don't like people who ... who ... stubbornly want to go their own way. One has to socialize with many people. I'm favorably disposed toward you, and with this grand affair you've partly made up for it again. Everything is fine here. Again, I'm satisfied."

Although he was bothered by the schoolmaster manner and had to laugh about the crazy circumstance of being praised by precisely this man at this particular time, a feeling of shame remained uppermost in his mind. It was really a dirty trick. Now that he was married himself, he could understand it better than before. And it had been perpetrated by a man who was a friend and a host at the same time!

Geber tried to talk past his feelings, and showed a great interest in the timber contract. He inquired how and if it would be possible at a later date to get a railroad through the *djati* forest that was to be exploited.

That completely rehabilitated him in Lugtens's eyes. It was just the thing for him: someone who didn't understand some business or other that he, Lugtens, was completely informed about, and who showed the correct interest so that he could enlighten him in the full glory of his superiority.

"The plan shouldn't originate here."

"But doesn't it have to be approved by the local government?"

"That doesn't mean anything. It's Parliament that decides where the railroad will run."

"That's no trifle to...."

Lugtens looked at him.

"It is no trifle, mister! I don't deal in trifles. I mustered all the help I could get in Holland and ... we'll see."

Fortunately, they were inundated by a stream of guests, some of whom stopped and talked to Lugtens. Geber escaped. It was getting to be too much for him, now that the heat was increasing. He would quietly slip to his room and try to sleep in spite of the noise that rose along with the temperature.

He was awakened a few hours later by Rose. He slept so soundly that it took a lot of effort. When she finally succeeded, he looked at her dully, his eyes red from fatigue. He was in an unpleasant mood.

"Cut it out," he muttered and turned determinedly onto his other side.

But she persisted in her soft, amiable way, just as if she were dealing with a child. "Wim, Wim, Willem! Get up now. We're having *rijsttafel* in a minute. You can always go back to sleep afterward. Wim, Willem, Wim! . . . "

"Damn it!" he cursed. "Stop it, will you. It drives me crazy!"

She had to laugh because she had succeeded. He got up and rinsed his face and wrists with cold water.

Rose was right; he had to be present at the table as much as she had to. The nap had refreshed him quite a lot after all. When he appeared among his guests in a white suit, he was somewhat like a fish out of water, someone who didn't share the prevailing mood. He hadn't had any of the champagne that had been flowing freely since ten that morning, nor the noontime gin and bitters that the men had started on at eleven sharp. Even after a glass of wine at the table, Geber still hadn't caught up with the men around him.

For the second time being out in the country had proven to be too strong for Lugtens, and he had allowed himself to be seduced again during the warm morning hours. And just like the first time it had fooled him. He wasn't dancing now but holding forth and tried to be witty. He wasn't successful.

Nevertheless, people laughed at his vulgar pleasantries: many did so out of respect for his position, others for the pleasure of seeing the man who always thought himself to be so distinguished showing his real nature for once, and the young people laughed just for the fun of it.

"In a minute he'll start jumping around again," somebody said.

"He's already started," whispered another, "with his tongue."

"You'll see him prancing around with that too pretty soon," a third one responded with a deep voice that almost everyone could hear.

They nearly choked from laughing and that latest quip made the rounds of the guests and, of course, had the success that could be expected under the circumstances. Geber wouldn't participate, and he smiled forcibly because he was the host after all. He saw that Rose could hardly eat from laughing so hard that tears came to her eyes, and saw Clara casting dark and contemptuous glances at her husband. It was all very unpleasant, he thought, very unpleasant.

But he couldn't escape it. Lugtens kept on talking—first about the party, then the host, then the hostess.

The young people at the other end of the table were grumbling now.

"He's pulling the rug from under us."

"There's nothing left for us to say."

"Just as much of a hog as he is in business."

Lugtens didn't hear any of it. Shiny with sweat and unsteady of eye, he tried to add force to his voice and tried very hard to keep his sentences from tumbling over one another. But he plowed on until the end, which came as a relief to everybody.

The guests cheered. There were still some young people who intended to put in a word, and nothing in the world could persuade them otherwise. When they had finished, Geber, who had remained perfectly normal and sober, thanked everyone with a few friendly words. He did it so well, so simply and unaffected by wine or liquor that he received two smiling nods: one from Rose and one from Clara. Rose thought that her husband was really different from all the rest, and so did Clara.

Another evening of dancing and gambling followed, and again the music blared through the night. But this time everybody was so excited that no one went to bed, neither the dancing couples nor the card players. Tomorrow was Sunday. Everybody had counted on that. They'd sleep late when they were back home.

At last it ended!

It had been wonderful, a great pleasure, very pleasant, great fun, generous, genial—whatever you want, but when the long, long row of carriages headed down the driveway away from Kuningan and onto the main road back to the city, the family and guests silently sent up a countless number of "Thank God's"

Only Geber and Clara weren't rejoicing. Lugtens's own big carriage was one of the first to be brought to the front of the house. Sad and out of sorts, Clara had thrown herself into a corner and forced herself to be friendly and smile at her sister Lena, at Uhlstra, Rose, and the other nieces and nephews. She had greeted *him* twice with her eyes through the opening in the hood at the back of the carriage. Then they drove away.

13　How the "Children" Amused Themselves

Things didn't get any merrier on the way back. The parade of carriages continuously raised great clouds of dust that shot up from the horses' hoofs and literally powdered the passengers.

When Markens and his wife arrived home, he was surprised and she worried when they didn't see or hear anything from the children.

"They're asleep," one of the servants said.

That was precisely what was odd: they never slept at this time of day.

They went into the bedroom and indeed the boys were snoring lustily behind the mosquito netting.

"Did they go to bed late last night?" Mrs. Markens asked.

"No."

"Have they been up at all this morning?"

"No."

"But, my God! they must be sick," she shouted. "Oh, what heartless people! They would rather let my poor children die in their sleep than go get a doctor!"

Markens followed her back to the bedroom and they opened the mosquito netting. A stench of liquor and tobacco assaulted them. The boys were sound asleep, their faces red and their eyelids swollen. They had their shoes on, were still dressed, and were incredibly dirty. Fred had a scratch on his forehead and Ed, who had bled from his nose, was not fit to be seen.

The parents were crushed and watched silently for a moment. Then Mrs. Markens began to cry and wailed that she couldn't go on living like this, that she couldn't go away for a minute and that all the servants had to be dismissed. She wanted to call the maids, scold them, and send them packing. She wanted to have the "children" undressed and washed, but Markens was against it.

"Let them sleep," he said indifferently.

And in fact that's what she preferred. She was too tired to

deal immediately with problems again. She didn't think she was strong enough to handle the problems of a household. Someone with her delicate constitution should never have to concern herself with all those unpleasant things. He'd heard that tune before and let her go on. He had heard it for so many years.

She loved to go out. She could take a good glass of wine better than other women. At home, alone in her room, she sometimes drank more than she could handle. If he'd ever check the quantity of port and Madeira that was used in his house, presumably with his knowledge, against the amount written on the bills. . . . Besides, she liked to play whist, and didn't care at all what time of night it got to be. She was mentally strong enough, and her constitution robust enough to do all of that, but she'd always been too weak to take care of a household with a couple of children. And by complaining long enough she had even managed to get several women to claim they believed her. He couldn't care less. He had learned to listen to it silently, aware that contradiction or reprimand would get him nowhere.

"What could they've been up to?" she finally asked after she finished complaining about herself.

That's what he had been wondering all that time.

"God only knows!" he answered with a sigh.

"I didn't give them any money and everything is locked up."

"We'll hear more about it, I'm sure. There's nothing we can do about it now."

She totally agreed with him on that too. She went to bed and fell asleep immediately. Though he was dead tired too, he couldn't sleep. He was haunted by the sight of the young drunkards, his children, already wrecks of society. Was he guilty? He tried defending himself. It didn't help. His weakness. . . . that was no excuse. He didn't want to use that common notion that was used by everybody whenever they were guilty of anything ugly. He was too intelligent for that.

There was already a *tamu*.

Barely asleep, Markens was angry, but when he heard that it was a policeman, he thought anxiously of his boys. Here we go!

Just as he walked onto the front veranda Uhlstra drove up and jumped from his carriage with one leap onto the veranda.

When he saw the policeman he kept quiet, and the official looked searchingly at Markens, who stood there in the grandeur of his official position.

"You can say what you have to say."

"The assistant resident ordered me to inform you of my report to him this morning."

"Go ahead, I'm listening."

"I was called last night because some young men, led by a few adults and aided by native soldiers, smashed up a *toko* in the Chinese quarter."

"My sons must have been there."

"Two of my scoundrels too," Uhlstra sighed.

It did Markens good to have a fellow sufferer from the upper class, and especially a man like Uhlstra, who wasn't easy on his offspring, at least not very often.

"What else?"

"They beat a Chinese."

"Oh well, that's possible," Markens said with a dignified face as he shrugged his shoulders. "That can't have amounted to much."

"It damn well did," Uhlstra said nervously. "They beat him to death!"

Dazed and pale, Markens looked at him.

His two guilty sons came out of the bathroom. They were clean now and were wearing fresh *baadjes*. Their young, handsome faces, already betraying a precocious degradation, were indifferent. Together they approached calmly while looking up at the same time, facing the men brazenly.

"What did you do last night?" their father asked with an angry face.

"I don't know," Freddy said.

"I don't know either," Eddy said.

"Where did you go?"

"Early in the evening we went for a walk with some friends. The Uhlstras and Lugtens's, and some others."

"And then?"

"Then we went by the club. There were only a few people because of the big party at Kuningan."

"And then?"

"César Jansen and some other guys were there. They gave us brandy with lumps of sugar in it. Then they went for a walk with us."

"Where?"

Uhlstra was nervous about Markens's question. He had questioned his two youngest children similarly and until now they had given the same answers, just as if it had been arranged.

"I don't know, Pa," Freddy said.

"I don't remember anything either," Eddy assured him.

"Really Pa, nothing at all."

The men looked at each other. Mrs. Markens, afraid of what she heard, had come closer without saying anything.

"It's clear," she said now, coolly and haughtily, "that a few adult, good-for-nothing fellows made the children drunk. It's a disgrace."

She was overjoyed when the policeman shared her opinion.

"I think so too, Ma'am."

Uhlstra and Markens nodded. They thought it was the only way to reach a solution without dishonor for their own children.

Furtively looking down at the floor, with sinful expressions on their faces, the Markens boys were the very picture of innocence as they glanced stealthily at each other, inwardly exulting that it was going so well.

They didn't try to get anymore out of them.

"That's enough," Markens said. "You can go to your room."

And Eddy and Freddy, their mischievous faces calmly controlled like experienced actors, entered the house together like well-drilled soldiers, with the story in their heads exactly as they had agreed on with César.

But once they were inside, out of sight and hearing, they stormed up the stairs like madmen, howling with laughter. Upstairs, they turned somersaults on the veranda to their room and grabbed a young *babu* who was carrying a load of clean laundry. In their licentiousness they almost pulled her *kabaja* off and rolled around on the floor with her, without consideration for anyone or anything.

"It'd be best to get to work right away," Uhlstra said. "The sooner there's an end to this mess the better."

"That César's really getting to be a mean creature," Markens said.

"We should try to get him out of town."

"I'll be glad to do my part. A guy like that would completely ruin our children."

Markens knew that there wasn't much left to ruin in his children, and that many adults were in prison for far less than what these boys were already guilty of, but what could he, as father, do?

"It won't be easy though. Mrs. Jansen...."

Now the woman of the house joined the conversation indignantly.

"Mrs. Jansen should be given a choice of having that nasty kid put in prison or thrown out of town. She's an old woman, that's true, but I don't feel sorry for her. It's *her* fault that that César's like that. She spoiled him rotten."

Markens was no philosopher, but at that moment he did think very philosophically about the contradictions in a person who, totally blind to his own faults, makes merciless judgments about quite similar flaws in other people. Uhlstra turned away so he would not show the angry expression on his face. He kept silent because his urge to tell Mrs. Markens the truth about this was so strong that he would have done so if he had uttered even one word.

It was the talk of the town. Everybody had a different story, but they were all very exaggerated.

Lugtens had begun by beating his two oldest sons with a dog whip until they screamed and asked for *ampon*. Then he locked them up in the carriage house for a while.

After they had used their money and influence to bring the family of the murdered Chinese around to letting things be, and after the police would no longer interfere, they combined their efforts to spread counterrumors. All the respectable people disseminated them in public. There was no dead Chinese at all. The young people and children that had been mentioned before had only watched when several of those Buginese soldiers,*

---

* The Buginese were a people from southern Celebes (now Sulawesi), an area bordered to the east by the Gulf of Bone and to the west by the Straits of Macassar. They were a martial people as well as renowned mariners. Robbery and other feats of daring were once considered socially acceptable activities particularly by Buginese nobility. Because of their martial nature, the Buginese

who always *rampassed* when garrisoned, had looted a small *toko*. Among the people who were helping to spread the opposite story were several who indignantly contradicted the previous false and slanderous gossip, even though they knew perfectly well what the truth was. The only one who suffered terribly from this knowledge was Markens.

Freddy had hit the Chinese on the head with a piece of iron. He was the murderer. It was too much for Markens. Though he was originally a proletarian and though, both in terms of his household and his wife's good family, he had always been nothing more than Etienne's husband, he had already shown once—though too late—that he was capable of action. Now he did it again, and he was amazed when it proved to be nothing more than a persistent kind of daring.

"The boys are going to Holland," he said, after he had told her everything.

"That's impossible," she answered, not at all impressed by the announcement. "They can't go to Holland alone."

"I didn't ask what you thought about what they can do alone or not. I know what they do *here* alone!"

"But I thought.... My God, I have.... "

"It's not a question of what you think and what you have. The boys are leaving on the first boat. I've taken appropriate measures and nothing whatsoever can change them."

"So you arranged everything without me."

"Yes, I did it without you and I will make many other arrangements without you. Far too long I've been stupid enough, in fact, wrong, to leave things to you that I should have done myself.... so what you think about this doesn't matter; it will happen! And what you 'have' only counts insofar as the boys' wardrobe is concerned. They can't travel without clothes."

She sensed how much ground she had irrevocably lost, but at the same time she knew what was left and how to take advantage of it. That very same day she visited one *toko* after another and bought and bought! There were so many suitcases and trunks stuffed with goods, some completely useless in Europe, that it seemed as if Freddy and Eddy were going to a desert island for many years.

---

were often recruited by the colonial government for troops, but they were notorious for creating mayhem and murdering.

The boys were happy. They didn't care where they were going. These days it would be pleasant anywhere but in the Indies. They had escaped all the difficulties and dangers. The only ones who punished them, and mercilessly, the only ones who had no *kasian*, the ones who were completely incorruptible and unpersuaded by anything, were their schoolmates, the boys from the highest grade who knew exactly what had happened. Furthermore, they were fully aware of Freddy's and Eddy's long list of past sins and had finally concluded that they had gone too far. And that conclusion, confirmed by more than one beating and by daily confrontations that consisted of a variety of surreptitious punches and unpleasant words, that conclusion was much worse for a boy than anything else in the world.

14 Comings and Goings

When this peculiar aftermath of the party at Kuningan was fortunately over, things went back to normal for a while. And yet there was something different from before, busier and more serious. Uhlstra traveled to the outer possessions for a long time, while Lugtens was making an inspection trip along the coast. Geber was somewhere else in Java looking after the interests of the timber contract that had come through. In the meantime his estate was being managed by his brother-in-law from Tji-Ori, who restored the bridge over the *kali* with bamboo, though only temporarily.

The only one who went to his office day after day like a machine was Twissels. He stayed late, very late in the afternoon, with the result that in the evening he yearned for a card game. He now spent three evenings a week plus Saturday evening at the club, but what to do about those other three evenings which, unfortunately, were still left?

Rose had come down, even though her increased size made it difficult. Mama Tjang was definitely on the verge of dying now, and she thought it would be "too bad" if she couldn't be there.

They were all in the room again, just like before. The old woman, even more wizened and emaciated than before, was lying motionless on the *baleh-baleh* with the beautiful mosquito netting. The children gawked at her curiously, but only little Lena, "her child," as she always said, stood close to her. The old woman was breathing with difficulty. She was dying, but still struggling hard to live, and she was fully conscious. Now and then she said something.

"I can see them going, all of them!"

"What's she saying, Clara?" asked Mrs. Uhlstra.

"She sees us go, *kasian!*"

"I see them all going to the big pit . . . one . . . two . . . three . . . four. . . . "

"She sees us going into a pit," Mrs. Lugtens explained, and

though that in itself didn't mean anything, all of them shuddered at the thought, their fingertips cold from nervousness. Mama Tjang's deathbed and words scared them, but they didn't want to admit it to each other as yet.

"What's she counting anyway?" Rose whispered. She felt another life in her and was even more afraid of death than the others, who were equally superstitious and fearful of what a dying person says.

"What did you say, Ma?" little Lena asked, to please cousin Rose. "What are you counting?"

"All of them ... all of them.... They're going in ... two ... now Lugtens.... that's good ... seven ... not my child.... She passes over it.... God holds her."

They looked at each other with fear, and they couldn't hide it from one another any longer. It was dark in the room. There was a small flickering light that made the shadows dance grotesquely on the white walls and the mosquito netting.

Rose, who was usually so calm, couldn't take it anymore and stole quietly away. She could no longer listen to those dreadful words about everyone going into that pit. Gradually the others left too. The children walked along indifferently, whispering to each other and making fun about going into a pit. Giggling, they used their heads and hands to show how they would shoot into it head first.

Only little Lena stayed behind; her big eyes watched the ugly old mask she was so familiar with and that she never thought was ugly. She listened with great interest to the constant repetitions issuing from the toothless mouth that was taut from the forced breathing and went in and out like a suction cup gripping and letting go again. Once more the now dulled, black eyes opened. She looked at her child, and tried to put her hand on the blond curly hair. Lena helped her when she realized what Mama Tjang wanted but could no longer do herself.

Outside in the bright sunshine of the pleasant backyard, the *glatiks* and other little birds hopped quickly up and down in the aviaries, the *badjings* played tag through the shimmering green of the coconut trees and the *perkututs* let the ten or twelve full tones of their call drift away softly and dreamily. The women's fears quickly disappeared. They shuddered for a moment, but were immediately caught up in busy conversations about the *tokos* and the *gundang*, or about what had or hadn't happened lately.

The children had wandered over to the horses who were stamping in the stable, or to the monkeys who, startled and afraid, flew shrieking into the bars, looked back nervously, and raised their eyebrows and bared their white teeth. It was life as usual. Perhaps ten minutes later little Lena came out of the room with a pale, sad little face, tears in her big blue eyes and a trembling underlip. She was ready to cry again.

Mrs. Lugtens and the others noticed it immediately. They were startled, and the indifferent chatter of their daily chit-chat ended with brief cries of alarm. They crowded into the room to the *baleh-baleh* with the beautiful mosquito netting where Mama Tjang was lying as dry, as bony and withered, and as taut and stiff as someone who has just died but had already been mummified while still alive. A momentary, noisy exhibition of sadness followed, and it spread at once to the two *babus* who leaned against the wall and put their faces against their raised arms. They cried loudly, but their wailing could not be understood. Only "*mati*," with the "i" drawn out in a monotonous cadence three or four times, could be clearly heard now and then. But it ended quickly. There was no real sorrow over the loss. The old native woman, who had so often seemed to be dying, had already been "written off" for just that reason.

Lugtens was glad. When he arrived home a week or so later and his wife told him that Mama Tjang was dead and buried, he said flatly:

"So much the better! Then we're finally rid of that nuisance."

When he said it he was holding little Lena's hand, glad to be back again only because of the child, who was the single person in the house he liked to see. She pulled away angrily, and looked at him full of reproach. Oh, that's right, suddenly flashed through his mind, and at the same time he was afraid that she might again say something as unpleasant as she had previously done when she spoke about his own mother.

"Ah, well, I meant to say," he went on, pulling his head back, apparently indifferent, "that she's better off."

"Yes," his wife agreed, "she was always sick."

"But she did have some fun too," little Lena said, thinking of the old woman's contentment at the stories she told her in Malay.

Lugtens and Clara remained silent. It was not a subject to return to while the child was present. She already had greater influence than they realized. They dared to say and do anything in the presence of the other children, they didn't really count! But little Lena did.

"Rose has a girl," Mrs. Lugtens went on.

"So I heard."

"Everything went very well. Geber is at Kuningan."

"I heard from him. The business is coming along very well. Anything else?"

"Lena says that he looks bad. I went there a day or so ago, when he wasn't home."

Lugtens shrugged his broad shoulders.

"It'll pass," he replied indifferently while he went to his room.

Rose's baby bore the unmistakable stamp of Mama Tjang, something the young mother didn't like at all. She was already terribly disappointed that it wasn't a boy. She had counted on it, since all the *dukuns* she had consulted during the last three months had assured her by all that was holy that it would be a boy. Now it was only a girl. Nothing made sense anymore! If she had only had a light complexion, or had at least been somewhat fair and blond like Aunt Clara's children, then she could have consoled herself after the disappointment. Little Lena— this child also had to be named after Mrs. Uhlstra—was rather dark at birth and she seemed to get darker every day! Dejected, Rose had brooded about it. She wasn't that crazy about Willem, lord no, but Aunt Clara certainly loved Lugtens a whole lot less.

So all of that was pure nonsense. It couldn't be the cause. And she couldn't stand to think about differences of fertility, constitution, or sensitivity between her and her mother's sister, in other words differences to her disadvantage. It had to be Geber's fault, she thought. He didn't have a strong enough personality: not a man to leave his mark on his offspring. That had to be it!

She had recovered again by the time Geber returned.

He appeared to be markedly thinner and paler, but she paid little attention to that. What she noticed more was his greater cheerfulness and gaiety. His mother-in-law, who was temporarily staying at Kuningan to do the housekeeping, noticed it too. He talked excitedly about business: everything was going extremely well! He displayed dutifully a great deal of paternal love, took his child in his arms, kissed it, thought it was beautiful and sturdy, and kissed Rose by way of gratitude for the living present. He behaved exactly as he ought to, according to Mrs. Uhlstra's feelings, and he rose in her esteem. Perhaps that's why she paid special attention to him and noticed that his face had changed.

"You know," she said to Rose at bedtime, while helping her take care of the baby, "I don't think that Willem looks too well."

Rose didn't answer, busy as she was with her baby, who struggled fitfully to find the best way to take her first nourishment. She nodded affirmatively to her mother, but without great interest or conviction. Her attention was on the child and she didn't want to speak because the baby might choke. Mrs. Uhlstra, fully aware of that possibility from a great deal of personal experience, answered herself:

"He's probably tired from the trip."

But the next morning Geber didn't look like someone who has recovered from his fatigue. It was etched sharper on his face and Rose would have had to be blind not to see it. She asked him if he felt well and he answered matter of factly:

"A little feverish sometimes. But otherwise there's nothing wrong with me."

"I'd rather have you see a doctor," Mrs. Uhlstra said.

"Maybe you're right. I don't sleep well."

"Then you should certainly talk to the doctor. It's a real problem."

Again it was Mrs. Uhlstra who said it, not very convincingly, but lightly, as if to keep the conversation going at the breakfast table. Her mind had been influenced by having been married to a man like Uhlstra, and she reduced a lot of things in life to a common cause.

"Willem looks betul bad," Rose said now too, when Geber had left for work. "I don't know what that is, not sleeping well, because I always sleep very well. It isn't serious, is it, Ma?"

"Oh no," Mrs. Uhlstra said with a mysterious laugh. "It's nothing at all! Your father had it too."

And Rose, in her simplicity, said:

"Gosh Ma! I never heard anything about that."

Her mother was amused. She thought it was so funny that she laughed until she shook softly.

"Just wait until you're fully recovered," she said, "then you'll see that he'll be able to sleep well again."

15 Suicide Fantasies

A few days later Geber went to town on business. Twissels received him in his office. He was by himself in a room that had been partitioned off from a larger one. Near his desk were three other ancient ones, lasting reminders of his predecessors. Nobody used them, but no one was allowed to take them away, either. Abandoned, they were falling apart just as his own would one day after he had permanently retired from the company.

The landowner, used to living in the fresh air, thought that it stank of dust and old paper, moisture and stray cats, of everything that was dirty. Twissels didn't think so. On the contrary, he felt exceptionally well in that atmosphere. For years he had spent most of his daylight hours there. He had started as a common employee and risen to supervisor, and from being poor, he had become rich there. He enjoyed being in that office, and when he entered it in the morning he sniffed its distinctive odor with more pleasure than someone else could possible receive from smelling the finest aromas.

"Sit down," he said to Geber, showing him a chair beside his desk. "I'll be done in a minute."

And with his nose on the paper and his glasses almost touching the lines and columns of figures, he checked an account. Now and then he made a note on a piece of paper or called to an employee on the other side of the partition in a high-pitched voice and asked for information.

"How's everything at home?" he asked politely when he was finished with his work.

"Very well. You ought to come over for a few days."

"Too busy," Twissels squeaked, brushing his hair back and straightening his glasses with both hands. "Much too busy nowadays. Stay here today and we'll play cards tonight."

But Geber had promised to be home, so when there was no possibility of one person going or the other staying, they discussed the business for which Geber had come. All the paperwork was brought out and they got busy bouncing figures back and forth.

One hour followed another and as they worked, their total profits rose and rose from adding up the results—some real, some planned—of the combined businesses, agricultural contracts, transports, product sales, and anything else the *kongsi* had a hand in here and there.

"Nice, isn't it?" Twissels said with his soft feminine laugh, and he rubbed his long, dry hands between his bony knees. "Damned nice!"

"Yes," Geber said and sighed. "It's magnificent, I have to admit."

"Stay and have *rijsttafel* with me here in the office."

"No thanks, I have other business to take care of."

He wouldn't have done it for anything in the world. He would not have been able to eat in that impossible atmosphere. He was already queasy just from being there.

Geber did indeed go to the doctor, whom he found home at dinner time.

"Have you had trouble with this before?" he was asked.

"No, only lately."

"Is there anything in particular that is troubling you?"

"No, nothing doctor."

That wasn't true, and he was aware now that the doctor couldn't help him, either. Why didn't he tell the truth? Why didn't he say that that miserable image of suicide haunted him all the time? During his trip it had returned for the first time one evening on board the coaster. It couldn't have been the surroundings, because it was delightful at sea with the silvery moonlight and the gentle refreshing breeze. He, a landlubber, thought it particularly beautiful. Suddenly, without transition, that damned idea came over him again. It was preceded and followed by pessimistic notions and a dazed indifference. That this idea had come back so unexpectedly gave him quite a shock. He thought frequently about it for the rest of the trip.

What could cause such a senseless repetition? He had a lot to do. He had been on his feet in the forests all day long in order to size things up, make an estimate, and so on. Tired as he was, he had driven twenty-eight miles to town in the afternoon in a stagecoach. He had eaten a steak and had a drink. By that time it was ten o'clock and very quiet in the hotel, because there was a concert in the theater. Geber thought that he could still go and listen for a while, got dressed and went to the theater where he met some friends and acquaintances. He went into the loges to say hello to their wives and chat with them. During intermission he was surrounded by people, not just because he was rich, but because he was well liked. People thought that he was a good and sympathetic person. Very old *sobats* from twenty or more years ago came up to him with friendly smiles of recognition and outstretched hands, saying "I'll be" and "Hello there, fella" or amicably "Well, I'll be damned." All showed a sincere liking for him.

"Come on," said the local commander who, when he had only been a second lieutenant, had known Geber. "Come home with me for an hour or so after the concert!"

As always, he was easily persuaded.

Two others went along because, they said, Geber did. Hence they got into a card game again until Geber climbed into his carriage at two in the morning. He was so exhausted that he was already asleep before the carriage stopped. He sleepwalked his way to his room and undressed with the feeling, the certainty, that he kept thinking about before he was entirely asleep, that against his habit he wouldn't get up early the next day.

It was as if someone had awakened him. Suddenly he was wide awake without any trace of sleepiness or drowsiness, but clear-headed and clear-eyed. Automatically he looked around the strange hotel room as if he had an urge to investigate who or what had awakened him in the middle of his sleep. There was nothing to be seen. On one side was the screen between him and the faintly shining night light, on the other, the lightly transparent shadow of mosquito netting on the white wall. The *gardu* struck four in the street. Everything was still and quiet.

He thought it was strange to wake up all by himself after such a hard day and after having been so sleepy earlier.

It was best to try and sleep again. He closed his eyes, but opened them quickly. . . . There was that idea again! It took shape now, he saw it himself, saw the familiar spot, and the gun he held in his hand. At the same time he saw his body, arm flung out, dead. When he did close his eyes it suddenly loomed up like a beautiful, idealized painting, full of light and color, but with extraordinary, fantastic, and sharp hues that came at him like the monstrous little men and strange animals in the odd imagination of children when they close their eyes before going to sleep. He surely wasn't a child anymore, and it wasn't that he was afraid of such trifles, or that he was superstitious; he only thought that the repetition was strange and disquieting. Why did the idea of suicide come to his mind so often? He wasn't planning on it, was he? He couldn't be seriously considering it. When it was discussed in company he always disapproved of it. People with a wife and children are especially guilty when they do something like that, he would say. They weren't honoring their obligations. But even if they didn't have a family, it was still an irresponsible act.

He closed his eyes and saw it again. He looked it over and smiled. It was beautiful. So artistically drawn with its softly receding perspective so fine and deep, and its tone especially so magnificently rich ... something like this was almost unimaginable: he had never seen it in reality. It took all the horror away from both the contemplated and completed acts, which were now combined within one outline. Form won over meaning. And anything outside that depiction faded away toward vague and sad hues, dirty gray and dull yellow. Was that life and the other death? His thoughts were on the old track again. What did he get out of life? He wore himself out in swampy, stinking, and suffocating forests in order to ... earn a little more money than he already had. And for what? What was the use? At home a mechanical life of indifference, and a wife who would always remain a stranger to him, even if she had twenty of his children. He could trudge through life like just another kind of coolie, civilized and well off! Just as he had done previously, and completely against his former notions, he returned to the theory that regarded life as a house that you leave when it no longer pleases you. And it no longer pleased him, not now! As he saw it, life was a horror of boring redundancies, of needless and useless misery. He had wanted to exchange Rose for Clara, but was that really what he was missing? It seemed unlikely to him.

He would still be in the same position he was now; a little more cheerful perhaps, but that was all. Other than that, the same misery: man's antlike work! Again he recalled the representation of the idea that had remained real in his mind. It was radiating beauty and light, and fading softly away.

The cannon shot at five o'clock, followed immediately by the sound of the *gardus* beating their blocks, made him jump up. Suddenly it was all gone, but when he ran his hand across his forehead and over his bald head, he felt the cold sweat. That was some kind of night again, he thought while he yawned and threw open the windows.

On the road and in the courtyard of the inn, the day's activities had already begun in the dark. He leaned on the window sill and watched, yawning so often that he shivered. Not even two hours sleep after such a day!

That would never have happened to him before. What was the matter with him? Were his nerves shot? Was something wrong with his digestion? Thinking about suicide and not being able to sleep must have one and the same cause. He didn't think that it could be explained in any other way. People talked about heredity, and his maternal uncle had shot himself through the head many years ago. But he thought that too ridiculous to consider.

The unpleasant night didn't bother him. On the contrary, he was more cheerful and lively than usual, with an inclination for a good glass of wine and a stiff drink. Yet people everywhere asked him if he was sick, and he would laugh and answer that no ox was healthier than he was. But he did present a very convincing picture of illness. It was a strange, inexplicable indisposition that had been the cause of everything he had experienced lately, even his extraordinary excitement and loquacity in unfamiliar company, something that was otherwise so uncharacteristic of him.

He was thinking it over after returning from his business trip to Twissels. He couldn't tell that doctor everything about his impulse to commit suicide! Probably no doctor would ever be able to help him. For God's sake, he sighed. Come what may.

16 Geber and Clara

A month or so later a family council was held at the Uhlstras.
They all agreed that there was no doubt Geber "had something."
The business went well. The profits of the *kongsi* were fabulous.
Prices to be paid for the spice harvests they had already contracted to buy were sharply up on the European market, while
harvests in the Indies were greater than expected. On the other
hand the prices for the products they had to deliver to the
colonial government at a high fixed rate were down. In Holland
the decision had been made in favor of running the railroad
through their forests. It was raining gold from all sides, and it
also fell generously on Markens to whom they owed so much
and to whom they hoped to owe even more.

"The best thing would be for you to go to the mountains for a
month or so," said Lugtens, who was part of the family council.

"I've told him that so often already," Uhlstra said, "but he
doesn't want to. He says he has his hands full with the
business."

"It's true, he has worked hard, but now the worst is over."

"But I can't go," Rose said. She was several months pregnant
again and, thinking that she meant that, her mother said:

"You can still go."

"Not that, Ma. I really can't leave the plantation. When Willem isn't there, everything goes wrong."

"But Henri can help you."

The young Uhlstra, also there, looked at his father, who was
rubbing the hard stubble of his short gray beard. He had done
what he could. During Geber's absence he had come to Kuningan each day from Tji-Ori in order to keep an eye on things,
but everything had always been done already by Rose, who was
very knowledgeable and loved to play boss on a plantation.

A few times Henri had pointed out something to his oldest
sister that he thought should be different, but she would have
none of it. They got into a big argument just as they had often

done in the past when they were still at home with their parents. It was the usual disagreement between the oldest sister and the oldest brother and was without further consequence and didn't damage their affection.

"Everyone has his own opinion," was Uhlstra's advice, "and Rose has hers."

"It isn't my opinion, Pa, it's my husband's."

She'd never give that short shrift. She subscribed to the generally current opinion in the Indies that the husband was the tukang, the boss. He was at the head of the business as an absolute ruler, and what he wanted or said was the way it would be. Furthermore, she was the mistress, and her brother better not meddle with that. Period!

"As far as Geber is concerned," Lugtens said in an authoritative tone that annoyed Rose, "I'll make it clear to him that he has to go."

Seeing that Rose was about to answer disagreeably, Mrs. Uhlstra cut her short.

"Well, yes," she said. "It's also in his family's interest. What if he has to go to Europe all of a sudden, what then? Huh?" she said in a typical Indo-European way, pulling a face. "Huh, Rose, what then?"

That really was a sore point and Rose was quiet. No, she didn't want to go to Europe; anything was better than that.

"It's still better if he has someone with him," Lugtens said.

Everybody was silent. They entirely agreed. Though he was not bedridden or in need of care, Geber's depression made it necessary for someone to go with him for company.

"It's close to vacation time," Lugtens continued. "My children could use some cool mountain air."

"You want to send the children with Geber?" Rose asked incredulously.

"I hope you don't think I'm crazy," he answered rudely.

"But what then?"

"Well, your aunt, of course! She will go with the children."

Rose pulled her lips in and her already big eyes got bigger. For a moment she wanted to say that such a thing was impossible.

But she couldn't! And what did it really matter. She didn't believe at all that Willem was still fooling around with Aunt

Clara, but even if he was. . . . of all such things it would be the least offensive!

That night Rose was back at Kuningan with Geber. His face and body had grown very thin. His eyes glistened, but he was very cheerful, except when he was momentarily distracted. A letter from Lugtens arrived; it was very lengthy and neatly written.

For a moment he looked dreamily at the flame of the lamp, then the old mocking smile appeared on his face.

"It seems that, no matter what, all of you want me to go to the mountains."

"It's for your health," Rose answered, continuing to look at the red silk change purse she was crocheting for her father's birthday—the same gift every year.

"Lugtens wants his family to go with me."

"Yes, he said so this morning."

Geber understood now that it was a put-up job, and it bothered him. With his elbows on the table and his chin cupped in his hands, he looked at his wife sitting opposite him. Her head was bent and he could only see the wealth of coarse, bluish-black hair that partly glistened in the light, and with here and there short hairs curled up that had split when she put it up. It framed part of her heavy face; only the small, tilted-up stump of a nose and the edges of her ears stuck out. Below her face, the bright white *kabaja* pulled tightly over the fleshy mass of her shoulders, allowing her skin and the white outline of her camisole to shine through. Was it really true that she had consented? Could she not care at all that he was going to stay with Clara somewhere inland? He knew that he didn't love her, not in *that* way. But if she had once had a close relationship with another man and he knew about it, as she knew about his relationship with Clara, and if it had been proposed to send her to the mountains with that man for a month. . . . No, he was really free of prejudice and most other nonsense, but never in his life would he have given permission for *that*.

And she kept working quietly on the red purse calmly and amiably, without looking up, turning and working the crochet hook, forming holes by continually pulling the thread through other holes.

"If you don't like it," he said at last, " . . . I don't care. I'd rather stay here!"

And he would. He dreaded it, knowing what the consequence would be. And though that might be pleasant in itself—he had always disliked it. As long as he lacked the opportunity, it meant nothing. Yet it seemed as if some strange coincidence always gave Clara and him an opportunity.

"You better go," Rose said. "As I said, it's for your health. Otherwise we might have to go to Europe."

He knew what that meant to her. And he couldn't go away for such a long time either.

"Nonsense! Lugtens wrote about that too. It's enough to make you sick."

"Everybody says it, and it's true, you don't look well."

It made him nervous and he no longer laughed mockingly. He rarely did lately. She looked up.

Kasian! she thought. No, she didn't approve of it. She didn't have much feeling for him either, but if he had said straightforwardly that he didn't *want* to go with the other one, then she would have thrown the little purse on the table and, though worried about the housekeeping and the plantation, she would have gratefully said that she would come with him. Tomorrow, if need be.

Geber himself would have liked it better if she had said she would rather go with him than have him off alone somewhere with Clara. He would have written Lugtens that very same evening that, under the circumstances, he preferred to be spared the bother of children, and that he was going alone with Rose.

Kasian! she thought, he looked so weak.

"Don't worry about going," she added. "I hope it does you good."

Cursing her silently, he got up, went to his office and sat down at his desk.

Such indifference . . . ! Really hopeless! Everything bounced off that easy-going disposition and smooth, immobile, dark face that was like a Buddha! Rose bent her head over her work again and continued to crochet, but her mouth was trembling at the corners. The crochet hook became entangled for a moment and everything became red before her eyes. They must have cooked it up in advance, she thought. It was a dirty trick on Clara's part!

Pulled by six horses, Geber and Clara rode to the mountains in the family carriage. Between them, the children, and all the stuff loaded front and back in tied-down suitcases, the carriage was full. They both thought of it just as Rose had. Clara saw in the strange trip that Lugtens had literally ordered her to take, the execution of a deliberate plan of Geber's. He saw it as the result of a calculated trick of a woman.

They kept up appearances during the first few days at the inn. Geber experienced the pleasant influence of a change in climate. He slept comfortably, and that calmed him down.

Clara amazed him; she was normal, friendly, and was casual without the least reticence, but also without any provocation. He thought it wonderful that she behaved like that! He could watch her while she was busy with the children—well dressed, small waisted, and quick as a young girl—and never think anything of it. He could let his eyes wander for the sheer pleasure of it, the way one looks at a flowerbed or at the sea, without asking what there really is to be admired.

Desire occurred to him suddenly, quietly insistent, without his trying to think it away. The children had gone to a spring with the servants, and after breakfast they walked slowly from the building onto the front veranda. While talking to her he went into his room and, while answering, she followed him.

He didn't feel so bad about it as he had before, he only felt the same discouragement, dissatisfaction with himself, a concern for an uncertain future—he didn't know what to call it or what it was that overcame him the most.

17   What People Said about It

They both received good news from home. All was well at Kuningan. Rose, who now dreaded his return, wrote that he really didn't need to hurry, and that he should stay until he had completely recovered.

At first they had been the only guests at the inn, but now that they were staying longer, other people came, and it restricted the freedom of movement Clara and Geber needed. They could meet someone at any moment when they came out of a room, so they had to be careful. They thought that they were, but they weren't.

The new guests whispered suspiciously, and one morning when the children were playing on their side of the yard, they called little Lena over and questioned her.

"Who is that man you were just talking to, honey?" a proper and highly respectable young woman asked.

It was Geber, as she well knew, but that wasn't the point.

"It's Uncle Willem," little Lena said.

"And do you love Uncle Willem?"

"Oh yes! He's always very nice to us, and to Mama too."

"Oh, well! That's very nice. Now I understand why you love him so much."

"Yes," the child confirmed in the steady tone of voice she had always heard from Lugtens.

"And your mommy certainly loves him too, if he's so nice to all of you."

Little Lena nodded her blond curls very earnestly, and as if to avoid the impression that her mother might be ungrateful for Geber's friendliness, the child added innocently:

"Every afternoon after lunch Mama goes to Uncle Willem's room to talk to him and keep him company."

Two other older ladies, who were also listening attentively, looked at each other fixedly, pursed their lips, and slowly pressed their chins on their chests, with an expression of forcefully controlled indignation about someone else's scandal.

"Well!" the proper, very respectable young woman continued in a sweet, cajoling voice and with an extremely friendly look on her face. "Mama must be tired in the evening when she hasn't slept all day."

"She sleeps in the afternoon too, sometimes in Uncle Willem's room."

"Do you want a piece of chocolate, dear? How long have you been here? Would you rather be here or at home? Do you want to see an album with nice portraits? Or a picture book? "

Little Lena was showered with sweets and with nice stories that she listened to admiringly, all of it coming from the proper, very respectable young woman, who didn't want the child to remember what she had said. And little Lena, though intelligent and sharp, was still naive and innocent, and the ploy was completely successful.

In the meantime the heads of the two other women turned from one side to the other at that new revelation. They rolled their eyes as if they were looking for something to crawl under and hide or to cover themselves with because of the shame of someone else's scandal. And when Lena had gone back to play with the other children they looked at each other. All three of them nodded silently at first as if to say "nice business" and "what do you think about that?" Then they put their heads together and, in whispers, let loose the name calling and backbiting.

The pebble rolled right along. The whole town knew of the scandal that same day, and the guests took it home with them gratefully, as the most wonderful thing that had happened to them. The news traveled on in coaches, by mail, and was carried on horseback across the mountains. On its way it circulated among the plantations, the houses of small towns, and in the clubs. It was one of the many Indies family scandals, one of the best "daily specials."

Geber and Clara had no idea about what was happening when Clara found him very early one morning in a chaise lounge on the front veranda. His face frightened her. During the last few weeks he had completely recovered. He had gained weight and was as quiet and calm as before. Now all the beneficial effects seemed suddenly gone. He looked pallid again, his eyes glistened, and his face showed traces of illness, just as when they had left home.

"What's the matter?" she asked, upset about the change.

"With me? Nothing. . . . For the first time I slept badly again. . . . It'll pass, I hope."

"I hope so too. You look so pale it frightened me."

"Oh well," he said, reassuring her, "you shouldn't be frightened by that. One person does so sooner than another. I seem to pale very quickly."

"It's no joke, Wim. Something's bothering you, but you suppress it."

"Not really."

"Why won't you say it? Not even to me?"

"Oh come on," he lied, "it's really nothing. Have the boy bring me some coffee, then I'll take a bath and everything will be fine again."

She got the coffee herself so that it would be better than it usually was. That day she took care of him as if he were sick.

He accepted her thoughtfulness with a smile, though he didn't need it. If Rose had done the same, he would have been secretly angry and would have said out loud that she shouldn't be so foolish. Now he felt a pleasant, quiet gratitude.

It had happened again. It was even worse. That night he had suddenly awakened to both his vision and the melancholic, indifferent view of life that always came with it as if they belonged together. He had submerged himself in his own thoughts as if he were dreaming profoundly, and not for a few minutes, but for hours, hours he had heard struck quite clearly. And something had been added that hadn't been there before: something that sounded like a steady voice in his head. It seemed to urge him on, and persisted in his thoughts with a clear message for him: he had to do it.

He hadn't been able to hide his torment from her. She hadn't believed his denials, and in her own mind she was sure that he was sick. When she saw that he didn't want to say anything for the moment, she didn't persist. Not until the afternoon did she return to it. It was during a mood of indifference and release of tension, like the one when he confessed his affair with Clara to Rose. Lying on his back on the bed, arms over his head and staring up to the *tenda* with eyes wide open, he told her everything about the strange idea that pursued him, his nightly torments, increasing insomnia, and the misery of his strained nerves.

"Have you told the others?"

"No, Clara, you're the first one."

"Not the doctor either?"

"No, not him either."

"Then I'll tell him."

He was silent, all the while looking upward as if lost in thought. Softly he started to talk to her, pouring out his feelings about the strange thing that was pursuing him.

"Please understand," he said, "that the usual reasons don't apply to me. I've not been hit by disasters, have no worries, no debts or grief. It's true that we should be man and wife but, as we know from experience, the situation doesn't sadden us overwhelmingly."

"No," Clara said, sighing deeply, "that certainly can't be the reason, and not now anyway."

"That's right," he agreed. "And any other cause, pain or illness, for example, is also out of the question."

She knew little about the sinister subject, and shiver after shiver ran down her back. He had been familiar with the idea for so many months that he spoke quietly about it, like someone who has looked at it from all sides.

"I know of no other reason," he continued in a resigned and monotonous tone of voice. "There is nothing whatsoever that exercises an overwhelming influence on me. Nothing, I'd say, that could rob me of my freedom of action."

"No," Clara agreed, again with a sigh, but without a particularly clear notion of what he was arguing.

"No, Wim, that's true. That's what's so terribly crazy."

He suddenly sat up and turned his drawn face toward her so quickly that she was frightened, and grew pale herself.

"You said the word! There is a reason. It couldn't occur without a reason; otherwise it would conflict with my personality."

"What do you mean?"

"There has to be an excuse," he continued, letting his head fall back again into the hollow it had made in the pillow. "An excuse! After what I've said there remains only one.... You mentioned the word, Clara. I have to be crazy, or on the way to becoming crazy!"

"That's nonsense," she protested. "You argue as intelligently as anyone ever could, and then. . . . No, that's nonsense."

He shrugged indifferently.

"Still, it's true!"

"It's not true, Willem," she maintained. "You're simply sick."

And when for a moment she saw the mocking smile on his face she added:

"I mean physically ill. That's why I'll tell the doctor. Let him examine you seriously, and prescribe a new regime."

She spoke angrily, excitedly, which was very unusual for her. She could have imagined anything, except such a terrible thing. Again he made the indifferent gesture.

"If I tell a doctor, I know what he'll ask. They all do."

"But that's good. He should. . . . "

"He'll ask if there have been other cases in my family."

"Not that, Wim," she said, frightened. "It's not true, I hope?"

He nodded slowly.

She sat motionless on the edge of the bed, her hands resting on her knees, so upset she couldn't think. She had only one image in her mind: little Lena.

"It's true. As far as I can determine there are two: my grandfather and later an uncle. Well, you understand, that's too silly to talk about."

She listened in amazement. Why was that so silly? On the contrary, wasn't it the only natural and understandable answer?

"It's doctor's talk, you know. What in the world could those people, who lived a half a century or more ago, have to do with me."

Clara didn't answer. She wanted to cry out of grief and pity for him. Suddenly she remembered the night of the big party at Kuningan and she mentioned it.

"Remember when you were lying fully dressed in a chaise lounge and you were very startled when I called you?" she asked.

He put his hands over his face, and his head nodded slowly up and down in the pillow.

"That was the first time."

She remembered it vividly and became afraid. She looked at him with fear. She felt certain that a permanent obstacle had come between them, and that there would never again by anything between them as man and woman. Whatever she had felt

170

for him in that way could never be revived. The fear of the great unknown, death, had suddenly gripped her, and while he was lying there with his hands still covering his face, she couldn't make herself pull them gently away and console and comfort him. In her pity for him she felt an urge to do so, but what prevailed was the fear and shuddering which seized her at the thought of the terrible things he had told her with such appalling calm. And so they remained silent together for minutes, until there was a knock on the door.

Geber got up and opened the door just a little, afraid that a servant would look in and see who was with him. The boy held out two letters to him and, because he could only see the address (his) of the top one, he accepted them both, and closed the door immediately. But inside he saw that the other one was for Clara. He recognized Mrs. Uhlstra's handwriting.

It bothered him that the servant had given both letters to him at that hour.

"It must be a mistake," he said, by way of excuse.

At the time it didn't bother her that much. Her mind wasn't back to trivialities after she had been taken so terribly unaware by everything he had told her. She kept thinking about it with the increasing conviction that he was beyond help, that today or tomorrow he would die by his own hand. Filled with sadness and dislike she took the letter and automatically tore the envelope open. She unfolded the letter in the same manner and saw that it was from her sister Lena. The plain heading: "Clara," startled her. What did that mean?

> Return immediately with your children. Everybody is scandalized by your behavior up there with Geber. It is terrible to do things like that without thinking about the disgrace you bring to your family and to your children. Come back at once. Lugtens could hear about it at any moment, and then there would be a disaster for all of us.
>
> Lena.

She looked at him while he was still reading his letter that had been sent by Twissels.

"Amice," Twissels wrote:

> This serves to inform you of the very annoying gossip which is circulating here about you and Mrs. Lugtens, and which has also

come to my attention. As you will understand, I am doing my best to contradict this slander as I'm obliged by our long and friendly relationship, both in as well as outside business. In the meantime I deem it to be in everyone's interest for you to return as quickly as possible to your plantation and for Mrs. Lugtens to return to her home. You will oblige me with an immediate answer and excuse me for not hesitating, in the interest of our mutual affairs, to acquit myself of this, for me, unpleasant duty. I count on your complying with my very urgent request, in order not to seriously endanger a cooperation which is extremely necessary for our business.

Yours, Twissels.

Geber was very indignant about it. That was a man who lived with a housekeeper and even had the nerve to allow her on his front veranda, a man who would do anything as far as sexual matters were concerned.

"He doesn't write about that," Clara said, after she had read the letter, while Geber had become quite indignant and had given her his opinion to that effect.

"He only talks about business and he is probably right."

"You're not planning to do it, I hope."

Clara looked at him and said:

"Dear Wim, I don't believe there's any alternative."

"But I won't do it," he continued, now completely enraged, while she was calm and depressed. "I'll...."

She handed him her sister's short note, which he read in an instant, and which had the result of suddenly deflating his excitement.

"It's terrible!" he said sadly. "Yes, I understand now too... we have to!"

"We certainly do."

"We would have to anyway, now or in a week or two. It's really all the same.... a little longer or shorter."

She was deeply moved. Having sat down on a chair, she looked up at his pale, sad face. Her eyes were full of tears, and she asked him in her soft, cultured voice, trembling from restrained sadness:

"Not that, Wim! Say you don't mean that."

He bent forward, put his hands on her beautiful shoulders and kissed her forehead, the way a brother might kiss his sister.

"Don't worry, Clara, I didn't mean *that*. It won't come to that. I don't feel like going to Kuningan, you can understand that! I dread it. But it will *djadi* when I'm back in the groove. My God, there's no other way."

She took heart, and her own conviction of what was necessary allowed her to regain control.

"It certainly has to be done, and the sooner the better."

They hadn't mentioned with a single word how amazed they had been at first when they realized that everything was common knowledge and that it had grown to be a subject of public conversation in town.

After all, it didn't matter anyway!

18 Clara at Home Again

When she arrived home with the children, Lugtens was waiting for them on the front veranda. During the drive home she only had one thought: What's going to happen? What was in store for her?

Trembling and pale, and straining to control herself, she saw him, fat and heavy, come down the stairs toward the carriage door.

"Well, there you are," he said, trying to make his voice sound friendly, which wasn't customary and didn't really work. At the same time he put his hands out for little Lena, lifted her suddenly out of the carriage and kissed her three times firmly and expansively.

"You look well," he said, "roses on your cheeks. As if you're just back from Europe."

He quickly looked at the others and also at his wife. Then he said as if reproaching her:

"The roses didn't blossom that much on you."

"I didn't go there to have fun, what with taking care of the children and a sick man!"

"Yes," he answered in a milder fashion, though he also particularly noticed those last words. "What's the matter with that man?"

"I don't know, the doctor doesn't know, and I don't believe he knows himself."

"And now?"

"Exactly the same. At first he recuperated quite nicely, but then he became just as sick and pale as before."

Thank God, she thought, the danger had passed! Whatever people might have said, *he* didn't know, he hadn't heard anything. And with her return home ordinary existence, with its domestic worries and demands, began once again, as if nothing had happened.

The next day there was quite a row with Mrs. Uhlstra. The older woman had come to give the younger one a piece of her mind, but Clara wouldn't stand for it. Once, years ago, she had submitted to it, but she wasn't about to do that again.

"Good God!" Mrs. Uhlstra shouted at the first indication of resistance, "people should know what you are!"

"They ought to take a look at themselves," Clara said, ashen but ready for any attack or defense, her head high, and with an expression of determination.

That did it for Lena. She slapped her fat thighs with both hands with a resounding smack.

"What did you say, you hussy? You mean me?"

"Or anybody else."

"What have I.... Good heavens!... What have I ever...?"

"No, not that, Lena. You can rest easy as far as that is concerned."

"That's not true! Even if Uhlstra was as awful as that husband of yours, I still wouldn't have done a thing like that. At first he was your husband's friend and now he's also my son-in-law!"

"Perhaps there'll be a letter from Holland tomorrow, saying that he's somebody's brother-in-law over there! What do I care."

"And your children?"

"My children?" Mrs. Lugtens exploded angrily, "they'll make themselves happy or unhappy, but not because of me. But at least I won't make them unhappy by marrying them off for money or to have them provided for."

They argued back and forth from every possible point of view until tired, their stock of invectives and reproaches depleted, they came down to gentler terms and in the end made peace with tears in their eyes. But this time Mrs. Lugtens had won. Self-reproach was still lingering in her sister's heart when she arrived back home.

Uhlstra was waiting for her impatiently. He had been the first one to hear the gossip and, very upset, had come home with it. His wife had made him believe that it was slander, but she would have Clara come back immediately and talk to her about it. It was easy to make him believe anything as far as that was concerned! Not that he had been a paragon of virtue in his youth, Lord, no! He had been born in the Indies, his complexion didn't differ from that of a native, and he had been surrounded by *babus* and houseboys who had taught him to walk and to talk. He was totally familiar with native smells and habits, and had been a real *njo* in his behavior. He thought that native women were beautiful, and Lena embodied the ultimate of what he considered attractive: a pretty Indies girl who had been raised according to what he believed to be European standards. And by the time he married her he had entered enough items in the native ledgers to remain completely faithful to his wife without any inclination for anyone else. He couldn't have said what caused it, but he didn't like full-blooded European women. Among males, he would voice his opinion about it. Although he had no personal experience, none whatsoever, he claimed that they weren't physically clean, and he supported his notion with very specific remarks about what they did and didn't do. He was completely alien to intrigues, and unforgiving as far as marital infidelity was concerned. That's why he was so afraid now. What if it were true! If the family name had been compromised by his friend, his sister-in-law, his daughter. . . .

"Just as I said," Lena announced as she stepped out of the carriage and went inside. "Not true at all."

"Thank God!" Uhlstra said with a deep sigh. Rubbing his stubbly beard vigorously, he added: "How do people come up with such outrageous gossip?"

"Well, you see dear, things are going too well for us. That's what it is, nothing else."

He shook his head, and his face looked as if the malevolence of the world had overwhelmed him.

"We'll have them come up from Kuningan and give a party."

"I thought of that too, but it won't work."

"That's right. . . . because of Rose. . . . "

"That too, but that would still be possible if it had to . . . but Clara told me that Willem is sick."

"I thought he was getting better."

"Not at all. He's just as sick and miserable as before. Worse even."

His heart went out to his old *sobat*.

"*Kasian!*" he said compassionately. "What can be the matter with that poor guy."

"I asked Clara. She said that his spirit is sick or something like that, and that she's afraid for his mind."

"Damn it, that's very bad. You and Clara don't seem to understand how bad that is."

"I think she's exaggerating, but she did say how scared she

was, that he acts so strangely at times. She's afraid that some day he'll commit suicide."

He looked at her with fear and alarm.

How could she say that so calmly, he thought, ignorant as he was of the hatred she harbored for Geber.

"I'll go and see him some time, Lena."

"That might not be a bad idea."

"And if I see that it really is something like that, I'll have him watched night and day."

A dark little hall in the house of a Chinese. In front was a small, very ordinary *toko* with a few *laku* articles and a lot of old, unsalable stuff. Behind the dirty primitive display window with its small glass panes set in sloppily painted brown frames, a Chinese *nona* sat with a baby at her breast. She was dozing dreamily, her dull-yellow face dangling from her thin neck. She had big, lusterless eyes and marked features, and was happy just being a mother: lazy, not doing anything else. A Chinese man was sitting on a bench in front of his door, his *kabaja* was open and his moon face glistened. He was leaning forward with his hands clasped around a raised knee. His bare chest and stomach were folded into heavy layers, like a fattened pig.

At this late afternoon hour it was quiet and bright in the town's Chinese quarter. The sun shone fiercely and monotonously on the white walls with the whimsical black streaks of dust that had been blown up from the street. The small low shops, crammed with colored *kains* and cottons, were very dark toward the back. The shopkeepers were quietly doing their accounting; one was calculating his earnings and the chance of having something left over; another his losses and how he would go bankrupt. Some of them were folding something, from a need to be doing something, or were running their hands along the smoothly starched pieces of white cloth with a merchant's love for the wares that earn him a living. But the heat surmounted everything, and anything in the small alley that contained moisture, anything that was decaying in nooks and crannies, produced strange, fetid odors that might strike a lone European passing by as unpleasant, but that would have been familiar and pleasant to the natives and the Chinese, an atmosphere in which they were born, raised, and lived.

The long white shape of the arm-swinging figure who came around the corner into the alley was barely noticeable against the dazzling walls. The contrast came rather from his quick movements in all that stillness than from a difference in color.

In nervous agitation Twissels swung his tall narrow frame into the house of the Chinese. The man got up, closed his *kabaja*, and pulled down the legs of his wide cotton pants that had been rolled halfway up his thighs for coolness. He ran after Twissels, past the startled woman behind the counter who was completely taken aback.

"You know you can't come in here like that," the Chinese man said obsequiously but with determination, like someone who seriously intends to resist.

"Quiet, *ba!*" the high voice squeaked shakily. "Call Mr. Lugtens."

"I'm not *branie.*"

"Call him at once, otherwise I'll do it."

"It really isn't possible, sir. He just arrived from the other side."

"I don't care. Call him at once, I said."

"I really don't dare. What if he gets angry! And he has company, sir. It's a European. . . . "

"*Ba,* I didn't ask about that, and I don't care either, but call him immediately."

It couldn't be helped. The fat Chinese man, sighing and grumbling to himself, disappeared up the stairs in a side wall, the hard soles of his feet stamping and shuffling on the steps.

Twissels heard some muffled noises upstairs, though he could distinguish Lugtens's gruff commanding voice. Then he heard heavy footsteps, and against the light from the hallway appeared Lugtens's powerfully hewn head with a peculiarly drunk expression, but also angry.

"Whadya want?" he asked rudely.

"Geber's dead."

"Goddamn it!"

Lugtens's face grew pale from the shock, became serious, and he was totally himself again.

"He has . . . ," Twissels whispered softly, with a gesture to his forehead.

"Goddamn it," Lugtens repeated disconcertedly while rubbing his hand over his eyes. "That's terrible!"

He hastily went back up the stairs, returned in a few minutes, and walked out of the house and into the street. They walked down the middle of the road, the blazing sun on their backs.

As if one thought of such trifles! What did it matter that Twissels had suddenly shown that he knew about the secret excursions Lugtens sometimes made at noon from his office? When he went into a big *toko*, as if he was doing business, and returned later through the hallway from the little shop in the Chinese quarter opposite the white wall. He didn't think that anyone was aware of it, but now it was clear that almost everybody knew about his sins, his secret jaunts, the only weakness of somebody who never smoked or drank....

"What happened?" he asked, because the apparently common knowledge didn't bother him at the moment. He was first and foremost a businessman, and Geber, as a member of the *kongsi* that used people to earn money, was part of a very important business.

"I'm not sure. Uhlstra sent a man on horseback from Kuningan with this note."

The two men stopped and looked at the small piece of paper that had been written with a nervous hurry and said no more than:

"Last night, despite our surveillance, my son-in-law shot himself through the head. Take care of his affairs."

They looked at each other uncertainly, not knowing what to think of it because they didn't know anything about such things.

"That damned man!" Lugtens said spitefully. "How's it possible!"

"That's what I'm wondering too," the other man sighed delicately with his high, reedy voice.

"He really fooled us with this one."

"With that timber business, definitely! He was the only one who knew all about it."

They kept on walking until they came to Twissels's office which they entered silently. Lugtens looked up intently at Twissels's slight head rising about his own sturdy one and, barely able to control himself, his face distorted, he said sorrowfully: "He was such a good guy, Twissels. I loved him so much, so very much! He had something...that I loved....I don't know why, but I loved him more than...than...."

He couldn't think of a comparison; he loved so little.

But Twissels nodded very seriously. He understood all too well. It was one of those ridiculous things in life, he thought, one of those illogical questions of sympathy that controlled even an unfriendly man like Lugtens, so that he, of all men, felt the deepest affection for the man who had given him the worst deal.

"Yes," he said, shaking his head with a sigh. "Yes, it gave me quite a shock too."

Dutifully, they continued talking like this for a little while, also about the suicide. He must have been sick and, therefore, insane. It was their first explanation as well as their final one. Privately they were thinking the same thing, yet neither wanted to come forward with it so soon, until at last Twissels said, with some hesitation in his voice:

"What if we make some kind of rough estimate?"

"All right, as far as that's possible."

"Yes, no special reason, you know. Of course we'll go there in a little while."

"Of course."

"I just thought that Uhlstra might want to know something about the state of affairs."

Lugtens nodded; he had spoken the short eulogy, the old *sobat* had been buried, and life's affairs had become "the state of affairs."

It was true that Geber had been watched since Uhlstra had been at Kuningan. They had been quite surprised by his visit.

"Are you coming?" Geber asked. He was just about to take a look in various places of his plantation and thought that Uhlstra would be interested.

"Thanks. But I'll keep Rose company until you get back."

"Gosh, Pa!" Rose said with astonishment. "Aren't you even going to look with Wim?"

She didn't understand it at all. She felt that Papa was such a good man, and her brothers and sisters agreed with her. But he wasn't someone who would stay around for small talk if the men could talk about business. And now this! Geber looked suspiciously at his father-in-law. He also thought that there was something behind it. Nothing bad, one couldn't suspect Uhlstra of such a thing, but still something that they didn't want him to know.

"How's Willem doing lately?"

"Oh . . . well . . . not too well, I think. He's not really sick. . . . I don't really know."

She leaned back in the rocking chair. Due to her awkward state, she was sitting on the edge, trying to find some relief in every possible way. She was broader than ever and a picture of quiet vitality.

Uhlstra was sitting on the other side of the table so that the large round white marble surface was between them. He tapped his riding whip against his shoe; his right foot rested on his left knee. His bearded face was darker where the shadow from the pith helmet fell, and brighter on the other side from the light that came from beyond the veranda. It was a darkly handsome face with the abundant black and brown flecked with white and gray. He looked down shyly at the tapping of his whip and then up into his oldest daughter's eyes, eyes that could have been his own.

In the distance Geber walked along the *djoar* avenue to his new plantings. A little stooped, somewhat old in his posture, and walking uncertainly without will or resolution.

Uhlstra had felt courageous at home, but no longer. He could only act according to what he knew, how could he do otherwise! He saw in Rose a loving woman who loved her husband dearly in all respects. She had a child by that man and when asked when her second one was due could indeed answer "soon." She was his daughter, they were his grandchildren, and Geber was his son-in-law, an old friend and neighbor.... Where had the time gone?... And now he had to tell her that Willem was walking around thinking about suicide. He had to tear Rose's domestic life rudely apart—an existence he thought was so good and peaceful—in order to warn her and try to save Geber by protecting him against himself. Uhlstra felt as helpless as a child. He *couldn't* say it; he wouldn't have said it even if he could have earned ten plantations with it.

"What's the matter, Pa?" Rose asked.

He looked again at his interesting shoe. Tick, tick went his riding whip.

"Nothing, nothing! I just came by to see how you're doing."

She didn't believe a word of it.

"Willem looks bad," he continued kindly. "Let him come with me, he has to.... "

But she got angry.

"Well, Pa, that's very nice of you. You think Willem is sick, and now he has to go to town and be under a doctor's care. And of course he'll play cards with you until three or four o'clock in the morning until he's fully recovered. What about me?"

"It's true, dear, it's true. I really didn't think of that right now."

"That's nice of you!"

"But you're always so healthy!"

"Oh, that's it! So I don't count. Great! Wim eats well and drinks well, he's always on the go, but he looks wan and is losing weight. I'm sure that's not so good, but to exaggerate it like that, and think nothing of taking him with you and leave me all alone here.... "

Rose started to cry, from anger really, and Uhlstra, who was completely befuddled by now, came up with one stupid excuse after another, each one making things worse. They were still quarreling when, out of curiosity, Willem had turned around and come back.

"I didn't want to leave you alone," he said to Uhlstra.

Looking angrily from under her long, curly lashes, his wife had seen him coming.

"When Pa is with me," she exploded, "he's not *alone*, as far as I know."

Geber looked at her with amazement, dumbfounded even. He had never heard anything so strange. He saw that she had been crying and said simply:

"You're right. Excuse me, I didn't mean it like that."

"But you say it anyway. Pa too, you know. They're worried because you're not well, they want to ask you to stay with them. . . . to recuperate, and leave me on my own here. Nice, isn't it? That's the way they are at home nowadays. . . . "

"Don't talk about it anymore," Geber said soothingly. "I wouldn't do it anyway," and to his father-in-law: "How did you come up with that?"

Uhlstra was glad that he could go back, though without any results. Despite his complaisance, he was a strong and courageous man, but this was no job for him. His wife had been amazed when he, so *branie*, had immediately volunteered to go to Kuningan. She was waiting for him with impatience and curiosity. She saw it on his face already when he dismounted.

"And?" she asked. "How did it go?"

But Uhlstra, embarrassed by it, didn't answer, and she continued:

"I bet you didn't say anything."

"I didn't, because Rose was already in a bad mood."

"Mood! . . . But it still has to be done, dear. I'll do it, all right? I'll have the horses hitched."

In her heart she thought it was nice that he hadn't been able to do it. She didn't reproach him either; on the contrary, she loved him all the more for it.

"God!" Rose exclaimed, waddling to the front of the house when the well-known carriage drove up. "Believe it or not, there's Mama!"

She understood at once. It became clear to her, as it did to Geber, that there was something Papa had wanted to say but hadn't been able too.

Mrs. Uhlstra wasn't very friendly to her son-in-law. That man gave her more *susah* than all her children put together. She disliked him now, and Geber could see that in her dark face.

"How are you?" she asked in a tone that gave the words the impression of a sharp reproach. It sounded like: "Creep, there's always something going on with you and it's never anything good."

"Fine!" he said with the mocking smile she couldn't stand. He knew very well what was behind the interest in his health, and he didn't want her to derive any pleasure from it.

"Very well, Mom! Only pure imagination says I'm not well. I've never been so healthy."

She looked up at his colorless thin face that contrasted so sadly with his words, but she felt no *kasian*. Nice son-in-law! Now it was only Rose, but if the other girls also had to have such *lakis* she would pass up being a mother-in-law, thank you, no matter how desirable it was.

"Rose," she said, when she was alone with her daughter in one of the rooms, "I have to talk seriously to you, dear."

"Yes, Ma," Rose answered. She knew that whatever was behind all the secrecy would come out in the open now.

"Your husband's crazy!"

A loud burst of laughter, the likes of which hadn't sounded through Kuningan for a long time, filled the room with its joyful sound. Rose shook from it, alarmingly so. "Oh Ma!" she managed to gasp, "Oh Ma!" and again she burst out laughing. "Your husband's crazy!" And she said it with the straightest face!

But the laughter made Mrs. Uhlstra feel terrible.

"Quiet, Rose, don't laugh! It's *betul, betul!*"

"But Ma!" Rose said, a bit indignant now. "Why do you think that?"

She never watched Geber. During the day she saw little of him and, therefore, didn't pay much attention to him. She was too busy with the little one, her housekeeping, and the domestic affairs of the plantation. They hadn't slept in the same room for quite some time. Tired from all the activity during the day, she went to bed immediately after dinner, and always slept soundly; she never heard him at night.

"It's really true, Rose. You've got to have him watched. He's walking around with very nasty things in his head."

"How's it possible! I think the things in your head are a lot nastier."

"*Sudah*, if you don't believe me. But I'm telling you it's true. He's very sick in his mind and if you're not careful, he'll do away with himself. Pa wanted to tell you that this morning, but he couldn't get it out. And he knows, it's *betul, betul* true. That's when I said: 'I'll have to warn Rose.' "

The young woman became serious. So that was it! She had to have her husband watched in order to prevent him from taking his own life!

"How do you know about it? He hasn't tried it, has he?"

But Mama didn't want to let on about that, and she talked past it, contending that Uhlstra had said it and that he knew all about it.

Rose wasn't indifferent, but she wasn't shocked either. She would have her husband watched by the old *mandur*, who had served him almost like a personal servant. She knew immediately what to do, but other than that it appeared that she either didn't really believe the soundness of the suspicion or didn't totally realize the importance of the matter.

At home the next morning Uhlstra asked worriedly and compassionately: "Lena, how was she?"

"Well," his wife lied, not wanting to tell the truth, "as you can imagine, she was terribly saddened."

Before two days were over Geber understood what had happened. His old servant behaved very strangely, as strangely as only a native can in such circumstances. Whenever Geber was at home and looked up, he always saw the old man's eyes resting on him with an expression of great astonishment before he turned them quickly and conspicuously away, or it was Rose he caught observing him secretly.

"What is it?" he'd ask her in an unfriendly manner.

"Nothing."

"You were looking at me."

"No, it's nothing."

But it seemed to him that they made a point of displaying their intention very clearly.

Nothing easier though than making certain.

"Hey, old friend," he said to his servant after a few days, "why are you following me everywhere?"

The man feigned utter amazement. He had a face typical of an old Javanese who has had a good life, with a potbelly from his lazy existence as well as bulging cheeks below the wrinkles around his eyes. But the expression on his face was so simple and imperturbable that Geber, who knew the man well and was used to him, shook his head about it.

"I'm not following the *tuan*."

"I know you too well and too long; you think you can fool me?"

For a moment the Javanese thought without answering.

"You can't, right?" Geber continued. "You've been ordered to keep an eye on me, to see if I'll do something to kill myself. Who told you to do it?"

"The *njonja*, *tuan*. But I won't do it, because *tuan* would never kill himself. *Tuan* is too rich and too smart for that."

He now knew what he had wanted to know. Clara had talked! The rest didn't matter to him. She was the only one he had told about the utterly miserable existence he endured during most of the day and night, and she hadn't been able to keep her mouth shut. Hardly back, and she had blabbed to her family. He couldn't trust Rose in that respect and now it was clear that he couldn't even trust *her*.

Alone in his room he concluded that it was all annoying and sad. Sure, he would shoot himself—that had been settled for some time. He faced the end of his life without fear: on the contrary, the agitation, the disquieting nervousness that occurred before and after his visions had vanished since he had reached his decision.

And now those visions kept on recurring. As soon as he was alone and no longer occupied by his work, his mind seemed to be drawn forcefully away from all that enveloped him toward that single, ever-recurring notion of image and color, compared to which life and the world were disagreeable heavy burdens. It was a difference in beauty and purity, in light and delicacy, like the difference between the white feathery puffs of cloud in a summer sky before a child's eyes, and the dirty city slums on a fall day to the eyes of a hungry beggar. No, he was going to check out, that was already quite certain. Now that Clara had betrayed him, it was definitely settled. On the one hand he was pleased. Wasn't she the only bond? He didn't feel anything for his child. He didn't like children in general; he had never paid any more attention to little Lena than to her brothers and sisters. Love for children was an unknown feeling to him, one that, at best, he feigned on occasion when it suited convention.

Now that last tie had been broken and nothing stood in his way anymore. Ideas and principles had yielded to the persistent drive of the sure and idealized image; bonds had proven to be weak; because of the size of his fortune, obligations had been rejected with a shrug—only his special feelings for Clara had made him yield time and again. That was over now. She had shown herself to be no better than the rest of them. He hadn't felt any sexual desire for her, it had been totally destroyed after his return to Kuningan by his overwrought imagination working in another direction. His affection for her kind had been purified. But it was gone for good now, thank God!

He had prepared everything.

His letters to the *kongsi* with his final accounts, calculations and statements; his letter to Rose, simple with a casual word of apology and a reference to fatalism; and one to his lawyer for the settlement of his affairs.

He had put everything in order and written it all in his room during the evenings, by the pleasant light of the big office lamp over his large old-fashioned desk. It was so peaceful and quiet! A powerful feeling of rest and relaxation came over him, as if a hand that usually held him fast had opened and let him go, giving him a feeling of wonderful relief.

He had fixed a date. Rose would deliver her second child, which would go well again according to all calculations. Her mother, of course, would come to "take care" of the house-keeping in the beginning, and then a date would be set for Mrs. Uhlstra's return. Rose would be better then, and when that day came, it was his.

21   A Tragic End

It went as if the world's events were under his command, exactly as he had imagined. A blond baby boy arrived who completely occupied Rose and her mother, who were both elated with joy. And just as he had figured, the discussion about the day of return followed four weeks later. The Uhlstras, father and children, had also come in the meantime, and Mrs. Lugtens had visited as well. She and Geber were very formal with one another. The idea of suicide had been entirely forgotten. Uhlstra was staying at Kuningan the day before his wife, whom he had come to pick up, was to return home.

That evening, after the women had gone to bed, he was talking with Geber over a brandy and soda on the front veranda. It was always about business, an easy-going chat that lasted until quite late. Misery was the last thing on anyone's mind.

Geber was secretly getting excited, but outwardly he remained calm. With a loud "Sleep well!" Uhlstra's brown big fleshy hand pressed his own warmly and strongly. Thank God he was gone!

Not that Geber had anything to think about—solitude was the only thing that attracted him. Otherwise, he acted normally, put out the light in his room and turned on the night light. But in that twilight he lay awake on his bed, smiling and full of longing for the phantasmagoria that rose before his closed eyes, more glorious and sparkling than ever. And next to it, in ominous discord, was the sad contrast of the boring insignificance and dull misery of real life.

It was almost four o'clock when he got up, calmly and soundlessly. Everything was dead quiet in the house. He softly opened the door of his room and went outside. The moon was dazzling, as sharply edged in white as it is during a freezing Norwegian winter night. His hand didn't tremble when he lit the candle in the porcelain holder in the bathroom. Neither did he think that he was there for the last time. He didn't think about anything, but acted with the great calm certainty of a machine.

In the same way he went back into his room and dressed neatly and carefully. Although he would normally walk around on his plantation in a pair of white pants and a *kabaja*, or at the utmost a light jacket, he now put on a clean shirt and a black jacket, making the difficult knot in his tie with care, as if he were going to a party.

He didn't laugh as he did it; he didn't think it was funny to dress up that way under these circumstances. He continued neatly and earnestly, more carefully than he had ever dressed before.

He put the letters and documents on the table in front of the window, so that they would immediately catch somebody's attention.

Everything was ready. He looked around the room by the light of the big lamp he had lit. Not for a second did any emotion touch him. He only looked to make sure that he hadn't forgotten anything. No, nothing!

From a dresser he took a handsome inlaid pistol that he had bought for a lot of money once, years ago. He had examined it often lately, but he checked it again. Before loading it he tested the trigger, it worked quietly and smoothly. He put the gun into the pocket of his jacket, looked through his pince-nez briefly at the addresses of the letters on the table, and left, walking softly on tiptoe to avoid making any noise on the wooden stairs by the window behind which Rose and the little ones were sleeping.

The watchman struck half past four.

Geber strode firmly along the path through the rice paddies. His very distinguished clothes and the stiffness of the collar around his neck gave him an instinctive sense of being well dressed, and he walked up straight now instead of stooping slightly. He walked on to the small wood by the river. He already saw it in the moonlight, silhouetted sharply as a dark mass against the pale violet sky. The sweetish smell of rotting foliage wafted toward him from the dark shady path. But he knew what he was doing.

He had ordered a wide bench built there with short legs. It had remained unpainted and he would see its gray outline in the distance in the spots of light that fell between the leaves onto the new planks.

As if he were lying down for a quiet nap, Geber carefully lowered himself with his back onto the bench. He hung his hat on a protruding peg, afraid that it would get dirty on the ground. He studiously moved his head so that it wasn't pulled back too far, but remained in a preferred forward position. The circles of light that came down amidst the leaves wandered over him, gilding spots on his uptilted blond beard, and shone on his bald head. He thought he was lying in the correct position now and put the gun against his forehead, paying strict attention to where he felt the impression of the cold little "o" of the muzzle.

Only a dull crack followed, and it didn't carry far. The arm fell back along the body that briefly tensed and then lay very still. The flecks of light between the softly moving leaves now wandered over the still, pale face and over the drops of blood that flowed slowly from his head, dripping down and spreading color over the gray unpainted wood.

They didn't miss him immediately at Kuningan.

Not until breakfast did Rose speak to her father, who was all dressed to go home with his wife.

"Where's Willem?"

"I think he's looking after his work first."

They thought so too; he would have done that first in order to have time to talk for a while before his in-laws left.

"It's strange that he isn't here yet," Uhlstra said a few hours later when a suspicion rose in him for the first time. He immediately felt it grow into the conviction of truth, and turned white from fear.

He didn't wait for an answer this time, but went to the front of the house where his carriage had been waiting for him for quite a while. The coachman brought the horses a step or so closer, thinking that the moment of departure had come.

Uhlstra called the mandur, the clerk. . . . They were all waiting for orders; they hadn't seen the tuan. Rose and her mother followed him, suddenly alarmed because of Uhlstra. They looked at each other, and trembled silently.

"Oh God!" Rose burst out, crying. "Ma, he's committed suicide. It's terrible!"

It didn't matter that her mother started to argue against her own conviction. Rose kept on repeating it, sobbing and wailing from a sorrow that suddenly welled up with great force.

The letters in their big white envelopes lying calmly on his son-in-law's table sent cold shivers down Uhlstra's spine. His big hands, trembling badly, grabbed at them and mixed them up trying to get a hold of the one addressed to him. He couldn't get the envelope open, he was shaking so badly from nerves, and he almost tore the letter in half.

There was no doubt anymore. The indications were clear; they were faced by a carefully planned and executed act. With big steps in the hot glare of the sun, Uhlstra's heavy figure trudged along the path through the *sawahs*. Now and then he nervously stumbled over his own feet. Led by the *mandur*, half a dozen Javanese were half trotting, half running behind him with a *baleh-baleh* on their naked shoulders.

They could head straight for their target, and found the body with thousands of ants hurrying over it. The face, which had changed very little, was ashen and taut. It was as if death wanted to show what life had so carefully hidden from others, as if death wanted to apologize by giving a reason: the narrow, waxen face, wasted to a shadowy black, expressed such mental suffering, such aberration, that even a man as casual as Uhlstra was overpowered.

Pressing his silk neckerchief against his mouth with a trembling hand, and with big tears rolling down his cheeks for his friend of so many years, he stood in front of the bench by the body, leaning on his heavy cane. The Javanese squatted down behind him on the other side of the path, while the *mandur* stood up straight, looking aside with a compassionate, *kasian* face.

"Poor devil!" Uhlstra whispered to himself, shaking his head repeatedly, and swallowing constantly because of his tight throat. With a gesture of his head he beckoned the men. They put the *baleh-baleh* against the bench and, dropping his cane on the ground, Uhlstra bent down, slid his big strong arms carefully under the long skinny body and moved it cautiously, as if he were handling a child.

Everything was in an uproar. Work in the fields and stables had stopped. The rumor spread like wildfire over the plantation; the native population came from everywhere, and many were genuinely sorry because Geber had always been good to them.

Rose, completely overwrought and suddenly overpowered by a feeling of love that she had never felt while Geber was alive, carried on like a madwoman. Pale, hair hanging loose, and wringing her hands, she wailed over the body and talked to it as if she were crazy. Uhlstra's deep voice could be heard now and then, kindly reassuring and consoling her until her mother, somewhat angrily and abruptly, took her away. There was no time for much talk or prolonged sadness. Action was needed.

As soon as the short time necessary to announce the event was over, sympathizers came from everywhere. So many Europeans attended the funeral on the plantation that everyone was astounded. Things went quietly and, as Geber had requested in one of his letters, there were no speeches.

That evening the three of them were sitting in his room. Lugtens, Twissels, and Uhlstra compared Geber's figures with those of the company. They agreed almost perfectly and, being a rough calculation, it was quite amazing. The men stared at them with admiration, unable to understand such a dualistic working of a mind that, on the one hand, permitted proof of a normal intelligence and, on the other, led irrevocably and persistently to aberration and an insane misjudgment of life.

"No, nobody can fool me like that," Lugtens said dogmatically. "Anyone who can keep up with his business like that is dealing from a full deck, and does a good job too."

"Absolutely," Twissels conceded, lifting his small head high like a cock that wanted to crow. "His things are in fine shape."

"I can't understand it," sighed Uhlstra.

But it was true. Uhlstra had immediately seen it when he arrived first at the body, and in his heart he stuck to his conviction but ... his mind doubted. What he used to consider his "common sense" told him that the others were right, and he rejected the possibility that a thorough performance of one's work could go together with any kind of insanity.

They guessed some more. Uhlstra mentioned heredity, and, as if that was the most common answer, something self-contained and not connected to a harmonious working of the mind, they agreed on that. Well, certainly, it was hereditary; it ran in the family; nothing could be done about that; it was another kind of kismet that explained everything and nothing at the same time. *Habis perkara!*

They established Geber's share in the total profits of the *kongsi*. It was a magnificent sum. Even if one didn't add anything else, Rose was a wealthy woman, but augment it with her own fortune and with Kuningan, and she and her children were rich.

Lugtens's sharp eyes looked mischievously at the blurred, tired features of Twissels's pale face.

"It's very nice," he said, raising his harsh voice, "very nice for the short term. But the man is dead and buried, and this is the end of it for his widow."

Twissels raised his eyebrows and pursed his lips. Feeling very uneasy he twisted his head back and forth because he understood where it was leading. And for the sake of decency he didn't dare say much.

"Together with the rest it's splendid," he pointed out, his voice running up to the highest pitch.

"Oh yes! But we have nothing to do with the rest now. Hence, as far as our business is concerned, I would like to add another hundred thousand."

The other men were silent. Badly cornered, and with a hangdog look, Twissels's face dropped, because he was embarrassed by the situation; Uhlstra was also embarrassed and was rubbing his beard as diligently as usual.

"What do you say, Uhlstra? You're the oldest."

"I . . . well, see. . . . of course, gladly. But she's my daughter. . . . "

Lugtens brushed that objection away with a short imperious gesture.

"And you, Twissels?"

His eyes were cast down and he was drawing little lines on a piece of paper. He was disgruntled about the thirty-three thousand that he had just been taken for so unnecessarily. Smiling painfully, he said:

"Well, if you two approve . . . then, of course. . . . I agree to it."

The two other men looked at each other. Lugtens's fat shiny face showed amusement. They understood that allusion to the power of the majority, but they casually let it go at that.

Rose wept loudly but forgot quickly, as they say. Otherwise Geber fared like anyone else who leaves an opening; it was filled. It was agreed that Rose could not stay on the plantation. She was very disappointed. At first she considered taking on one of her younger brothers, and Uhlstra also thought that it was a good idea. But the young man had said "No thank you. I'll gladly work for strangers, but to be a supervisor for Rose— nothing doing!"

In the end Uhlstra bought the plantation from his daughter for what he had once offered Geber, half a million, and he came with the check in his pocket. Why should he buy on time and pay interest? It wasn't necessary. Now, unconstrained, his younger replica could be the manager there.

No one else was taken into the *kongsi*. The trio continued to work quietly outside their regular businesses, earning more with the first than with the latter. When one deal had been accomplished, another one would already be negotiated. Markens's help remained necessary and they treated him very generously so that, in spite of everything, even he began to have something left over.

The rapidly changing Indies society had been transformed in the meantime. People left with their fortunes, other people came to try and make theirs. Sick government workers departed and healthy ones returned; the endless replacement of retirees with newcomers continued on and on. Not many people stayed, the unlucky ones and the bad ones disappeared into the *kampongs* and the slums. The not-quite-lucky ones stagnated at a certain level and couldn't advance, nor did they want to fall back.

The question was asked with amazement hundreds of times in these small social circles, Why didn't people like Lugtens and Twissels go to Europe? They were so rich! One could understand about the Uhlstras; they were genuine Indies people. Each year civil servants became more and more annoyed that Markens, with his high lucrative position and well-deserved pension, remained in office. Why didn't such a man leave the colonial service!

They did talk about it among themselves sometimes, and they would have gladly gotten out of it for a year or so, if the three privately employed members hadn't been of the opinion that they had too good a thing going and that it was a "sin" not to take care of it themselves. It was like a hobby to them. Self-made men that they were, they had taken hold of work, and now that they had made it, work had taken hold of them and they couldn't let go of it anymore. And Markens thought that whoever gets up loses his seat. At last, after so many years of service, he was beginning to have some money and that really cheered him up despite his many domestic sorrows! The reports from Holland about his boys were very unfavorable. It took all his influence and a great deal of trouble for the man who had his power of attorney to avoid having them sent from one school to the next. When he thought about what to do with his two sons, when he thought about that. . . . no, they wouldn't get him out of the service so easily!

"Why should we go to Europe?" Lugtens asked when Clara, who wanted to go, told him how the ladies had made it sound very appealing. "We get everything here too. It just takes a little longer, that's all. We're even getting a railroad now!"

He had to laugh about that. If that railroad ever paid to the stockholders what it had brought in for the *kongsi*, they would be well off!

"We'll have a big party for the opening."

"Oh yes, for men only."

"For you too. And I have another plan. An opening celebration is all well and good, but it's a little too good for ordinary folks."

"What do you want then?"

"We should run a special train. I'll throw an outdoor party the likes of which have never been seen in the Indies."

The idea possessed him. It was to be a royal affair, really grand, and the idea of a party appealed to Clara too, not because of the train, but because she had changed so much to her disadvantage after Geber's death. His death had bothered her less, because she was convinced that sooner or later his suicide was inevitable. Now that he was dead, a bond seemed to have been cut, one she hadn't felt before, but which surely must have existed. She had become a flirt in the most ordinary sense. She was already at an age when a lot had to be hidden at the dressing table. She did that with tact and discretion, and knew how to present herself so that she was attractive to men. And that's what she worked for now, without much restraint.

For many people Lugtens's plan, which had already become common knowledge, cast a shadow over the general opening festivities of the railroad. Would they be invited to the big outdoor party for which a special train would be put into service? Many people were depressed by the possibility of being passed over. They were so very lofty and rich, those people! Nobody could measure up to them. And when the great day dawned, the special train was waiting for its first run on the new tracks in front of the platform in the new railroad station. The passenger cars shone with green and brown newness; the locomotive up front, quietly making steam, stood there in black distinction, its brass rims shining like gold. The smell of fresh paint hung under the gay, gray-yellow awning and rays of sun beamed through its iron lattice work. Everything looked fresh, neat, and friendly, as if it had just been taken out of a giant toy box and arranged with care.

The guests, already excited, climbed up the carriage steps. Most were dressed in bright white that was relieved here and there by the colorful red and blue of the women's ribbons and bows.

The foremost first-class car was occupied by Markens, Lugtens, Twissels, Uhlstra, and the three wives. They were seated facing the small crowd of spectators, the clerks and officials who had been left behind on the platform and were wandering around or standing in small groups smoking cigars. They sat there in distinguished inaccessibility, as a truly separate kind of people, far above the rest.

They had never felt as important as they did in that compartment of the special train. And it seemed to them that the glory of their fortune had never glittered as much. Never had they been so much on top of the world. And when the steam whistle answered the bell, and the train pulled out of the shadow into the sun on the long iron track, the people who stayed behind looked after the travelers with envy and admiration. How rich and happy these people were, they thought.

Glossary

Unless otherwise noted, the words are Malay. Modern Indonesian spelling is different from Daum's. The old spelling tj is now c, dj is j, ch is kh, nj is ny, sj is sy.

ajo   an exclamation meaning something like "come on," "let's get going."

ampon (ampun)   mercy, forgiveness, pardon. *Minta ampon* means "to beg forgiveness."

ariet (more commonly spelled *arit*)   in Java this referred to a curved, sickle-shaped knife for cutting grass.

atap   thatch; a roofing material made from the leaves of various palms.

ba   abbreviation of *baba*, a word that referred to Chinese born in Indonesia.

baadje   is the Dutch diminutive of the Malay word *kabaja*, a kind of white cotton jacket.

babu   Javanese for a female servant who might have various functions.

badjing   tropical squirrel.

baleh-baleh   a bench to sleep or rest on.

bandjir   violent flooding of rivers.

betul   can mean "straight" or "right," but is used here primarily in the sense of "really" or "quite."

bingung   bewildered, confused, mixed up.

bosen (or *bosan*)   to be fed up, get sick of something, feel distaste.

brani (branie)   to be brave, daring, plucky.

budjang   generally means a "bachelor" or single man, but it can also refer to a servant.

djadi   here primarily meaning "to succeed," "it'll work," "it'll happen"; it can also mean to become, to be born, or to grow.

djati   a tall tree that produces the "djati wood" or Javanese teak.

djeruk   the generic term in Javanese for citrus fruit.

djoar (normally *djuar*)   the *Cassia siamea* or *Cassia florida* tree; a tall shade tree once used a great deal to line roads because of its rapid growth.

djuragan   commander, shipmaster (of a native vessel), hence "lord" or "master."

dukun   native doctor, herbalist, medicine man.

gardu   a guard, also used for guardhouse.

glatik a rice-eating finch.

grobak Javanese for a two-wheeled ox-drawn cart, which had some sort of roofing to protect the goods that were being transported.

gudang warehouse, or any place where goods are stored.

habis perkara means "that's it," "that's final," "basta."

kabaja (or *kabaai*) a woman's loose jacket which reaches just below the hips. Its front is open and has no buttons. To close it one uses the *kerosang*, three brooches connected by a small silver chain. It has long, narrow sleeves. A *kabaja tjina* was worn by men, especially the Dutch, and was a loose cotton jacket with an upright collar.

kain a piece of batiked cloth similar to a sarong, but wider, and in a more traditional style.

kali Javanese for river.

kampong is Malay for a village. In Javanese it can also mean a neighborhood or section of a city, or a compound (a single house). Javanese uses the term *desa* for an independent hamlet. The Dutch used *kampong* most frequently.

kasian (or *kassian*) literally means to feel pity, sympathy, mercy. It was a very common expression used by Dutch colonialists for anything they felt sorry for. Comparable to the Spanish *pobrecito*.

kètjo (or *kètju*) a gang of thieves or robbers; a robbery.

kondé a traditional hair style of Indonesian women. The hair is pulled back tight and worn in a chignon in the nape of the neck.

kongsi originally a Chinese word, it meant a secret society or a secret syndicate and came to refer to any kind of partnership or organization. Here it refers to a secret business partnership or syndicate.

krabu an earring; often a large stone set in a circle of small stones and attached to the ear with a screw.

kris the Indonesian dagger.

kwee-kwee a kind of cookie.

laki husband.

laku to be wanted, desired, to be in demand.

malieng (commonly *maling*) thief.

mandi room the room where one takes a bath, not a room with a toilet.

mandur from the Portugese *mandador*, refers to a native overseer.

manga is the mango fruit (*Mangifera indica*).

mati dead.

nassi cooked rice.

njo (from *sinjo*) a male of mixed blood, a Eurasian.

njonja "madame" or "lady"; refers to a married woman of high social rank. *njonja besar* great lady.

nonna (*nona*) Javanese for an unmarried European woman, hence "miss" or "young lady." It is also used here to indicate an Eurasian woman.

obor   Javanese for torch.

padi   in Java refers to rice still in the field.

palang pintu   a wooden crossbar; *palang* refers to any kind of crosspiece or bar, and *pintu* means a door, gate, or entrance.

parang   the Indonesian machete.

perkara   from Sanskrit, meaning "matter," "affair," or "concern."

perkutut   a kind of turtledove.

pindjam sepuluh rupia   *pindjam* means "to borrow," *sepuluh* is "ten," and *rupia* refers to a monetary value, here meaning the Dutch guilder. Hence the phrase means: "I would like to borrow ten guilders." Today the *rupia* is the official Indonesian currency.

pisang   banana.

rameh-rameh   the word means literally "lively, loud festive goings on." Hence here something like "a day of noisy fun" for the bachelors.

rampas   to take something by force, to loot.

rijsttafel   Dutch for a main meal eaten by the colonials. It consists of rice, a large number of sidedishes, and a variety of condiments.

rudjak   a salad made from unripe fruit that is diced and mixed with vinegar, hot peppers, and sugar.

rugie (commonly *rugi*)   loss, damage, injury (other than physical).

sajang   "It's a pity."

sambal   a condiment made with crushed hot peppers as a base and a host of other ingredients; it is used to flavor and accompany meals.

sawa (or *sawah*)   irrigated rice field.

sedekah   here meant to refer to a religious meal or banquet.

sinjo   a boy, either a European or the son of a European father and a native mother. Often abbreviated as *njo*.

sobat   a word from around Batavia, from the Arabic *sahabat* (a term also used in Malay), meaning a friend, a companion.

sudah   done, finished, "that's over with," "let it be."

sungu mati   an expression used to insist on something or affirm something; it is somewhat like "to be sure," "I *mean* it," "I'm sure."

susa(h)   trouble, difficulties.

tabé   means "Greetings"; it can be used as our "hi," but it was originally intended (as it is in the text) as a courteous word to open a conversation.

tamu   a guest, a visitor.

tempo dulu   literally "time before," hence the past. The Dutch colonials used it often to indicate "the good old days."

tenda   canopy (of a bed).

terlalu   very, too much, exceedingly.

terus   direct, to go straight at something, forthright.

tikar   floormat to sit on.

tjap   a seal, mark, trademark, stamp. Generally used by colonials to indicate something particular, authentic, inimicable.

tjientjang (more commonly *tjintjang*)   colonial usage, meaning that someone has been cut to pieces.

tjilaka   Javanese for unlucky, bad luck, misfortune.

tjotjok   to agree with something or someone, to belong together, to "click."

toko   a shop, usually run by Chinese, that often contained the most amazing variety of goods.

tong-tong   a large, hollowed-out block of wood that hung in the *gardu*. The guard struck the hours on it during the night.

trimakasi banjak   a formal way of expressing gratitude for a favor; literally "many thanks."

tuan   "mister" or "sir." Used particularly by the native population when addressing a European.

tuan tanah   *tanah* means earth, soil, land, hence *tuan tanah* is a landowner, a planter.

tukang (tukan)   a workman, but in the sense of someone who knows a trade, such as carpentry. A *tukang* is not an unskilled laborer or coolie.

tutup   to close, cover, hide. Here meant in the sense of a cover-up to prevent exposure.

warong   small shop or eating stall.